Praise for Kate Carlisle's Bibliophile Mysteries

If Books Could Kill

"Carlisle's story is captivating, and she peoples it with a cast of eccentrics. Books seldom kill, of course, but this one could murder an early bedtime."

—*Richmond Times-Dispatch*

"The mystery plot is lighthearted and cozy but with depth enough to keep me guessing.... The eclectic cast of characters kept a smile on my face throughout the book."

—Gumshoe

"Excitement bounds off of each page! This twisty tale will keep you guessing until the very end. I feel like Brooklyn is an old friend and hope to meet her again in another mystery." —The Romance Readers Connection

"Brooklyn's uncommon occupation drives the well-constructed and smoothly executed mystery. Offbeat secondary characters contrast nicely with the more levelheaded Brooklyn." —*Romantic Times*

Homicide in Hardcover

"A fun, fast-paced mystery that is laugh-out-loud funny. Even better, it keeps you guessing to the very end. Sure to be one of the very best books of the year!"

—*New York Times* bestselling author Susan Mallery

continued . . .

"Who'd have thought book restoration could be so exciting? When Brooklyn Wainwright inherits the job restoring the priceless copy of Goethe's *Faust* from her murdered mentor, her studio is ransacked, she's stalked, and the bodies pile up around her. Is it the famous *Faust* curse? I'm not tellin'. But, trust me, you'll have fun finding out."

—Parnell Hall, author of the Puzzle Lady Mysteries

"Beautiful and brilliant Brooklyn Wainwright thought bookbinding was a low-risk occupation, but she soon discovers her mistake in Kate Carlisle's smart and sophisticated page-turner."

—Leslie Meier, author of *Valentine Murder*

"Brooklyn is my kind of detective! She loves books, wine, chocolate—and solving mysteries! Kate Carlisle has crafted a fabulous new series with great food, great books, and lots of fun." —Maureen Child, author of *A Fiend in Need*

"Welcome to the fresh and funny world of bookbinder Brooklyn Wainwright. A delicious mix of San Francisco, book restoration, and a lingering counterculture beset by murder. Who knew leather and vellum could be so captivating!"

—Jo Dereske, author of the Miss Zukas Mysteries

"A cursed book, a dead mentor, and a snarky rival send book restorer Brooklyn Wainwright on a chase for clues—and fine food and wine—in Kate Carlisle's fun and funny delightful debut."

—Lorna Barrett, author of the Booktown Mysteries

"Saucy, sassy, and smart—a fun read with a great sense of humor and a soupçon of suspense. Enjoy!"

—Nancy Atherton, author of the Aunt Dimity Mysteries

Other Bibliophile Mysteries

Homicide in Hardcover
If Books Could Kill

The Lies That Bind

A Bibliophile Mystery

Kate Carlisle

OBSIDIAN
Published by New American Library, a division of
Penguin Group (USA) Inc., 375 Hudson Street,
New York, New York 10014, USA
Penguin Group (Canada), 90 Eglinton Avenue East, Suite 700, Toronto,
Ontario M4P 2Y3, Canada (a division of Pearson Penguin Canada Inc.)
Penguin Books Ltd., 80 Strand, London WC2R 0RL, England
Penguin Ireland, 25 St. Stephen's Green, Dublin 2,
Ireland (a division of Penguin Books Ltd.)
Penguin Group (Australia), 250 Camberwell Road, Camberwell, Victoria 3124,
Australia (a division of Pearson Australia Group Pty. Ltd.)
Penguin Books India Pvt. Ltd., 11 Community Centre, Panchsheel Park,
New Delhi - 110 017, India
Penguin Group (NZ), 67 Apollo Drive, Rosedale, North Shore 0632,
New Zealand (a division of Pearson New Zealand Ltd.)
Penguin Books (South Africa) (Pty.) Ltd., 24 Sturdee Avenue,
Rosebank, Johannesburg 2196, South Africa

Penguin Books Ltd., Registered Offices:
80 Strand, London WC2R 0RL, England

First published by Obsidian, an imprint of New American Library,
a division of Penguin Group (USA) Inc.

First Printing, November 2010
10 9 8 7 6 5 4 3 2 1

Printed in the United States of America

This book is dedicated with love, affection, and gratitude to my brother, James Carlisle Beaver. Jimmy, my favorite memories of San Francisco are the times I've spent there with you.

Acknowledgments

My thanks and acknowledgment go to book conservator Jeff Peachey for generously granting permission to use his name and his bookbinding tools in my books.

Many thanks, as well, to the wonderful San Francisco Center for the Book, where book geeks like me are welcomed and encouraged by the generous staff and talented teachers. Any resemblance between SFCB and my own fictional BABA is entirely coincidental. I'm also indebted once again to book artist Wendy Poma for her help and inspiration.

I am grateful to my plot group, Susan Mallery, Maureen Child, Christine Rimmer, and Teresa Southwick, for their friendship, advice, and support. Great thanks, also, to my literary agent, Christina Hogrebe of the Jane Rotrosen Agency, for her guidance and enthusiasm, and to Executive Editor Ellen Edwards, for her encouragement and consummate skill with words.

Finally, I owe a debt of gratitude to the librarians and booksellers around the country who continue to spread the word that Brooklyn and bookbinders are hot stuff, indeed. Thanks to you all.

Chapter 1

Layla Fontaine, Executive Artistic Director of the Bay Area Book Arts Center, was tall, blond, and strikingly beautiful, with a hair-trigger temper and a reputation for ruthlessness. Some in the book community called her a malevolent shark. Others disagreed, insisting that calling her a shark only served to tarnish the reputation of decent sharks everywhere.

Since I had business with the shark, I arrived at the book center early and parked my car in the adjacent lot. Grabbing the small package I'd brought, I climbed out of the car and immediately started to shiver. It was dusk and the March air in San Francisco was positively frigid. I seemed to be in the direct path of a brisk wind that whooshed straight off the bay over AT&T Park and up Potrero Hill. Huddling inside my down vest, I quickly jogged to the front entrance of the book center and climbed the stairs.

I almost whimpered as I stepped inside the warm interior and rubbed my arms to rid myself of the chills. But looking around, I grinned with giddy excitement. It was the first night of my latest bookbinding class and I, Brooklyn Wainwright, Super Bookbinder, was like a kid on the first day of grammar school. A nerdy kid, of course—one who actually looked forward to spending the day in school. I couldn't help myself. This place was a veritable shrine to paper and books and bookbinding arts, and I had to admit, grudgingly, that it was all due to Layla Fontaine.

As head fund-raiser and the public face of the Bay Area Book Arts Center, or BABA, as some affectionately called it, Layla had her finger—and usually a few other body parts—on the pulse of every well-heeled person in the San Francisco Bay Area. She was willing to do, say, or promise anything to keep BABA on firm financial ground, no matter how shaky the legalities seemed. Hers was a higher calling, she claimed, right up there with Doctors Without Borders and Save the Children, and anything was fair game in the nonprofit sector. While that might've been true, the fact remained that Layla Fontaine was a snarky, sneaky, notoriously picky, manipulative bitch.

But Layla had one true saving grace, and that was her pure and abiding appreciation of and devotion to books. She had an extensive collection of antiquarian treasures that she displayed regularly in BABA's main gallery. And miracle of miracles, she'd managed to turn BABA into a profitable enterprise and a prestigious place to visit and contribute one's time and money to.

Most important, she had brought me on staff to teach bookbinding classes here, and she'd also hired me privately to do restoration work on her own books. In exchange, I suppose I was willing to give her the benefit of the doubt when it came to her questionable behavior. Yes, I could be bought. I wasn't ashamed to admit it. After all, a girl's got to make a living.

I walked through the foyer, where artists' brochures and postcards and flyers and all the local free press papers were stacked, then entered the main gallery. The room was large with a dramatically high ceiling and skylights. Two ramps led down to the lower gallery, where glass display cases showed off the best works of the visiting bookbinders and artists. In the center was an unusual mix of ancient art and new technology, including an antique printing press and a large freestanding eighteenth-century cast-iron paper cutter with a thirty-inch blade. Next to these was BABA's latest acquisition, a computerized guillotine that could cut cleanly through six inches of compacted paper.

The lower gallery was surrounded by the upper level, conveniently referred to as the upper gallery, which ran the perimeter of the room. Here were the main display walls and two large alcoves filled with bookshelves and comfortable seating areas.

Strolling through the upper gallery, I spied Naomi Fontaine, Layla's niece and BABA's facilities coordinator. She was busy assembling a new display of children's vintage pop-up books.

To my left, on the main display wall, a number of darkly dramatic, steampunk-style wood-block prints were hung. On another wall, tall shelves of beautifully bound books were available to study or purchase.

Off the main room were three long halls that angled off like spokes on a bicycle wheel. Down these halls were classrooms, offices, mudrooms, a number of individual workrooms, the printing press room, and several smaller galleries.

"Hi, Naomi," I called out. "Is Layla in her office?"

She bared her teeth at me. "She's in there and she's in rare form today. Good luck."

"Thanks for the heads-up," I said, wondering, not for the first time, why Naomi Fontaine stayed with BABA. She would never get the respect she deserved from her aunt Layla and would always stand in her shadow. Naomi was a true bluestocking who, in another era, might've been just as happy as a cloistered nun. She was pretty in an understated way, and talented enough, but she was a mouse. Shy and a bit obsequious, she lacked the dynamic personality it took to appeal to the high-society types with whom her aunt Layla hobnobbed.

Still, it was wise to keep on Naomi's good side. She was

the person to talk to if you wanted to get anything done here. If Layla was the brains behind BABA, Naomi was its heart and soul. She had her faults, but everything ran smoothly because of her.

I crossed the gallery and walked down the north hall toward Layla's office. I was anxious to show her the restoration work I'd done on a rotted-out copy of a nineteenth-century illustrated edition of Charles Dickens's *Oliver Twist*. She'd given me the decrepit old book to restore, and if I said so myself, I'd done a fabulous job for her.

Layla planned to use the book as the centerpiece for BABA's two-week-long celebration of the one hundred seventy-fifth anniversary of Dickens's publication of *Oliver Twist*. She was calling the festival "Twisted." Layla was always throwing lavish parties to celebrate obscure anniversaries such as this one. Anything to drum up sponsors and visitors to BABA.

I was grateful for the work and figured that as long as Layla was willing to provide me with books to restore, I was willing to believe she had a heart buried somewhere in that size double-D chest of hers.

As I reached the end of the long hall leading to Layla's office, I could hear voices, loud ones. Her door was closed but the angry shouts penetrated through the thick wood. I was about to knock when the door flew open. I jumped back and missed being hit by an inch.

"You'll be sorry you crossed me, you bitch," a furious man declared, then stormed out of Layla's office. I stood flat against the wall as a handsome, well-dressed Asian man stomped past me, down the hall, across the gallery, and out the front door.

I took a moment to catch my breath, then peeked around the doorway to make sure Layla was all right. She sat at her desk, casually applying red lipstick and looking as if she didn't have a care in the world.

"Are you okay?" I asked.

She glanced at me over her mirror. "Of course. Why wouldn't I be?"

"That guy sounded like he wanted to wring your neck."

"Men." She waved away my concern, swept her cosmetics into her top drawer, then stood and rounded her desk. She was dressed in an impossibly tight, short black skirt and a crisp white blouse unbuttoned to show off her impressive cleavage. In her five-inch black patent leather stilettos, she looked like an overeducated Pussycat Doll.

"Give me the book," she demanded.

I hesitated, feeling a bit like a mother wavering at the thought of handing a beloved child over to a stern East German nanny. Yes, the woman might make sure the child was fed, but she wouldn't *love* it.

"Brooklyn." She snapped her fingers.

I don't know why I faltered. The book belonged to Layla. Aside from that, she was my employer. I exhaled heavily and carefully handed her the wrapped parcel, then had to watch as she ripped the brown paper to shreds to find the *Oliver Twist.*

"Oh, it's perfect," she said greedily as she turned the book over and back. "You did a good job."

"Thank you." *Good?* I did a *great* job. If I said so myself. She'd given it to me in tattered pieces and I'd turned it into a stunning piece of art.

She stared at the elegant spine, studying my work; then she glanced inside and stared at the endpapers. Turning to the title page, she murmured, "No one will ever suspect this isn't a first edition."

I laughed. "Unless they know books."

She glared at me. "Nobody knows that much about books. If I say it's a first edition, then that's what they'll believe."

"Probably," I conceded.

Then she jabbed her finger at the date on the title page. I tried not to wince but I could see the dent she'd made in the thick vellum. "It says right there, printed in 1838. The year he wrote it."

"Right," I said slowly. "But that doesn't mean anything. We both know it's not a first edition."

Her left eye began to twitch and she rubbed her temple as she leaned her hip against the edge of her desk. "True. But no one's going to hear the real story, are they, Brooklyn?"

Her tone was vaguely threatening. Was I missing something?

"Are you saying I should lie about the book?" I asked.

"I'm saying you should keep your mouth shut."

"But what's the big deal? The festival is all about this book, and it's got an interesting history."

To me, anyway. The story went that, back in 1838, Charles Dickens was doing so well with the serialization of *Oliver Twist* that his publisher went behind his back and published the manuscript, using Dickens's pseudonym, "Boz." That first edition included all of the illustrator Cruikshank's drawings.

Dickens was displeased because he'd intended to use his real name once the book was published. He was also unhappy with one of Cruikshank's drawings in the book, calling it too sentimental, according to some accounts. He insisted that the publisher pull that edition and revise it to his specifications. It was done within the week.

A true first edition of *Oliver Twist*, written under the pseudonym of Boz, with Cruikshank's unauthorized drawings, was beyond rare.

Layla's book had Charles Dickens listed as the author on the title page, and the Cruikshank illustration was missing. So while the book was valuable, it didn't count as an official first edition.

"I don't want you going around telling people about this book, do you hear me?" Layla pushed away from the desk, drew herself up to her full height, and glared down at me.

She was only an inch or so taller than I, but it was a good attempt at intimidation. "For the purposes of the festival, this book is a first edition, got it? I want to rack up some high bids on this baby."

I looked at her sideways. "So you want me to lie."

"Isn't that what I just said?"

"It just seems like the real story would be more interesting to people."

"Jesus, do you ever give up?" she asked. "Nobody cares about your stupid book theories, and if you like working here, you'll say what I tell you to say. *Capice?*"

I sucked my cheeks in, something I tended to do whenever I wanted to chew somebody's ass but needed to hold my tongue instead. After a long moment, I gritted my teeth and said, "Got it."

Casually slapping the exquisite nineteenth-century volume against her hand, she said, "That's what I thought you'd say."

"You know what?" I turned toward the door. "I've got to go get my classroom set up."

She pointed her finger at me as though it were a gun and she'd just pulled the trigger. "Good idea."

I rushed out of her office and made it back to the central gallery before the urge to strangle her took over.

Naomi caught one look at my face and snorted. "Glad I'm not the only one she's picking on today."

"Yeah, lucky me." As I headed toward my classroom, I couldn't decide what annoyed me more: the fact that Layla hadn't given me enough props for my work, or the idea that I should lie about the whole first edition issue. The lack of props won out. I'd done a spectacular job of restoring the book but she was just too screwed up and snotty to say so, more than that pitiful "good job" comment she'd grudgingly given me. I would have to think twice if she offered me any more restoration work.

But Layla was forgotten as a sudden bone-deep chill

settled over me, as if someone had just walked on my grave. My mother used to say that, but I never knew what it meant until this moment.

"Well, if it isn't the black widow herself," a woman said in a familiar high, whiny tone that was purported to cause dogs' ears to bleed. "Wherever she goes, somebody dies."

Minka LaBoeuf.

My worst nightmare. To think I'd been so happy to be here only a few minutes ago.

I turned and glared at her. "So maybe you ought to leave, just to be on the safe side."

"Very funny," she said, tossing back her overly processed, stringy black hair. "I should think they'd be afraid to let you in here with your record."

I ignored that comment, just as I ignored the cheap, fuzzy black angora sweater she wore that was causing tiny black hairs to stick in unattractive clumps on her face and neck. "What are you doing here?"

"I'm an instructor now," she said, jutting her pointy chin out smugly. "I ran into Layla at the book fair in Edinburgh and she offered me the position."

"What?" I might've shrieked the word. I couldn't help it. Minka was the world's worst bookbinder. She destroyed books. She was like the bubonic plague to books. Why in the world would anyone hire her to teach bookbinding? "You've got to be kidding."

But she was no longer looking at me. I turned at the sound of scuffling footsteps behind me and saw Ned, the printing press guy, frowning at us. And when Ned frowned, what little forehead he had completely disappeared. He wasn't completely unattractive, if you liked that haunted, confused look in a guy. Minka did, apparently.

"Hi, Ned," Minka said, her eyelashes flitting rapidly.

"Huh," he said as he scratched his pasty white muscle-free arm.

Was Minka actually flirting with Ned? I'd been teaching classes here for years and I'd seen Ned maybe four times. Each time, he'd said exactly one word to me. That word was *Huh*. Seriously, that was his only vocabulary.

Ned could work magic with the ancient printing press BABA used, but that's where his social skills ended. He was probably a sweet guy, but he worried me. Today he wore a T-shirt that read "Can't Sleep. Clowns Will Eat Me." That might've been funny, but I was pretty sure Ned believed it.

"I like your shirt," Minka simpered.

"Huh," he said, then turned and walked away, disappearing down the hall.

"Nice talking to you, Ned," I said, but I wasn't sure he heard me.

Minka's snarl returned, signaling she was ready to go another round with me. But it was not to be.

"Minka, darling," Layla cried as she rushed forward and gave Minka a big hug. "I thought I heard your voice."

Not surprising, since yapping puppies in the next county could have heard Minka's voice.

"I'm so pleased you could join our faculty," Layla gushed, winding her arm through Minka's. Then she turned to me and her green eyes gleamed with amusement. "Don't tell me you two know each other. Isn't that perfect? Brooklyn, you'll be able to show Minka around. I know you'll make her feel comfortable and welcome here."

Minka smirked in victory. Over her shoulder, I saw Naomi roll her eyes. Good to know it wasn't just me who thought that would have been a really bad idea.

I gave Minka a look that made it clear that hell would freeze over before I would show her anything but the back door. My former good mood plummeted even further as I realized I'd have to spend the next three weeks trying to avoid both Layla's caustic bitchiness and Minka's toxic stupidity.

I thought of Minka's first words a minute ago, about people dying whenever I was in the vicinity. I hoped her words wouldn't come back to haunt us all, but with so many volatile personalities to deal with, I had to wonder how long it would be before one of us turned up dead.

I just hoped it wouldn't be me.

Chapter 2

Avoiding Minka's gaze, I turned to Layla and tried to smile. "I'll have to take a rain check on that tour. Right now, I need to set up my classroom. See you all later."

I walked with purpose across the gallery and down the south hall to my classroom. I hoped I'd be able to avoid Minka for the next three weeks but she was like a noxious cloud. Really. If I got within a few hundred feet of her, I tended to suffer flulike symptoms. I supposed I'd be forced to hide out in my classroom from now on, like a sniveling coward.

I stopped at the glass display case outside my room and found the posted schedule of classes for the month. Sure enough, Karalee Pines's name was crossed out and Minka's name was written in. She would be teaching a three-hour limp-binding class two nights a week for the next month. My own comprehensive bookbinding class was four nights a week for three weeks. The possibility of seeing her six times in the next month made my head hurt.

Safe in my classroom, I unpacked my tools, then placed the stacks of decorative cloth I'd brought on the side table. I'd found some beautiful printed paper at the Edinburgh Book Fair, from a vendor who specialized in handmade Japanese prints. These would be used by my students for book covers and endpapers.

Looking around, I took a quick inventory of the book

presses and punching jigs. The jigs were clever, handmade contraptions made with two pieces of wood screwed together to form a V-shaped cradle. A thin space at the apex of the vee allowed for the pointed end of a sharp punching awl to make sewing holes in folded signatures.

There were six standard cast-iron table presses, plus stacks of twenty or thirty iron weights of different sizes and shapes. The students would have to share the equipment, but that was rarely a problem since everyone worked at their own pace.

The door opened and Karalee walked in and closed the door. She was BABA's book arts manager and, along with Mark Mayberry, aka Marky May, the print arts manager, was part of the small permanent staff at BABA. They designed and ran the two main curriculums offered here.

"Hi, Karalee," I said with a tight smile. I didn't know her all that well, but we'd always had a good business friendship. Until tonight, anyway.

"Brooklyn, I'm so sorry," she said. "I didn't know Layla hired Minka until this morning. I was supposed to teach that limp-binding class, but Layla said she promised it to Minka. I swear, if I had any real authority, I would tell her to take this job and shove it."

"You can't do that, Karalee," I said. "It's okay."

"Well, if I'd known sooner, I would've tried to change her mind." She shrugged helplessly. "I've worked with Minka before and she's a mess."

"That's putting it mildly." But I was grateful to know I wasn't the only one who thought so. I cleaned a bunch of glue brushes in the sink and organized them in glass jars as we talked.

She tapped her nails on the worktable, plainly uncomfortable. "I'm just worried we'll lose students because of her."

I choked out a laugh. "You'd lose me if I had to take a class from her."

"You and me both," she admitted. "Damn it. Well, I don't want to lose you, so let me know if I can do anything to make things easier for you."

"Don't worry about it," I said. "I'll just stay close to my classroom and try to avoid her."

"That's so unfair," she said, nervously straightening the pile of colorful papers I'd fanned out across the side table a minute ago. "But look, I mean it. I want you to be happy. So just come running if you need anything."

I smiled at her. "Thanks, Karalee."

She walked out and I continued to clean up, then checked the room's supply of polyvinyl acetate, or PVA glue. This was the glue of choice for most bookbinders because it was water soluble and strong, while it allowed for flexibility and adjustments until it was left to dry completely.

"Meow."

I looked down, surprised to see a big yellow cat staring up at me. "Hey, Baba, how'd you get in here?"

"Meow."

I knelt down to stroke his lovely thick coat as he rubbed himself against my ankles. Baba Ram Dass was his full name and he was BABA's official mascot. The cat had been in residence for as long as I'd been coming here.

"You're welcome to stay until someone starts sneezing," I said.

"Meow." But his look said, *I'll stay as long as I feel like it.*

"I think we have a deal," I said, standing up. I grabbed a sponge and wiped down the sink counter in the corner as my first students began to file in. They greeted me, then chose seats around the high, wide worktable that dominated the center of the room.

Within ten minutes, the table was filled with twelve chattering students who talked among themselves and fiddled with the tools I'd laid out for them.

I introduced myself and gave a brief background of my

bona fides. "Okay, that's me. Let's go around the room and have you give your names and backgrounds. And tell us all what you hope to get out of the class."

Five of the students were graphic artists: Sylvia, Tessa, Kylie, Bobby, and Dale. I recognized Tessa and Kylie from previous classes they'd taken with me.

There were three librarians: Marianne and Jennifer, who worked together at the main library in Daly City, and Mitchell, a muscular, tattooed Desert Storm veteran who had returned home from the war and decided to become a librarian because, as he said with a shrug, "I like books."

"You've come to the right place," I said, chuckling.

Mitchell added that his sister was a librarian and she thought books and binding would be good therapy for him after the war. "She was right. I've got the books part down. Now I'd like to try my hand at binding."

The next person was Cynthia Hardesty, a tall, buxom brunette who introduced both herself and her husband, Tom.

"We've been on the board of directors here for three years," she said. "Layla finally insisted we take your class. She holds you in such high regard."

"Yes, my dear, she thinks you're a pip," Tom said. He was tall and lean, though not quite as tall as his wife, with thinning hair and a bit of an old-world aristocracy vibe about him. I pictured him in an ascot and smoking jacket, drinking cognac with Lord Peter Wimsey or Jay Gatsby.

"Isn't that nice to hear?" I said, even though my internal BS meter was ticking loudly, indicating an overload of crap, for sure. Especially coming from Layla. And why hadn't I been alerted that I would have two board members in my class? It meant I would have to be on my best behavior and that was never fun.

The last two to speak were best friends, Whitney and Gina, who talked over each other as they explained that they were always looking for interesting things to do together.

"We're newbies but we'll try to keep up," Gina said.

"I think it'll be fun," Whitney added brightly.

"I hope we'll all have a lot of fun," I said, then began to explain how the class would proceed each week.

On Mondays, we would start with a very brief explanation of the type of binding we'd be constructing. Each student would create a miniature version of the real thing. I held up some samples of the tiny three-inch books we'd make, and got "oohs" and "ahhs" from the women. The little books were always a big hit. By Thursday night, they would each have a larger finished journal in the same style. At the end of the three-week course, they all would've made six handmade books.

"How exciting," Whitney said.

Gina nodded vigorously. "I'm totally psyched."

"Good." I smiled at them, appreciating their fresh view of things. It would be a good motivator for everyone else, including me.

"This week, we'll construct a textblock of ten sections of sheets sewn through the fold onto three linen tapes and cased in cloth-covered binder's board. Any questions?"

"Uh, yeah," Whitney said. "Will you be speaking English anytime soon?"

We all laughed. I did tend to get caught up in the jargon sometimes. "I'll try to remember to explain things, but just in case, I've included a glossary of terms in each of your packets. You'll probably want to keep it close by for easy reference. Especially when I blather on about the lapped-component case binding, or when we discuss double-folio colored endsheets and half-cloth bindings. All that fun stuff."

Amid more scattered laughter (for which I was pathetically grateful), I began to go over the tools I'd given them, explaining how each one fit in the process of creating a book. Grabbing an essential tool, I held it up to show them. It was lightweight, about eight inches long, flat and white, and looked like a fancy tongue depressor.

"Okay, I'll just say this right out," I said. "This is called a bone folder."

There were the predictable giggles and snickers.

"Go ahead and laugh, get it out of your systems," I said, waiting for the reactions to die down. "It's a stupid name, but it makes sense. The tool is often made of bone, which makes it lightweight and durable. And it's used to crease a fold. Bone. Folder. Get it? If you all say it a few times, it won't sound funny anymore."

After the laughter faded, I went on to discuss the advantage of metal-edge rulers over wooden ones, and then I began my riveting discussion of the hazards of glue and the importance of recognizing paper fibers and grain direction. The grain should always run parallel to the spine of the book, I explained. Otherwise, the folds would appear ragged and uneven instead of smooth and rounded.

"Seriously," I said. "Fiber alignment can be very sexy. The whole subject gives me happy chills."

There were more chuckles and everyone seemed to relax a little more. I noticed that Baba the cat had taken up residence on the front counter and was curled up next to my soft leather tool bag.

Since the room had its own cast-iron paper cutter in the back corner, I gathered everyone around the machine for a demonstration. Depending on the way the paper was cut, a bookbinder could produce either a smooth edge to the paper or a ragged, uneven edge, based on the style of book one wanted to create.

As everyone took their seats back at the worktable, there was a knock at the classroom door.

"Knock, knock," Layla called out, then walked into the

room. She was followed by a petite blond woman I'd never seen before.

"I hate to interrupt the class," Layla said, "but I've brought you another student."

I secured the heavy, razor-sharp handle of the paper cutter and made my way to the front of the room. I didn't know anyone else had signed up for the class, but the more, the merrier.

"Brooklyn Wainwright," Layla said formally, "this is my dear friend and associate, Alice Fairchild."

A dear friend of Layla's? That was worrisome. But I smiled and shook hands with her anyway.

Her hand was small and smooth, and I felt like a clumsy giant next to her. "Nice to meet you, Alice."

"Alice has been with us over a month now," Layla said, her tone hushed and reverential. "She's our assistant director in charge of fund-raising and I don't know how we ever got along without her. She's doing a fabulous job."

"Congratulations," I said.

"Thank you." Alice's face was significantly more pale than it had been a few seconds ago. She continued to shake my hand vigorously, then realized what she was doing and pulled away. "It's great to meet you. Sorry for shaking your hand off. My stomach nerves are bouncing off the walls."

"Oh, don't worry about the class," I assured her. "We all go at our own pace."

"Oh, no, I'm excited about the class. I've never made a book before. No, I'm actually nervous about a new account I'm pitching tomorrow for the center. They could be a great asset. Matching funds, the whole deal." She whipped around and looked at Layla, then back at me. "Why am I going on and on? I warned Layla I'd start blathering."

Layla smiled. "You're not blathering."

Alice shook her head. "You're very kind, but Stuart says I talk too much when I'm nervous and he's right, of course.

Stuart's my fiancé." She held up her hand and wiggled her finger, where a large and absolutely stunning diamond ring twinkled and dazzled.

"Wow, that's a beautiful ring," I said.

"Thanks," Alice said, gazing fondly at her ring. "Stuart is still back in Atlanta, closing up his office. He'll move out here next month. He's great. And he's so smart. And when he says I talk too much, he's right. I, well . . . I'm doing it again." She laughed.

Layla smiled indulgently. "You're doing fine."

I wondered if my eyes were as big and round as they felt. I'd never seen Layla actually dote on anyone before. But I couldn't blame her. Alice was adorable, despite being friends with Layla.

"No worries," I said, and meant it. "We're glad to have you."

"I'll try not to talk everyone's ears off," Alice said earnestly. "But my nerves. Oy."

I laughed. I couldn't help it. She was sweet. I wanted to take her shopping and buy her a cup of hot cocoa. And it was weird, but I had an urge to rescue her from Layla's influence, just as I'd wanted to rescue the *Oliver Twist* from Layla's greedy paws earlier.

Layla, all cheery and upbeat now, said, "I can't tell you how thrilled we are to have Alice working at BABA. She's already highly respected in the arts fund-raising world, so now I want her to learn every aspect of the book world and BABA's place in it. She's met a few of the teachers, but this will be her first classroom experience. I thought I'd start her off at the top with your excellent master class."

"Thank you, Layla," I said, my BS meter still ticking at full capacity. "That's very kind of you to say."

Layla beamed at my humble appreciation of her words. I supposed, or hoped, that this was her way of extending a peace offering. I had no choice but to play her game, seeing as how she signed my checks.

"I'll leave Alice in your good hands, then," Layla said, and gave the class a queenly wave before whisking herself away.

As the door closed, I happened to notice Tom Hardesty staring at Layla's backside. Were those stars in his eyes? He looked like a teenager about to swoon over a rock star.

I stole a glance at Cynthia, whose look of sheer contempt was quickly replaced by mild interest.

Well, that was intriguing. Cynthia didn't seem to like Layla at all. It was no wonder, given the way her husband practically drooled over the woman. Very interesting, I thought. No, wait, it wasn't interesting at all. The last thing I wanted was to get involved in boardroom theatrics or BABA politics. And it could be job suicide if Tom or Cynthia knew I'd even noticed their reactions to Layla.

Alice looked up at me. "Thank you so much for letting me take your class."

"It's my pleasure. Always room for one more."

"Oh, I don't know about that, but I appreciate it. Layla can be a bit of a bulldozer, but I promise I won't slow the class down. I studied art and I love books, so I'm fascinated to learn more."

"Great," I said with a nod. "This is the perfect place to learn more. I'm sure you'll do fine."

"Thanks," she said, and leaned close to speak quietly. "But in the interest of full disclosure, I should warn you that ever since I moved here, my stomach has been going bonkers. I've been getting tested for everything but the doctors don't know what's going on." She rubbed her belly for emphasis. "I'm just telling you because I tend to run off to the ladies' room with alarming regularity. I'll try not to be too disruptive about all the comings and goings."

"Good to know," I said, biting back a smile. At least she was honest, and I appreciated her self-deprecating wit. And now that I'd had a moment to study her more closely, the name Alice suited her perfectly, from her demure white blouse to her straight blond hair and velvet headband.

Her cell phone beeped and she jumped, then checked the screen. She shook her head and shot me a beleaguered look. "Sorry. Stuart and I text incessantly. We're having wedding issues."

"You have my complete sympathy," I said, patting her shoulder. I handed her a set of tools and pointed to an empty chair. "Why don't you sit over there next to Tom, and we'll get started with sewing signatures?"

One hour later, I walked the periphery of the classroom, helping those who were struggling with the kettle stitch, the intricate nineteenth-century thread pattern used to sew linen tapes to signature pages. For some, the tricky part was drawing the thread through the paper without actually piercing the linen strips that would hold everything together. For others, it was keeping the thread tension even, as they added a new set of signatures to the previous one.

"Ack!" Gina cried. "I'm never going to get this."

"Yes, you are," I said, trying not to cringe at her wobbly stitches. "It's just a little tricky because the book we're making is so small. When we start on the journals, you'll have an easier time."

"I hope so," she said, unconvinced.

"Don't forget, you need to link each new stitch to the previous section's stitches."

"Oh, God, whatever that means," she moaned.

I went over to my bag and pulled out a thick manila file folder of reference material. After a quick riffling, I found what I was looking for: a close-up photograph of someone's hand, sewing the stitch.

"Oh," she said when I showed her the photo. "That's what it's supposed to look like?"

"Yes." Exactly as I'd showed everyone twenty minutes ago, but I didn't say that. For a lot of people, this was complicated stuff. I handed her the photo to use as a guide.

"It's pretty." She stared at the picture. "This helps a lot."

"Good. Hold on to that for as long as you need it."

"Thanks."

There was a low-level buzz and Cynthia Hardesty grabbed her cell phone. "I've got to take a quick break," she said, staring at her smart phone as she pushed her fingers across the screen. "I need to take care of some personal business."

Except she called it *bidness*. I wasn't sure why. Maybe she thought it sounded cool, but it really didn't. One thing that bothered me was that she didn't seem to take the class seriously. She was much too busy with her *bidness*.

"Would you mind if I ran out for a minute, too?" Alice said. "I've finished my sewing and I'm afraid Stuart might be asleep if I wait much longer."

"No problem," I said, taking a quick look at her stitching job. "You're doing really well."

"Thanks," she said, with a note of pride. "Be right back."

"Oh, can I be excused, too?" Whitney asked, her arm bobbing up like an overeager student's. She nudged Gina. "I need to make those reservations, remember?"

"Oh, right," Gina said, and winked at me. "She's got a hot date Friday night."

"Shh, don't jinx it," Whitney said.

"Go ahead," I said, checking my watch. "I need to talk to someone down the hall. But I should be right back."

"Are we taking a break?" Marianne asked, looking up for the first time.

"We'll be taking an official thirty-minute dinner break in a while, but if anyone needs a minute right now, go ahead. For those staying, please continue to work on sewing your signature pages."

"Before you go," Jennifer said, "can you show me how that loopy knot thing works again? I'm all thumbs."

"Yes." I stopped at her station and demonstrated the weaver's knot again, pointing out the importance of kinking the linen thread. Then I went around the room and showed each student the kink in the thread, just to be sure everyone was on base.

After Jennifer assured me she could do it on her own, I left the room and headed for Layla's office. For the last hour, my mind had been fretting about our argument over the *Oliver Twist*. I'd appreciated her making nice when she brought Alice into the class, but I was still anxious.

I'd formed a plan. I would ask her if I could buy back the book. Or, if that didn't appeal to her, I could call Ian McCullough, the Covington Library's head curator and an old college friend of my brother Austin—and my ex-fiancé. And when I say *fiancé*, I mean we liked each other a lot and tried to pretend it was love, but we both knew it wasn't. We're still great friends. Ian might have had a way of tracking down an actual true first edition of *Oliver Twist*. If he was successful, the Covington might consider it good publicity to donate the book to the Twisted festival auction. It went against the grain to help Layla Fontaine, but the last thing I needed was to have her blackball me in the book arts community because, God forbid, I had too many scruples.

Scruples. How boring!

I skirted the gallery, dark now except for the few pin spots illuminating the wood-block prints and a faint stream of moonlight seeping through the skylight.

From across the wide space, I saw a figure silhouetted against the window of the front door. It was probably one of my students making her phone call, but I couldn't tell which one. I didn't see any of the others who'd taken a break. They might've gone outside or down to the mudroom for some privacy. It seemed awfully quiet in here, even with two classes in session. Naomi's pop-up book display created odd shadows on the lower gallery wall. I shivered and wondered why they didn't turn up the heat a little.

The long north hall leading to Layla's office was even darker than the gallery. The lights were off, which was odd. Someone from the staff always worked late when classes were held, but both Karalee's and Marky's offices were dark. I had to feel my way along the wall as I walked.

I thought about Ned, who ran and maintained the printing press. He never seemed to leave and often closed up on the nights when classes were in session. Did he live in one of the dark rooms down the hall? Maybe it was the absence of light that made me nervous, but I couldn't help thinking that Ned was one of those guys you heard about on the news. *He was quiet and kept his yard clean. Who knew he'd stored the bodies of six ex-wives in his freezer?* You could never be sure about guys like Ned.

That wasn't fair. Ned was a nice guy. It was just too dark in here and my thoughts were turning morbid.

As I got closer to Layla's office, I could make out a thin line of light under her closed door. I hoped that meant she was still working in there. Maybe she didn't realize the hall lights were off.

"Layla?" I called.

There was no answer. Perhaps she'd already gone home. I took one more step and nearly tumbled over something on the floor.

I flailed my arms out to balance myself, then found the wall and leaned against it. "Damn. Who leaves stuff in the middle of the hall?"

I didn't know what it was, but it was something substantial. A bundle of laundry, maybe? I reached down to try to move it and heard a groan.

It wasn't a bundle of anything. It was a body.

Chapter 3

"Oh, my God." I grabbed my phone from my pocket and dialed 911. When the dispatcher answered, I cried, "Somebody's been hurt or—or . . ."

They're dead. I didn't say it out loud. I'd heard a groan. They had to be alive.

"I need your location, ma'am," the woman said.

I gave her the information.

"Are they breathing?" she asked.

"So far. I'll check to make sure." Duh, good idea. It was still so dark, I could barely see my own hands in front of my face, but my eyes were beginning to adjust. I hunched down and felt an arm, covered by a soft wool sweater, indicating it was probably a woman. Moving my hand up her arm, I felt her shoulder, then her neck. There was a weak pulse. She was still breathing.

"She's alive, but very weak," I said. "Hurry, please."

"We have a squad car in the area, ma'am," the dispatcher said. "Please don't panic. They're less than two minutes away."

"I'm not panicking," I said, standing. "I just can't see anything. Are you sending an ambulance, too?"

"Yes, ma'am. I'll stay on the line until the police arrive."

"Thanks."

The door to another office opened suddenly. Naomi peered into the hall. "What's going on out here?"

A sliver of light from her desk lamp cast her in shadow and did nothing to light up the situation in the hall.

"What are you doing in there?" I asked.

"I'm trying to work," she said, her tone petulant.

"Really sorry to bother you, but somebody passed out in the hall." Hey, I could be cranky, too. She wasn't the only one whose peace and quiet had been disturbed. "Can you turn on some more lights? I can't see a thing."

Naomi didn't move, just stared at the body. "What happened?"

"How should I know? Turn on some lights. This woman fainted or something." I was getting crabbier by the minute. I hated stumbling over bodies.

"Oh, my God." Naomi fumbled for the light switch on the wall outside her office door, but nothing happened. "Sorry, I guess the hall light's burned out. I'll have to get it fixed."

She flipped her office light on and opened the door all the way, and the hall was illuminated. She tried to open Layla's door, but it was locked. She skirted the body and tried Karalee's office. It was unlocked so she shoved the door open and turned on the light.

"How's that?"

"Much better." As I said it, I could hear a siren wailing in the distance. "Police should be here any second now."

"Is she breathing?" Naomi asked, still staring at the body.

"Barely," I said.

Naomi wrung her hands. "It's a good thing you found her. You probably saved her life."

"I just happened to come along," I said modestly, clasping my hands together. They felt tacky. I held them up to the light, then wished I hadn't.

Blood. My stomach twirled and my head started to spin. I really hated blood. "Idiot," I muttered. I couldn't help it, though. The sight of blood made me sick. I took deep breaths and stared at the woman on the floor. Since she was bleeding, she must've hit her head on something. Something sharp or hard enough to draw blood.

As I stared more closely at the woman, my insides took an even more unwelcome dip. That fuzzy black angora sweater looked alarmingly familiar.

"Oh, no." I inched back until my butt hit the wall.

"What's wrong?" Naomi demanded.

Icy chills slithered down my spine, worse than I'd ever felt before. God help me, I had just saved the life of Minka LaBoeuf.

The blast of sirens brought everyone out of the classrooms. I managed to keep the hall clear while Naomi ran to the front door and led the two police officers through the gallery to the hall. One officer looked around while the other knelt and checked for a pulse.

"Watch out," I muttered. "There's blood."

The officer kneeling looked up at me. "You found her?"

I nodded, then shivered and looked away.

"Okay, good job." He grabbed his walkie-talkie and called for an ambulance. He was answered by a squawk, then the dispatcher responded, "Ambulance en route."

"I'll wait up front," I said, and walked back to the gallery, where all the lights were now glaringly bright. Alice rushed over and met me.

"What happened?" she whispered. She looked even more pale than when she'd first showed up in class. "Is somebody sick?"

"Somebody's been hurt," I said.

Tom, Cynthia, and Gina crowded behind Alice.

"Who is it?" Tom asked, staring past me into the hall.

"Another instructor," I said, unable to utter Minka's name out loud.

"It's Minka LaBoeuf," Naomi announced from behind me. "Brooklyn saved her life."

I winced. "No, I didn't."

"Yes, you did," Naomi insisted, then added, "Brooklyn found her and called nine-one-one. Look, she's got Minka's blood all over her hands."

Oh, great. I knew she meant that in a nice way, but it really didn't sound good.

"I . . . I need to wash my hands," I whispered, staring at the dried streaks of blood.

"How did you get her blood on your hands?" Cynthia asked, her eyes focused on my outstretched hands.

Her tone carried a strong hint of accusation and I was about to shoot back something when Alice took hold of my arm and said gently, "Let's go wash your hands."

Just then, the tall, good-looking Hispanic officer whose badge read "Ortiz" zeroed in on me. "You found the victim."

"Yes, I did," I said. *Soldier up, Wainwright,* I thought, taking a deep breath and letting it out slowly. "She was passed out in the hall. I stumbled over her on my way to Layla Fontaine's office and called the police."

"Who's Layla Fontaine?"

"She runs this place," I said. "Her office is at the end of the hall. I think she must've gone home already."

"What do you do here?" he asked, taking notes.

"I'm just one of the instructors." I waved my hand toward Naomi. "This is Naomi Fontaine. She's the facilities coordinator for the center."

"But—but I didn't do anything," Naomi declared, her wide-eyed gaze whipping back and forth between Officer Ortiz and me. "I opened my office door and Minka was lying there, and Brooklyn was kneeling over her."

I shot her a look. "They already know that."

"It's okay, ma'am," Ortiz said calmly.

No, it wasn't. Was Naomi deliberately trying to throw me under the bus? Whatever happened to me being the big hero, saving Minka's life? You couldn't trust anyone anymore.

"Where's Layla?" Tom asked, looking around.

"She went home," Cynthia said through clenched teeth. "Brooklyn just said that. Try to keep up."

Someone was even crankier than I was.

The cop tending to Minka called from the hallway, "Can somebody turn on the hall light?"

"It's not working," Naomi explained to Ortiz.

He walked a few feet into the hall, stretched his arm up, and tested one of the exposed bulbs by twisting it. The hall filled with light.

"Now that's weird," Gina said, her eyes big and round.

Cynthia frowned in agreement.

Another blast of a siren announced the arrival of the ambulance. Two EMTs rushed through the gallery carrying their packs filled with equipment. I managed to corral the onlookers away from the hall to give the techs enough space to pass through.

Whitney walked over and joined us. "What's going on? I thought I heard a siren. Are we on a break?"

Gina grabbed her arm. "Girl, where were you?"

"I was on the phone," Whitney said defensively, then lowered her voice to add, "That skinny guy let me use one of those storage rooms down the hall so I'd have some privacy."

Was she talking about Ned? I looked around the gallery, but he was nowhere in sight.

"Somebody was attacked while you were gone," Gina whispered excitedly.

"We don't know that," I said quickly.

Officer Ortiz signaled me over. "We'll need to get everyone in one place and start some interviews."

"You can use my classroom," I said, then turned to Gina and Whitney. "Can you help me lead everyone back to the classroom?"

"You bet," Gina said. She gathered my people while Naomi assembled Minka's students and led them back into their classroom. Within five minutes, the area was cleared.

"You should go wash your hands," Alice murmured.

I scowled as I held out my hands. "I completely forgot."

"Do you want me to go with you?"

I smiled in gratitude. "No, thanks. I'll be okay."

In the small bathroom, I let hot water run over my hands. My stomach took another dip as the water turned pale red from Minka's blood. I wasn't sure what made me feel worse, the blood itself or the fact that it was Minka's.

And wasn't that a horribly uncharitable thought? Nevertheless, I used lots of soap and plenty of paper towels to clean and dry my hands completely, then tossed everything in the trash can.

And no, I didn't consider that destroying evidence. I hadn't done anything to Minka but save her life, sort of.

Back in the classroom, Officer Ortiz was trying to keep order.

"If anyone saw or heard anything," he said, "I want to talk to you first."

Everyone began speaking at once.

"Stop," he barked. "Did anyone actually witness anything specifically related to the assault on Ms. LaBoeuf? Raise your hand if you did."

I was impressed that he pronounced Minka's name correctly, although I always preferred to hear her referred to as La Beef. I should've felt more remorse that Minka had been hurt, but I was almost giddy. Not in a happy way, but more of a shaking, freaking-out kind of way. Maybe I was in shock. I'm sure the fact that someone had been attacked a few short minutes before I walked down that hall would sink in later.

Since nobody in the room could offer any real help, Ortiz gave up and passed around a sheet of paper, asking everyone to write down their contact information.

As the students took turns complying with his request, I asked Ortiz where the ambulance would take Minka. He mentioned San Francisco General Hospital, barely a mile away.

Somehow, the name of the hospital made Minka's injury sound even more life-threatening. "I don't suppose she just fainted and hit her head."

It sounded lame, even to me.

"She didn't faint," Ortiz said bluntly.

"Was she attacked?" Whitney asked.

"Are we all in danger?" Marianne asked.

"We don't know yet," Ortiz said. "Until we find out, I strongly suggest that you leave here in pairs or in groups. Don't let anyone walk to their car alone."

"Absolutely not," I assured him.

"Is class canceled?" Dale asked.

I looked at Ortiz, who shrugged. "Doesn't matter to me. We'll be here for a while, asking questions and checking the premises."

I glanced around. "Who wants to keep working?"

I was surprised to see everyone in the room raise their hands.

"I guess we'll keep going," I said.

On the drive home, I tried but failed to find some connection to all the strange events of that night. First, the Asian man had shouted and stormed out of Layla's office, followed by Layla giving me grief over the provenance of the *Oliver Twist*.

Then Minka showed up and ruined my day. And shortly after I started my class, Layla came in to make nice and introduce Alice Fairchild. That's when I saw the pathetic look of adoration on Tom Hardesty's face. Apparently he had the hots for Layla, a fact that hadn't gone unnoticed by his wife, if her expression of sheer contempt was any gauge.

Then there was the attack on Minka. Followed by Naomi's lame attempt to blame me.

And damn it, why did I have to be the one to discover Minka? My shoulders shook with dread as I recalled her statement earlier in the evening.

"Wherever she goes, somebody dies."

And sure enough . . . Okay, she didn't die, but tonight's attack was a little too close for comfort.

And that train of thought had to stop immediately. This was not my fault and I refused to feel guilty about it. And hey, Minka was a rude bitch for bringing it up in the first place.

Still, I wondered what this meant for Minka. How badly had she been injured? It couldn't be a good sign that she hadn't regained consciousness by the time the EMTs took her off to the hospital.

True, I didn't like her. To be honest, I pretty much despised her. She'd been a thorn in my side since the day we met back in graduate school, where she developed an unhealthy crush on my boyfriend and tried to physically injure me badly enough that I would drop out of school. There were other weird and creepy happenings during that time. A dead cat on my porch. My tires slashed. I knew Minka was responsible, but she was never caught.

So as far as I was concerned, Minka was not a nice person. And yes, on occasion, I'd wished her ill.

But the "ill" I'd had in mind was something along the lines of a large potato bug crawling up her nose and laying eggs. I'd never wished for her to die or anything. Basically, I just wanted her to go away and leave me alone.

I turned off Seventh Street onto Brannan, then waited until the oncoming traffic cleared and the security gate in front of my building garage opened. I quickly turned in and parked my car.

I had less stuff to carry upstairs than I'd brought down with me. Naomi had given me a key to my classroom so I could leave some of my cheaper, less dangerous tools and supplies at BABA. I was determined to keep the more lethal and expensive ones in my possession at all times. Thanks to my recent misadventures in Scotland, I hesitated to leave hazardous tools in a place that might not be completely secure.

The block-long brick building I lived in had been built as a corset factory in the twenties and retained some of the old quirks from those days. One of my closets used to be a dumbwaiter with ropes and pulleys to move supplies up and down. It was sealed off now, of course, but it still had steel walls, so I used it to store important documents and the occasional rare book.

Most of the windows in my apartment were original as well, and reinforced with old-fashioned chicken wire. The heating ducts were exposed. Those touches, together with the interior brick walls, gave the large loft-style living space the look and feel of the old factory.

I loved my apartment, loved the South of Market location that was a mix of converted industrial lofts like mine, small ethnic restaurants and shops, and decorators' outlets selling tiles and used brick and wrought iron gates. You could shop and dine in upscale luxury, then turn the corner and find a blighted, burned-out factory, waiting to be bought up and converted. The recession had slowed down some of the growth in the area, but I expected it to pop back any day now.

I stepped inside the service elevator and pushed the button for my floor. This lift was original, as well. It was wide enough to carry industrial-sized machinery, with a four-inch-thick wood plank floor and an iron gate that folded back to let passengers in and out.

As the elevator rumbled to life, I recalled again the angry words of the Asian man who'd left Layla's office earlier that night. Did he have anything to do with the attack on Minka? I should've mentioned him to the police. What if he'd come back to threaten Layla and Minka had interrupted him? I didn't know who he was, but Layla would know. And if she were his real target, I figured she'd be more than glad to give the police his name.

As the elevator stopped and the gate opened, I saw my neighbor Vinamra Patel peeking out her door. Everyone in the building could hear the old-fashioned industrial elevator when it was in motion, so we all kept an eye out for each other.

"Ah, Brooklyn," Vinnie said, waving me over. She wore overalls and high-top Converse All Stars, and her glossy dark hair was braided down her back. "I was hoping it would be you."

"It's me," I said. "What's going on?"

"Guess who went out to dinner tonight?" she said seductively.

"Really?" My eyes must've lit up because she laughed and grabbed my arm.

"Yes. Come in. I have leftovers packed up and ready for you."

I followed her like a puppy. "You guys don't have to feed me every night, you know."

Vinnie grinned. "But you're always so pathetically grateful, it's fun for us."

"Hey, I like to eat," I said in my own defense.

And my favorite neighbors knew it. Vinnie and her girlfriend, Suzie Stein, were wood sculptors. They worked at home, as I usually did, and their loft was filled with huge, oddly shaped hunks of wood and burl. Their sculpting tools of choice were chain saws, and a number of those were mounted on the walls. It was an artistic statement in itself.

Because of the sawdust and mess they made while working, they liked to dine out most nights. And they invariably brought home leftovers for their hungry neighbor. Me.

As I stared at their latest sculpture, a massive wooden pyramid with wings, two cats approached me, purring loudly as they rubbed up against my shins. I bent over to scratch their necks. "Hi, Pookie. Hi, Splinters."

"They love you so much," Vinnie said, smiling fondly at the cats. "You take such good care of them."

My gaze met Pookie's and she cocked her head as if to say, *Aren't you glad I can't talk?*

I sent her a telepathic message. *Yes, ma'am. I am.*

The last time Suzie and Vinnie left town, they'd left me in charge of their beloved pets. One morning, I walked out without feeding them. I remembered by the time I got to the garage and raced back upstairs to set out their food and water. But there had been a moment . . . okay, maybe five or six seconds, during which I'd actually debated whether or not it would make any difference if I waited until that night to feed them. In the end, my guilt got the best of me and I rushed back to meet their needs.

So yeah, I was eternally thankful that cats couldn't talk, because these two would have spilled their guts about my lackadaisical caretaking skills. And Vinnie and Suzie, who loved their pets to distraction, would never give me another bag of leftovers again.

I couldn't live with that.

"Have you seen our new neighbors?" Vinnie asked, shaking me out of my guilt trip.

"No," I said, straightening. "But I heard them moving in. Is it a family?"

"No, two lovely men," she said, her eyes twinkling. "A chef and a hairdresser. Aren't we lucky?"

I laughed. "The perfect neighbors."

"And your new class?" Vinnie said, leading me toward the wide bar that separated their massive living/work space from their kitchen. "It is pleasurable?"

"Oh, it's fine," I said. "But you'll never guess what happened tonight."

Suzie walked into the room just then, cracking her knuckles. "Let me guess. Somebody died."

I was taken aback. "Why would you say that?"

She flopped onto the couch and stretched her arms out. Her spiky platinum hair was still wet from her shower and she wore pink flannel pajamas and Bullwinkle slippers. It was possibly the most feminine outfit I'd ever seen her wear. "Just seems whenever you show up somewhere, somebody gets their bucket kicked."

"Suzie, stop," Vinnie said. "She teases you, Brooklyn."

"That's okay," I muttered. "Minka said the same thing."

"Minka?" Vinnie frowned. "Is she not the girl we revile?"

"She is. But she was attacked at BABA tonight and left unconscious. Somebody must've hit her over the head."

Suzie grimaced. "Oops."

"Yeah," I said, pacing now. "And the weird thing is, Minka said the same thing to me earlier this evening, that whenever I show up, somebody dies."

"You poor thing," Vinnie said. "Suzie, you are not to be mean."

"Hey, I'm a sweetheart," Suzie protested.

"Yes, you are," Vinnie whispered, "but Brooklyn is sensitive because people really do have a tendency to die when she is around."

"I'm standing right here," I reminded her.

Suzie snorted. "Yeah, Vinnie. I think she can hear you."

Vinnie gasped. "Now I am the rude one."

"No, you're never rude," I said.

"As opposed to me," Suzie said, "who's a thoughtless pig."

I laughed, as she'd meant me to, but the merriment didn't last as I explained what had happened. "I was the one who found her. I practically fell on top of her. She was still out cold when the paramedics took her to the hospital."

"Good heavens," Vinnie said.

"Freaky deaky," Suzie said.

"Yeah." I nodded, then shivered. "There was blood, so somebody must've attacked her. I've been trying to figure out who might've done it."

I told them about the irate Asian man, then mentioned how nasty Layla had been to me.

"That woman sounds horrible," Vinnie said as she walked into the kitchen area. "My money is on her as the culprit."

"Yeah, she's pretty awful," I said. "But she gives me work, so I can't be too critical of her. Well, I can, but I shouldn't. You know what I mean."

"Oh, yes," Vinnie said, nodding sagely. She opened the refrigerator and pulled out a shopping bag.

"Anyway, I stumbled over Minka on my way to see Layla, to apologize for our disagreement. I don't want her to be pissed off at me."

"Oh, balls," Suzie said. "Why should you care? She's a bitch."

"Language, Suzie," Vinnie chided. "But, Brooklyn, Suzie has a point. Why must you be the one to apologize to this foul woman?"

"I just want everyone to be happy," I said. Then I saw Suzie's eyes widen in horror, so I played back what I'd said. "Oh, dear God, I'm channeling my mother."

Vinnie nodded. "Yes, but your mother is a lovely woman."

I shook my head and tried to get back on track. "What I meant was, I wanted to make nice with Layla so she'd be happy and continue to give me work."

Suzie shrugged. "Can't blame you for that."

I sat on the edge of the cushy chair across from Suzie. "But Layla wasn't even in her office, and then I ended up saving Minka's life."

"Wow," Suzie said. "Bad luck. For her, I mean. Because, you know, she owes you big-time now."

"She doesn't owe me anything."

"Yes, Brooklyn, she now owes you her life," Vinnie explained. "This will not make her happy."

I made a face. "No kidding."

"No good deed goes unpunished," Suzie warned. "She's about to make your life a living hell."

Vinnie patted my shoulder in sympathy. "May the gods have mercy on your soul."

I rubbed my forehead, where a headache was blossoming to life. "Yeah, thanks for that."

Chapter 4

The following night, I arrived at BABA early, determined to pin down Layla first thing. I was still worried about her and I hadn't slept well. I wondered what she would think about my idea of buying back the *Oliver Twist*. She might laugh in my face. Maybe I would just keep my mouth shut. Layla could ruin someone's reputation with one perfectly tweezed eyebrow raised at just the right moment.

But I knew I couldn't keep my mouth shut about the book.

I drove around the block twice before I found a parking place three blocks away. When I walked inside BABA, I found out why the area was so congested.

It was happy hour. The central gallery was packed with people partying, laughing, and drinking. A full bar was set up along the far wall and guests were grabbing wineglasses as fast as the two bartenders could fill them.

It was the kickoff cocktail party for BABA's Twisted festival. I'd completely forgotten. This exclusive, by-invitation-only event was being held for BABA's major donors, the movers and shakers who contributed so heavily to Layla's coffers all year long.

I knew this event had been on the calendar for months, but it still seemed tacky to be throwing a party the night after someone was viciously attacked. I wondered, not for the first time, if Minka was still in the hospital or if they'd sent her home already.

The noise level was set at shrill, thanks to the rock music being piped through the sound system. Was it my imagination or was every man and woman in the room wearing black? They all looked artistic and wealthy and skinny. It was odd to be the most colorful person in the room in my navy jeans, white T-shirt, and moss green jacket.

I recognized some familiar faces. These were the San Francisco elite, the same people I'd seen barely two months ago at the Covington Library's gala opening of the Winslow Exhibit. The night my old friend Abraham Karastovsky had been murdered.

It made sense that the same people who supported the Covington would be BABA patrons and donors. They were all book lovers. I just wished I'd remembered about the party tonight. I would've dressed a little better.

Looking around, I wondered how many people in this room knew a woman had been assaulted down the hall just twenty-four hours ago. My guess was not many.

I had no doubt that this was another subject about which Layla would prefer I kept my big mouth shut.

"Yoo-hoo, Brooklyn," someone cried.

I turned in time to receive a fierce hug from Doris Bondurant, an old friend of Abraham's.

"Doris," I said, taking in the subtle scent of her Chanel No. 5. "It's so good to see you."

She grabbed hold of my hand. "How are you, my dear? I haven't seen you since Abraham's memorial service. A very unhappy day, I must say."

"Yes, it was," I said. "But it was wonderful to see you there."

"He was a good friend." She squeezed my hand tighter, then let it go. "And since then, I must admit I've been so distracted, I haven't gotten around to giving you the books I want you to restore for me."

"That's okay," I said. "Why don't I call you next week and we can arrange a time to meet?"

"Good girl," she said, patting my arm. "Now, what's going on in your life?"

Doris was a petite, wizened but feisty eighty-year-old, with a grip stronger than a truck driver's. She was one of the wealthiest women in the city, but down-to-earth and approachable, although I'd seen her pull the diva act when the situation warranted it. She laughed at my thirty-second recap of my excellent adventures in Scotland, then frowned as the lights dimmed behind me.

"Oh, dear, what is this now?" Doris murmured.

I turned and followed her gaze to the center of the gallery, where a pin spotlight was aimed at a podium and microphone setup.

Layla walked up to the podium, wearing a white off-the-shoulder spandex sex-kitten top with skintight black toreador-style pants. She wore all that with four-inch-spike-heeled black ankle boots. Her blond hair was piled high atop her head, except for several strands that had escaped to twirl coquettishly around her neck.

The crowd closed in, blocking our view.

"She's too damn old to be dressed like that," Doris groused. "And I'm too damn short. I can't see a thing over this crowd. What's going on, Brooklyn?"

I bit back a smile at her grumblings. "Looks like Layla is going to speak."

"I was afraid of that," she said dolefully.

Two men flanked Layla, but both were in shadow. I couldn't see their faces but she clutched their arms tightly and gazed up at each of them as though she knew them intimately. Then someone moved in front of me and I caught a glimpse of the man standing on Layla's right side. He was tall and powerfully built, with a ruddy complexion and sandy hair. Now I had a better view of Layla, too. Lucky me. She moved close to the microphone and the crowd hushed.

"I'm *tingling* with excitement," she said, her voice sultry as she rubbed up against the sandy-haired man. She pretended to shiver with delight, which made some of the crowd laugh and cheer.

"Oh, she's impossible," Doris murmured.

I wasn't a prude, but I heartily agreed. I hated that she used sex to stir up the crowd, and I hated the crowd for sucking it up. She made everything sound so icky. These were book people. Weren't they supposed to be smarter than the general public? I was severely disappointed in my people.

"It's my *extreme* pleasure," Layla continued, "to welcome to the Bay Area Book Arts Center the *incomparable* Gunther Schnaubel."

As applause rang out, I had to admit I was excited. Gunther Schnaubel was the world-famous Austrian artist who'd been commissioned to create a series of lithographs to commemorate the *Oliver Twist* anniversary. The lithographs would be auctioned off at the big party on the last night of the two-week-long Twisted celebration. I hadn't realized the artist himself would be on hand for the entire week. Maybe Layla had made him an offer he couldn't refuse.

I didn't want to go there. I was a Gunther fan, but if Layla kept rubbing up against him, I might change my mind.

Schnaubel acknowledged the applause with a brief smile and a wink for Layla, then waved to the audience. I couldn't help but notice he had huge hands. It was an interesting contradiction that many male artists who did finely detailed work had such large hands. I'd once seen an exhibit of exquisite miniature portraits done in the Regency style, and when I met the artist, I stared dumbly at his large hands. A woman standing near me had winked and slyly confirmed that the man's other parts matched in size.

In Gunther's case, the theory appeared to be true, as

well. He towered over Layla and looked to be made of solid muscle.

Meanwhile, Layla was still talking, explaining to the crowd how the silent auction would benefit the nonprofit Book Arts Center and also allow several scholarships to be given to underprivileged high school students who showed artistic promise.

She listed a few of the items that had been donated to the silent auction by both wealthy contributors and vendors who supplied paper and materials to BABA. Then she returned to the subject of Gunther Schnaubel.

"I don't mean to *gush*, but if you could all see how beautiful Gunther's . . . mm, *lithographs* are . . ." She cast another lascivious glance at his well-toned body. "Well, all I can say is . . . cha-ching!"

Over the roar of the delighted crowd, I could hear Doris make a *tsk* sound as she shook her head. I had to agree this was a "*tsk*-able" moment.

But Layla was on a roll. "And we're doubly—no, triply honored that Gunther has agreed to conduct three short hands-on demonstrations of his patented lithographic technique, and attendees will walk away with your own piece of artwork. And I do mean 'hands-on,' ladies."

The ladies and a few men tittered excitedly.

I checked my watch, then touched Doris's arm. "I'd better try to get through the crowd. I have to teach a class tonight."

"Good luck, dear," she said, looking around at the wall of people. "This reminds me of the time we crossed the Serengeti. I believe I'd rather take my chances with the wildebeests."

I laughed and promised to call her next week to discuss her books. As I inched my way through the crowd, Layla continued speaking, describing the highlights of the week, especially the closing night celebration. She named a celebrity chef who would prepare the menu, an award-winning winery owner who would select the wines, and the many spectacular items available to bid on at the silent auction that night.

"For instance," Layla said, "just to whet your appetites, we have a first edition, 1922 quarto of James Joyce's *Ulysses;* some lovely, rare Hemingway ephemera contributed by our own Zachariah Mason; and of course, the jewel in the crown and the raison d'etre of our Twisted festival, an exquisitely bound, *extremely* rare, 1838 first edition of Charles Dickens's *Oliver Twist*."

I stopped in my tracks, wincing at her announcement. Even though I'd made her think I would play along with whatever lie she wanted to put out there, it was grating to hear her actually announce the lie to a crowd of this size. For a moment, I had the worst urge to walk right up and call her bluff. Of course, I would be kissing my job good-bye, but it was more than my job at stake. If I defied Layla, I could kiss my reputation good-bye, as well.

I hated her for that.

There was another round of applause; then Layla held up her finger and the noise died down quickly. "And I know some of you will be enchanted by a *naughty* little 1887 British photography journal that contains *scandalous* nude photographs of members of Parliament cavorting with the ladies of Queen Victoria's court. That's right. We're not calling our festival Twisted for nothing, and I expect you all to be extremely *generous* with your bidding."

The crowd's laughs and whistles seemed to energize her and she licked her lips. More cheers and hoots rang out. Everyone seemed excited and happy.

Well, almost everyone. I happened to catch Naomi and Karalee rolling their eyes at each other in obvious distaste. I couldn't blame them, but they probably needed a reminder to be more discreet around this crowd.

And didn't that make me sound like Sister Mary Responsibility? Sometimes I really hated my inner disciplinarian.

Looking around for a way to move past the tight-knit group in front of me, I spotted my three librarian students near the front door. They appeared stranded and confused, until Marianne spotted me waving. She waved back and I knew they would make it through the crowd eventually.

Skirting yet another group of partygoers, I listened as Layla's speech drew to a close. She thanked a few of the biggest benefactors, then introduced Alice Fairchild.

"Alice, are you out there?" Layla glanced out at the audience, looking for her protégée. "Alice is BABA's newly appointed assistant director, and I'm thrilled to have her with us. Alice?"

I scanned the space but couldn't see her. Maybe she was in the ladies' room.

"Yes, I'm here," Alice called finally, sounding resigned.

I craned my neck and spied her standing next to a ficus tree in the corner. I wondered if she'd thought about hiding behind it. She sounded so stressed, I had to smile in sympathy. Was there some medication she could take to calm her nerves?

"Alice is just a bit shy," Layla said, her tone surprisingly maternal. "But I'm confident she'll do a fantastic job."

As the crowd applauded politely, I eased my way around the last group standing between me and the south hall. From here, I turned to watch Layla wrap up her speech. And that's when I saw Cynthia Hardesty dragging her husband, Tom, into one of the empty classrooms. She looked angry enough to spit nails and he looked clueless as she shoved the door closed. Had she caught him drooling over Layla again?

As I watched Layla from this vantage point in the hall, I could finally see the other man standing at Layla's left side, as he turned to survey the crowd.

I gasped.

The crowd burst into applause just then, so no one heard me wheezing as I rushed into my classroom, slammed the door, and sagged into a chair.

I couldn't catch my breath. My ears buzzed and my stomach wrenched dangerously. I was going to be sick. I needed to move, get away, but I was frozen in place. I began to panic and had to fight not to pass out.

I knew the man standing next to Layla Fontaine. Or I thought I did. Now I wasn't so sure. They were standing so close to each other that Layla's hawklike talons had embedded themselves in his thousand-dollar coat sleeve. They were so close that she had slipped her leg between his. So close that, as I watched, she'd reached out and groped his excellent butt.

The man with the excellent butt was Derek Stone.

Chapter 5

Yes, *that* Derek Stone. Was there any other?

God, he looked good. He appeared even taller than I remembered and his dark hair had grown a bit in the last four weeks. Four weeks and three days, to be exact. That's how long it had been since I'd seen him at the Edinburgh Book Fair.

Despite our best intentions, nothing of a physically romantic nature had happened between us that last night in Edinburgh. There was simply too much else going on. My parents were there, along with my best friend, Robin. I'd just won a prestigious award. And I'd been held hostage by a vicious killer earlier that afternoon. The police had wrapped up a double-murder investigation. Talk about distractions.

The next morning, Derek and I met for coffee; then he was called to Holyroodhouse Palace and I took off for the airport.

That was the last I saw of him. I'd thought at the time it was all for the best. Yes, he was far and away the most appealing man I'd ever met, but why would I get involved with someone I might never see again? It was a good question, one I spent many long nights arguing over once I was home. The plain fact was, I'd missed him every day. I missed his dry sense of humor and his intelligence, and I missed the way I felt with his arms wrapped around me. Would it have been so wrong to spend one night together, even if we never saw each other again?

And now, here he was in San Francisco, without any advanced warning. He couldn't call? He couldn't write? His e-mail wasn't working? Not that he owed me anything, but I thought we'd become . . . close. Close what? I couldn't say. Friends? Buddies? Lovers? No, unfortunately, not lovers. Not yet anyway. And seeing him snuggled up next to Layla just now, I was pretty darned sure we never would be.

I buried my head in my hands. I refused to cry, but I was sad, really sad. And I could feel another headache blooming.

What was he doing here? Besides being fondled and rubbed and drooled over by Layla Fontaine, of course?

Derek Stone and Layla Fontaine?

"Oh, God, no." My insides did a loop de loop and I groaned out loud. Just saying their names together made me want to hurl my lunch. They obviously knew each other. So what was my favorite British security agent doing with someone like Layla? She was poison; couldn't he see it?

I didn't want to think about it. But I couldn't help it. I couldn't get the picture out of my head, of her pressing up against him.

Now I knew how Alice felt with her sensitive nerves. I wasn't sure if my own would survive the night. And my heart wasn't doing so well, either.

I stood and paced. I knew I'd have to confront Derek eventually. I mean, he was here. At BABA. And the thought of him being here with Layla was more than I could bear. I would have to quit my class. It was completely depressing. And confusing. And infuriating.

"Damn it." I slammed my fist against the counter. Yes, I was furious. I was also in pain. It hurt to slam body parts against hard surfaces. But I was so angry. Angry at Derek, who hadn't had the decency to call me, not once, since I had left Edinburgh. And angry at Layla, who even on a good day was not exactly on my list of favorite people.

I let out a little shriek and perused the room. This was an impossible situation. My students would be here shortly. I had to get ready for class.

I gripped the edge of the worktable and tried to steady myself. I refused to panic, but it had been a long time since I'd felt this edgy and desperate.

No, I had to take that back. I'd felt almost exactly this way a few brief weeks ago, when I was accused of murder. For the second time.

Frankly, this felt worse. Last time, I knew I hadn't murdered anyone, so I was confident the truth would be revealed eventually. This was different. This was hideous. This was jealousy. And it sucked. It hurt. It made me feel stupid. It made me want to find that hole in the ozone and crawl through it and disappear. Or better yet, I could shove Derek through it and solve all my problems.

The door opened and I whipped around, half expecting Derek to walk in. But thank God, it was only Cynthia, Gina, and Whitney. I was ridiculously disappointed. Idiot.

"Hi, Brooklyn," Gina said merrily. "Cool party, isn't it?"

"I thought I saw you come in," Cynthia said, dropping her bag and jacket on her seat. Her hair was askew and her sweater and shirt were pulled up in back. I wondered if she'd gone a few rounds with her husband in the other classroom.

"I was going to run out and grab a glass of wine," Whitney said. "But if you're ready to start class, we're ready, too."

As Cynthia rearranged her clothing, she took a good look at me and frowned. "Are you okay?"

"Oh, sure," I said lightly. "I felt a little sick to my stomach but I'm fine. Probably something I ate."

"Wow," Gina said, taking notice for the first time. "You really don't look good."

"What every woman longs to hear," I said, forcing a smile. "I'm fine. I should go wash my hands."

"Do you want me to go with you?"

"No. I'll go in a minute. I just want to make sure everyone gets here."

"Honey, we're all big kids," Cynthia said. "We'll be fine on our own for a few minutes."

"Yes, Brooklyn," Gina said. "Go wash your face."

The truth was, I didn't want to leave the room for fear of running into Derek. But they were all watching me, so I threw them a grateful smile and escaped, racing to the ladies' room without seeing anyone.

As I washed my hands, I stared at myself in the mirror. Except for being a little pale, I looked fine. A little shell-shocked, maybe, but if you looked beyond the blank-eyed stare and the deathly pallor, I looked the same as always. That was my story, anyway. I pinched my cheeks a few times to get some color back. It wasn't working.

I placed a cold paper towel on my forehead and closed my eyes. I would get through this. Hell, there was a good chance I might not run into Derek at all. He didn't know I was working here, although he'd be pretty stupid not to. And he wasn't a stupid man. Except when it came to his taste in women, apparently. Layla was a stupid choice, just my opinion.

But that didn't matter. The point was, he hadn't cared enough to call me and say he was coming to town.

"So, it was nice while it lasted," I whispered. But it was over now. If I was being perfectly honest, it had never started, not really. Yes, we'd had a flirtation, a few kisses. A lot of kisses, actually, and some intense moments. He was a really great kisser. Lucky me. But now he was with Layla, and lucky her. If she was what he wanted, then who needed him? Not me. No way.

Oh, that was such a lie.

As I dried my hands, I tried my mother's old trick of smiling at myself in the mirror. If you stared long enough at yourself grinning like a loon, you could make yourself laugh. It always worked to cheer me up.

I wasn't cheered. I could barely manage more than a trembling sneer. When my eyes began to tear, I looked away and carefully blinked until the moisture evaporated. Then I tried on a neutral smile.

"That'll have to do," I muttered philosophically. In a year or so, I'd look back on this time and laugh at myself for making yet another horrible choice in men.

I tossed the paper towel in the trash and shoved the door open.

"Hello, Brooklyn."

Derek leaned casually against the wall directly opposite the restroom. He looked like an advertisement for tall, dark, and dangerous men. Oh, and dashing. I couldn't forget dashing.

I lost my breath for just a second, but I refused to faint. Refused to look even more stupid than I felt.

"Oh, hello, Derek," I said, marveling that my voice was so steady. "Isn't this a pleasant surprise?"

He pushed away from the wall and pulled me into his arms. I almost groaned.

"I was hoping I'd be lucky enough to see you here tonight." His breath played havoc with the sensitive skin under my ear. "Then I saw you in the crowd and knew I must be lucky indeed."

So much for avoiding him.

I shuddered; I couldn't help it. The sound of his deep voice combined with his languid British accent caused chaos to run unchecked through my body. His unique musky scent of leather with hints of citrus and rain forest was intoxicating. The slight brush of his lips against my ear was nearly orgasmic.

And I was pathetic.

I carefully backed away from him and plastered a smile on my face. "Yes, aren't we lucky? What a pleasant surprise. How are you, Derek?"

He winced. "I should've called, but I—"

"Don't be silly," I said, waving his words away. "You don't owe me any—"

He gripped my arms. "Brooklyn, I honestly didn't know I'd be coming until I got on the plane."

"Well, there you go," I said. "It couldn't be helped."

"You're angry," he said, studying me. "I don't blame you."

"Me? Angry?" Did I sound as shrill as I felt? "Just because you came to town without calling me? That's ridiculous. It's nothing."

"It's everything," he said, gently brushing my hair back from my face. "I've hurt you. I'm a damned fool."

I tried to laugh. "No way. It's all—"

"It's not all right." He frowned. "How can I make it up to you?"

"It's not necessary." I straightened my shoulders and smiled with purpose. "So, how are you? I didn't realize you knew Layla."

Oh, God, I didn't really say that. I just prayed I sounded nonchalant.

"We've met," he said flatly. "But I don't know her."

I raised my eyebrows. "Oh, really?"

"Yes, really. I hardly know the woman."

"Huh. It didn't look that way from where I was standing." *Ack! What was wrong with me?*

"Ah," he said, and a slow smile appeared.

"Ah?" So much for nonchalance. I was livid. "What's 'ah' supposed to mean?"

As his grin widened, I wanted to bite my own tongue off. And smack him. Hard. And maybe punch him in the nose.

"It means, my darling, that—"

"Excuse me, please," a woman cried.

I turned and saw Alice running down the hall toward us. Derek yanked me out of her path just in time. She whipped past and disappeared behind the ladies' room door. Whatever was wrong with her, I could relate.

"Well, it's been great running into you, Derek." I patted his chest, a tad more forcefully than necessary as I tried really hard to be affable. "But I have a class to teach, so—"

He grabbed my hand. "Easy, darling."

"Sorry." I pulled my hand away.

"I want to see you."

"That would be nice," I said in a vague, noncommittal way. Damn, I was good. "I'm pretty busy, but if you're hanging around BABA some evening, we might—"

"Brooklyn, please," he said, his voice edgy with frustration. "Look, I didn't expect to include myself in this assignment."

I paused. "You're here on assignment?"

"Yes."

"What's the assignment?"

He paused as well, then finally said, "I trust you to keep this to yourself."

"Of course I will."

He waved away the statement. "Yes, of course you will. You're as trustworthy as anyone I know." He took a step closer and bent to whisper in my ear. "Gunther Schnaubel has received death threats. My team is guarding him."

"He's in danger? Here?"

"Yes."

I looked around, instantly on guard. Then I remembered Minka. "Are we all in danger?"

"No."

"Are you sure?" I gave him a brief rundown of the attack on Minka. Although, I thought, there were any number of reasons someone might want to take Minka out, none of which had anything to do with Gunther. "The police warned us to be alert and not walk outside alone."

"That's always a good idea," he said, ever the security expert. "But Gunther's threats came from an extremely jealous husband. I doubt the man would come here and start attacking women."

"So much for that theory," I said, disappointed that we still had no clue as to who had attacked Minka. "But I can't believe you brought an entire team here just to guard one artist."

"Unfortunately, that one artist was caught in flagrante delicto with the daughter of the prime minister of a small European nation that I'm not at liberty to name. It's grown quite political and sordid and I wouldn't be surprised if they sent one of their army battalions to do him in."

"Oh, I see." I didn't, but I also didn't have time to force the issue. I was late for class. Besides, I was still angry. Yes, he hadn't known he was coming to San Francisco until he was on the plane. But what was his excuse for not calling during the rest of the four weeks? And didn't that make me sound like a shrew? "I've got to go."

"Wait." His jaw clenched. "Damn it, Brooklyn, I wasn't going to come to San Francisco."

I frowned. "You said that already."

"Yes, I guess I did." He began to pace in front of me, gesticulating as he explained in a loud whisper, "Gunther Schnaubel is a royal pain. He doesn't follow the rules. He's asking for trouble and he's going to get himself killed if he's not more careful."

"So you needed all your men here."

"Exactly." He looked relieved. "I knew you'd understand."

"Of course." Even though I didn't. I mean, I understood why he was here, but I didn't understand why he hadn't called. Oh, I suppose I could've called him, but the strategy of calling men never seemed to work for me. I guess I was an old-fashioned girl when it came to that sort of thing. But none of it mattered right now. I had a class to teach.

"I'm glad we talked." I checked my watch. "Now I really have to get back to my class."

"We're not finished here."

"No, of course not. But I do have to go."

The bathroom door flew open, and Alice stepped out into the hall. "Oh," she said, and looked from me to Derek, then back to me. "You're still here."

"I'll just be another minute," I said, feeling my cheeks redden. "Can you tell everyone?"

"Sure can," she said, smiling as she walked away.

"What time is your class over?" Derek asked.

"Ten o'clock."

"I'll be waiting."

"You don't—"

"I do."

I took a deep breath and exhaled slowly. That first rush of fury was draining away as I looked at him. After all, we weren't a couple. We were kissing buddies. Occasionally. Not exactly a declaration of couplehood. "This is crazy, Derek. You don't owe me an explanation. We're not—"

"Christ." He raked his hand through his hair in aggravation. "I hate this."

"Oo-kay." I wasn't clear on what it was he hated.

"I don't apologize," he said through gritted teeth.

"Why should you?"

"There," he said, pointing at me. "Right there. You're doing it again."

I looked at him sideways. "Doing what?"

"Making me feel like I ran over your dog."

"I don't have a dog." I was completely lost now. "What are you talking about?"

He laughed. "You're right. I've gone insane. But it's your fault."

"Mine?"

"Yes."

"Don't drag me into this," I protested.

He laughed again. "Damn it, I've missed you. I didn't want to. I was determined not to see you again."

"Well, thank you. That's really flattering. I'm so happy we had this conversation." I folded my arms across my chest. "And guess what? You don't have to see me again."

"Ah, but it seems I do." He urged me back into his arms and I almost whimpered. It wasn't fair. He kissed my neck, kissed my shoulder. "Damn it, you're even more lovely than I remembered. What was I thinking?"

"I have no idea."

He laughed, and the sound went a long way to refresh my spirit. "God, you'll be the death of me. Go teach your class. I'll be waiting."

Breathless, I rushed off, but made the mistake of turning around. He stood in the same spot, watching me, his eyes as dark as cobalt, his lips twisting sardonically. It was disconcerting and a complete turn-on. Part of me wanted to rush back and kiss him and another part of me wanted to slap him silly.

I couldn't believe I'd mentioned Layla to him. For one thing, I sounded like a jealous cat. But also, I was annoyed with myself for revealing what I was angry about. Women were never supposed to tell a guy what was actually bothering them, right? It was in the Official Rule Book. *If a guy doesn't know what's bothering you, then why should you tell him?*

I jogged down the hall but slowed when I heard two women arguing in one of the empty classrooms near mine.

"Keep your hands off my husband."

"Honey, it's not *my* hands you have to worry about."

"I know what you're doing, and it stops now."

"Oh, really?"

"Yeah, really," she said, then lowered her voice to add, "Or you'll be sorry."

"Oh, threats?" The woman laughed and I realized it was Layla. Her voice dripped with cynical delight.

"Yeah. Hands off, or you're a dead woman."

The door was thrown open and I pressed myself back against the wall. It was my ridiculous attempt to hide in plain sight, but it didn't matter because Cynthia Hardesty never looked my way. Layla followed a moment later, twirling a loose strand of hair around her fingers as she strolled leisurely back to the party.

As I walked into my classroom, I considered the scene I'd just overheard. I couldn't let Cynthia know I'd witnessed the argument, but I had the strongest urge to console her. I could feel her pain, having just experienced a meltdown over the possibility of Layla and Derek together.

I took a moment and mentally shoved Derek Stone into a box so I could conduct the class without going bonkers.

Within the first half hour, the party sounds from Layla's happy hour bash dwindled. Eventually all was quiet and my students were able to concentrate on practicing the kettle stitch they'd learned the night before.

This was only the second evening of class but the group was already beginning to meld nicely. As everyone worked, the personalities of some of the students rose to the fore. I'd like to think we were all getting used to each other's quirks and foibles, but some were more easy to acclimate to than others.

Cynthia and Tom, for instance, tended to bicker quietly over almost anything. The subject matter could be as trivial as the choice of covers for the books they were making. But I'd heard that argument with Layla and there was nothing trivial about it. Tom would have been wise to pay closer attention to his wife.

Gina and Whitney liked to talk, too, but at least they were entertaining. Both were pop-culture fanatics and proud of it. They told me what they'd seen on *TMZ* the previous night; then Gina showed everyone the GoFugYourself.com app on her phone. Kylie and Marianne both begged to see the latest red-carpet disasters.

Mitchell was a jovial man, cheerful and interested in the others' lives. Dale, Bobby, and Jennifer, on the other hand, worked quietly and kept to themselves.

When Alice wasn't texting her boyfriend, Stuart, or rushing off to the bathroom, she would absently rub her stomach while she worked. Fortunately, she was blessed with a self-deprecating sense of humor, so most of the students found her charming, despite her health issues.

When she walked back in from her latest bathroom run, I approached her and asked if she was okay.

She sighed and whispered, "Sometimes I think I was born without intestines. Food and liquid seem to travel directly from my stomach right down to my . . . well, you probably don't need the specifics."

"Ya think?" Gina whispered loudly, and everyone nearby laughed, including Alice.

"Maybe it's your diet," Whitney suggested gently. "My cousin is gluten-intolerant and he had to change his whole way of eating. But now he's fine."

"Oh, I'm getting tested for celiac disease tomorrow," Alice said. "Stuart read about it and insisted I see my doctor."

"Good idea," Gina said.

Alice sighed. "Sorry to disrupt the class."

I glanced around the room. Most everyone seemed to be concentrating on gluing their books properly. "I don't think you're disrupting anyone."

"Yeah, Alice, don't worry about it," Whitney said, waving away her concern. "We just want you to be healthy."

Alice blinked, clearly surprised. "You guys are so nice."

Just then, I caught Tom Hardesty casting a disgruntled frown at Alice. It wasn't the first time I'd seen him make that face, but I only now realized it was directed at Alice. Since he was a board member, there was no way I could tell him to knock it off. But I didn't like students being disrespectful of each other. I wondered if maybe Tom disliked Alice because she was such good friends with Layla.

It occurred to me that Cynthia Hardesty left the room almost as frequently as Alice did, in order to make and return phone calls. "Bidness," she'd whisper loudly, and walk out.

Tom never glared contemptuously at his wife when she slipped out. Probably because he was scared to death that Cynthia would catch him and spank him. And that was a visual I never wanted to conjure up again.

It was almost ten thirty by the time everyone was finished for the night. Following Officer Ortiz's orders, I put Mitchell in charge of making sure nobody left alone. As the students packed up their stuff, he went around assigning a buddy for everyone.

Then he turned to me. "What about you?"

I thought of Derek's promise that he'd meet me after class. "I have to clean up a bit, and I've got someone waiting for me. I won't leave alone."

"Are you sure?"

"Yes. My friend should be here any minute, if he's not already waiting in the gallery."

"Well, we're not leaving until he shows himself."

"Fine, let's go." I grabbed my bag and locked the door, then followed Mitchell, Sylvia, Kylie, and Alice into the gallery. I glanced around for Derek, but he wasn't there. My first thought was that he was in Layla's office. I hoped not.

"Give me thirty seconds," I told them, and ran down the hall to check. Layla's office was empty, but Naomi was still working. She looked up when I knocked.

"Have you seen Derek Stone?" I asked.

"No," she said irritably.

"Do you know who he is?"

"Yes," she said pointedly.

"Okay, thanks. Good night."

She muttered something I couldn't hear and I wondered what had put her in such a foul mood. Then I remembered she worked for Layla and let it go.

Walking back to the gallery, I refused to show that I was hurt by the fact that Derek was nowhere to be found.

"Let's go," I said.

"Change of plans?" Mitchell asked.

"Yeah," I said, and left it at that.

Maybe Derek and Layla had gone out for a quick drink. Or maybe he'd run off to guard Gunther. Yeah, Gunther. I preferred that scenario.

But I was still hurt. Again. I really needed to stop caring about that man.

Outside, the cold, foggy air hit me hard. I hunched my shoulders and huddled inside my down jacket as we all walked briskly to our cars. Alice's was parked almost directly in front of BABA and we teased her for snatching the primo spot. The rest of us had all parked farther away because of the party.

As we hiked down the street, the heavy fog made it impossible to see Potrero Hill, but I knew it was there. I considered swinging over to Goat Hill Pizza to drown my sorrows in takeout and my mouth began to water at the thought of the goat cheese and pesto combo. Last year, before settling on my SOMA loft, I'd looked at houses on the Hill. Some parts were still in transition, as real estate agents liked to say when working-class areas were gentrifying. But I still loved the cozy neighborhood feel of the area, with its Victorian homes perched on the sloping hills and the cool shops and parks. Best of all, besides superlative pizza, the Hill was the home of Christopher's Books, one of my favorite little bookstores in the city.

Another two blocks farther, we turned the corner. The street was dark and shrouded in fog that seemed to cling stubbornly to us as we walked through it. It was so thick, I didn't notice the man standing in the shadows next to my car until I was almost in front of him.

"Hello, darling," Derek said.

I jumped. He looked even more dangerous than usual. Maybe it was the fog.

"Are you all right, Brooklyn?" Mitchell asked.

"I'm fine," I said, staring at Derek. "Good night, gang."

"Good night," a trio of voices answered, and I heard their footsteps recede into the night.

"You waited," I said to Derek, tossing my bag into the backseat of my car and pulling my jacket even tighter around me.

"Of course I waited. I told you I would."

"I thought you'd be inside."

He scowled. "I tried waiting inside, but it became troublesome."

I chewed my lip nervously. "Layla?"

"Yes. Come here." He coaxed me into his arms.

"It's been a long night," I said, and covered up a yawn.

"And you're tired." He began to knead a pulse point at the junction of my shoulder and neck.

"Yes. I'm exhausted and just want to . . . oh." I was pressed up against him and he was doing miraculous things to my muscles. I would melt if he continued much longer.

"We can go for a drink, or dinner," he said.

"Oh, well, I could eat something." Thoughts of pizza returned and I smiled.

"That's my girl," he whispered. He was well aware of my ability to eat heartily anytime, day or night.

But was I really his girl? Did I want to be? After all, he didn't call, he didn't write, and he didn't want to see me again. And yet, he was here, and so was I. I certainly didn't want to be his port in the storm, but if he kept rubbing my neck like that, I would say yes to just about anything he asked.

"Darling, I—" His cell phone vibrated in his jacket pocket and he muttered, "Bloody hell."

I took the opportunity to step back, away from temptation. "Better answer it."

He stared at the screen, then looked at me, plainly conflicted. "I warned them not to call unless—"

"Answer it," I said again, then tried to move farther away to allow him some privacy. But he swung his arm around my shoulders and dragged me up against his solid chest.

I could hear yelling on the other side of the call but couldn't understand what the speaker was saying. Derek barely said a word but for a muttered expletive here and there. And with his clipped accent, even cursing sounded charming.

"I'll be there in ten," he said, then clicked off the call.

"New plan?" I said lightly.

"Yes," he said, "I must go kill Gunther Schnaubel."

"Hey, that's okay," I lied. "I should go feed my neighbors' cats anyway."

He laughed. I liked the sound of it.

I tried to convince myself that this was a good thing. I'd been seconds away from going to dinner with him. From there, I might've agreed to spend the night. Only a couple of hours ago, I'd been furious. Now I was ready to throw my panties in the wind, for heaven's sake. Things were getting serious and complicated, fast. For me, anyway.

I still didn't understand his relationship with Layla and I wasn't sure I wanted to. More important, I didn't know what to expect by getting involved with him, if anything. And now I wouldn't have the chance to talk to him about it. Not tonight, anyway.

So it was just as well that he'd received that phone call. It would give me some space to think about things. I needed to figure out exactly what I was getting my very vulnerable heart into.

He leaned his forehead against mine. "Tomorrow night, Brooklyn. I'll be here. We'll go to dinner and we'll talk. And I promise you, there will be no more interruptions."

"Okay," I whispered, grateful for the short respite. Twenty-four hours was plenty of time to think about stepping off a cliff, wasn't it?

Chapter 6

Wednesday night, I walked the periphery of the classroom. Earlier, my students had insisted on grilling me about why I happened to be wearing a cute dress when I normally wore jeans. I wasn't about to tell them I had a date with the hottest secret agent in the Western Hemisphere, but they guessed anyway. Well, about the date part. Who would guess he was a secret agent? Well, he wasn't really. Not anymore. Anyway, once my upcoming date was out in the open, I had to endure all their opinions and warnings and teasing. Then Alice mentioned that she'd seen my companion up close last night and oh, he was dreamy.

Dreamy. Who said that anymore?

Finally, though, they all settled down enough to concentrate on yet another of my fascinating lectures, this one on wood-block presses. I'd already given every student a small wood press to work with. The classroom had enough for everyone, thanks to Marky May, who had made them all himself.

Marky's presses were an ingeniously simple pattern, essentially two fifteen-inch blocks of smooth hardwood held together by two long wood screws, one on each end.

"To press your pages together, you place your textblock between the pieces of wood, spine side up. Then twirl the wing nuts to tighten until the textblock is held firmly. Could it be easier?"

I pointed out that the spine should stick up a little higher than the press itself so glue wouldn't drip onto the wood. "And make sure the linen tapes aren't pressed between the pages and the wood. They should lie on top. We don't want to get glue on any part of the tapes except where they're already sewn to the signatures."

"There you go, speaking in tongues again," Mitchell said, shaking his head in confusion.

"Sorry," I said, chuckling as I studied everyone's pressed pages. "Okay, everybody, look at Alice's press. See how the tapes are strewn over the block? That's what yours should look like."

"Teacher's pet," Gina teased, and they laughed.

Alice laughed along with them, then frowned as she rubbed her stomach.

"I was just kidding," Gina said, her forehead creasing in concern.

"No worries," Alice said, trying to wave away the pain. "It's just me and my nerves."

Whitney wiggled her eyebrows. "The good news is, when you rub your stomach like that, I'm blinded by your gorgeous diamond ring."

Alice held her hand up to the light and stared fondly at the ring. "It is pretty, isn't it? Stuart is so sweet."

"You're very lucky to have a nice guy," Whitney said. "You have no idea what's out there these days."

"Slim pickings," Gina agreed.

"Hey, I resemble that remark," Mitchell muttered.

Everyone laughed, then settled back to work.

"I could make these wood presses for the kids taking our classes," Marianne the librarian marveled, flicking her wing nuts. On the first night she'd told us that she planned to take what she learned here and offer book craft classes for kids at her library.

"That's way too much labor," said Jennifer, who worked

at the same library. "And the little kids won't be able to operate something like this."

"Are you kidding?" Gina said. "If I can do it, anyone can."

"It's true," Whitney said, elbowing her friend. "She's all thumbs and press-on nails."

I pulled a large binder clip off my stack of notes and held it up. "Two of these will hold a book in place almost as securely as a wood press."

Jennifer's eyes lit up. "Binder clips. How clever. Now that's more my speed."

Once they all had their signature pages firmly held inside the presses, I demonstrated how to apply the thin layers of PVA glue to the text spine.

"Dip the brush halfway into the glue, then swipe it liberally across the spine edges. You want to soak the threads completely. Be sure to daub the wet brush carefully between the pages so that everything is covered in glue."

I wandered around the room, watching them apply thin layers of adhesive to the compressed textblock.

"Something's wrong with mine," Mitchell said, scratching his head as he stared at his project.

"What happened?" I asked, walking around the table.

"I think I overglued."

"Wow, you sure did." I laughed. I couldn't help it. Glue was dripping down the side of the wood press and his linen tabs were drenched as well.

"I know you're laughing *with* me," he muttered.

"Absolutely," I said, grabbing a wet wipe. "Here, use this to wipe off the wood."

"You said a liberal application."

"I did," I said, shaking my head at the mess. "I also said to do it carefully. But I'll take the blame for this one."

"I like the sound of that," he said.

"We can fix this," I said, raising my voice so the entire

group would pay attention. "For the linen tabs, take a cotton swab dipped in acetone and wipe the linen carefully."

I demonstrated. "These tabs should remain dry and loose because they'll eventually be used to hold the spine to the covers. The last thing we do is glue them between the cover board and the pastedown."

Mitchell groaned at my incomprehensible explanation.

"Okay," I said, with a laugh. "Instead of trying to explain it, let me find an example to show you what I mean."

I grabbed two of my sample journals from the table at the front of the room and passed them around the table. The three tabs were clearly outlined beneath the pastedown.

"Ah," Mitchell said, peering at the inside cover. "I think I get it now."

"Good." I smiled and gave the book to Dale, who sat next to Mitchell. "Pass those journals around so everyone can get an idea of what the tabs are used for. Thanks."

I spent a quiet half hour working alone in the classroom while everyone took a dinner break. I munched on malted-milk balls and string cheese as I prepared another textblock for demonstration purposes.

Once the demo was set up, I did a little paperwork and balanced my checkbook, adding in the check I'd deposited that morning from Holyroodhouse Palace. It had been sent along with another children's book that Philip Pickering-Jones wanted me to restore.

While I was in Edinburgh, Derek had taken me to the palace, where Pickering-Jones, personal secretary to the British princes, gave me a shabby old book that belonged to one of the prince's girlfriends. He wanted it restored for her as a gift.

I knew I'd received the job only because I'd been in the right place at the right time. With the right British commander, of course. So I was shocked and pleased and honored that they'd sent me more work.

The book I'd received today was *Mrs. Overtheway's Remembrances* by the same beloved British author of the first book, Juliana Horatia Ewing. Pickering-Jones asked that it be restored in the same style as the first, making a matched set. Coincidentally, the two books were illustrated by George Cruikshank, the same man who did the *Oliver Twist* I restored for Layla.

"Small world," I murmured.

As students began to shuffle back into the room, I put my personal stuff away and pulled out my bookbinders hammer.

"It's hammer time," I announced, and everyone groaned. "Hey, these are the jokes, people."

Marianne raised her hand. "I hate to interrupt the jokes, but could you show me that weaver's knot again?"

"Fine, ruin my timing," I groused good-naturedly.

She wrinkled her nose. "Sorry, but I still don't get the kinky part."

There were a few chuckles as I cut a length of thirty-gauge linen thread from the spool. I ran the thread through my fingers several times, reminding them that it was an important step to take the twist out and get rid of any sizing or wax the manufacturer had applied to the thread. I reached for the long sewing needle and was about to show them how to kink the thread in order to make a knot when someone shouted out in the hall.

"Buzz off!"

"No! Don't go in there."

The classroom door flew open and Minka stormed in, followed closely by Layla and Naomi. Minka walked right up and shoved me. I fell back against the counter, hitting my hip bone.

"Hey!" I cried. Even knowing Minka for as long as I had, she'd caught me by surprise again.

"I suppose you think I owe you my life or something," she said belligerently.

"Nope. You don't owe me anything." I sidestepped her and backed away. I'd vowed never to be within arm's length of Minka again. She had a bad habit of belting me when I wasn't paying attention. On the other hand, with her head wrapped in a thick white gauze bandage, she didn't seem half as threatening as usual.

"Liar."

"I mean it," I said, balancing on the balls of my feet, ready to spring if she made a move. "If I could do it over again, I would've left you to rot."

"You bitch," she snarled.

"Back atcha. Now get out of my classroom."

"Just because you made a stupid phone call doesn't mean you're some kind of savior."

"I agree." I gestured toward my students, who watched with avid interest. "Now, I have a class to run, so amscray, itchbay."

"Because you're not," she continued, as though I hadn't said anything.

"I know. I heard you." That's when I noticed Naomi wringing her hands. Even Layla looked nervous. Fascinating. But not much help. To Minka, I said, "What part of *hasta la vista* don't you understand?"

Her scowl would've been scary if not for her tendency to spit when she spoke. "I can see the smug satisfaction in your eyes."

"Can you?"

"Yes, and it sickens me."

"Minka," Naomi said, tentatively reaching for Minka's arm, "you should thank God that Brooklyn found you in time."

"Oh, really?" Minka shrugged Naomi's hand away as her voice grew louder and more shrill. "So she can rub my nose in it for the rest of my life?"

A few of my students cringed as she shrieked the word

life. She sounded like a squealing rat, but I could sympathize. The thought that I'd saved her life made me just as queasy.

"But you could've died," Naomi said. I appreciated her attempts to be civilized, but she didn't know who she was dealing with.

"Oh, get real," Minka said to Naomi. "It was just a friggin' bump on the head."

"Is that so?" Naomi said, irritated now. "I heard you were still out cold until late this morning."

Minka rolled her eyes, then grimaced in pain from the effort. "Never mind."

"You probably shouldn't be here," Naomi said. "I'll bet your doctor doesn't even know you left the hospital."

Minka's nostrils flared but she said nothing. Naomi folded her arms in triumph.

"We're just glad you're back in fighting form, sweetie," Layla crooned, touching Minka's shoulder. "Now, don't you have your own class to teach?"

Why did Layla treat her so nicely? Professional courtesy among snakes, maybe?

Minka glared at me. I gazed back at her with what I hoped was a look of blasé indifference, though I wanted more than anything to stab her with my long, sharp sewing needle.

Finally, she shook her head in fury, stomped her foot like the frustrated cow that she was, then whipped around and clomped out. Layla rushed after her and wrapped her arm around Minka's shoulder. Naomi exhaled loudly, shot me a fulminating look, and left the room, shutting the door behind her.

I let out a breath I didn't realize I'd been holding. So much for gratitude.

"Wow, that was so rude," Alice said, shocked. She turned and studied my face. "Are you all right?"

"Yeah."

"Isn't she the girl who was knocked out in the hall the other night?" Gina asked.

"Yes, she's the one," Whitney said, then grimaced. "I remember that hair."

"What an ingrate," Marianne said, righteously indignant on my behalf. "She could've died if Brooklyn hadn't found her."

"What's wrong with her?" quiet Jennifer asked.

"She's just a royal bee-yotch," Whitney said, and the others agreed.

I smiled gratefully. I was growing more fond of my students every day. "So, where were we?"

"It's hammer time?" Mitchell said, causing more groans and a few laughs.

"Right. Everyone find their hammer in their tool packet." While they went through their packets, I took a minute to catch my breath. Minka was a menace to my health.

"Okay, everyone ready?" I asked, holding up my favorite tool. I'd purchased the new bookbinders hammer when I'd returned from Edinburgh last month. My old favorite hammer, a gift from my mentor, had been stolen and used as a murder weapon.

It was a long story, and I tried not to think about it as I prepared to demonstrate the proper way of rounding the spine of the textblock.

I had them remove their glued pages from the wood presses and test the glue.

"The adhesive should still be slightly tacky," I said, holding up my demo and touching the spine.

"The reason we hammer the spine is to round it out. A flat spine won't allow the book to lie nicely. You want to round it slightly. And you do it by pounding it with a hammer."

"Fun," said Kylie.

I demonstrated by holding up two different books I'd

made. "If you keep the spine flat as it is now, the book will plop one way or another when you open it. See? But a rounded spine will allow the book to fan open."

"Cool," Jennifer whispered.

"Now, hammering works best if you place the textblock flat on the table with the spine near the table's edge." I used the end of the worktable to demonstrate.

"I'm going to hurt myself, aren't I?" Gina whispered to Whitney.

I smiled at her. "No, you won't. These hammers are lighter and shorter than a regular carpenter's hammer, and the head is wider. That's because you don't need to apply as much pressure to this as you would to a nail to pound it into a wall. Your pressure to the book is more of a smack than a smash."

"Smack, don't smash," Gina muttered.

"You take the hammer and start pounding the spine with a pushing motion," I said, demonstrating. "You're effectively nudging the layers out to form a curved surface."

"I like it," Kylie said, clobbering the pages with her hammer. "I'm pretending it's my husband."

"This is fun," Gina said, pounding like mad on her book. "I'm so fierce."

"Easy," I cautioned. "Push, don't pummel."

"Oops," she said, and lightened the pressure of her thrusts.

"Now, turn the textblock over and do the same thing from the back side so it evens out. Do this several times, and you'll see the spine becoming rounded." I held mine up for everyone's scrutiny.

"As soon as you have the desired curve, place it back into the wood press and apply another thin layer of glue. That way, it'll stay rounded for good."

A twittering sound chirped. Cynthia grabbed her purse and found her cell. She checked the screen and looked at me. "It's bidness. Can I take a quick break?"

"Sure," I said. "Everyone knows what they need to do now, so proceed at your own pace and take a break if you need to. I'll walk around and check your work or answer questions if you have any."

For the next ten minutes, everyone worked quietly. Some people left the room, others came back in. I didn't pay much attention to the comings and goings as I stopped to ask Marianne and Jennifer about their library arts-and-crafts program. Then I made another pass around the table and paused at Mitchell's place.

"How'm I doing, boss?" he asked, grinning as he held up his glue brush.

"Much better," I said.

"Thanks," he said. "But I—"

A loud blast interrupted him.

Gina screamed and Whitney pulled her under the table.

"Oh, my God," Kylie cried.

"Calm down!" I shouted. "It's probably nothing."

But I knew that sound. I'd heard it more than once before.

"Everyone stay here." I ran from the room, closing the door behind me. No one was in the hall. I tiptoed to the entry and peeked around the corner. The gallery was empty.

"I'm right behind you," Mitchell said evenly. "That was a gunshot."

"I know." I turned and scowled. "That's why I told everyone to stay in the room."

"Oh, right. Like I'm going to wait in there while you're out here getting yourself killed."

"Men," I muttered.

"Yeah, we suck," he growled. "Come on."

We crossed the gallery to the north hall. I could see that Layla's office door was open. Light poured into the hall, illuminating a lifeless lump on the carpet.

"Oh, crap," I whispered. Déjà vu, anyone? I moved

closer, then stopped abruptly. Mitchell stopped directly behind me.

It was Layla. Blood trickled from a hole at the center of her chest, leaving a bright red stain in the middle of her stretchy white top.

My head began to swim at the sight of all that blood and spandex. I looked away from the bullet hole, straight into Layla's dull green eyes. She stared right back at me, but there was only emptiness.

Layla Fontaine was dead.

Chapter 7

"Jeez, what's with this place?" Mitchell wondered aloud. "You got bodies falling everywhere."

"Call nine-one-one," I said as I knelt to check her pulse. I couldn't blame him for asking the question. Every other night I was finding another body in the hall. It couldn't be good for business.

"Is she dead?" he asked.

"Oh, yeah," I mumbled, pushing myself up.

"Well, duh," he said, thumping his forehead. "I guess the bullet hole should've been my first clue." He pulled out his cell and made the call.

I brushed and straightened my wool dress, then leaned against the wall, staring off into nowhere. I listened to Mitchell speak clearly and dispassionately to the dispatcher. I was glad he'd followed me out of the classroom. Despite being a wiseacre, or maybe because of it, he was a good man to have in a crisis.

After a few seconds he covered the phone and asked, "You okay?"

"Yeah," I said, my back pressed against the wall.

"Don't pass out."

"Very funny."

"I'm not kidding. You look like you're going to faint. You can just walk away and go sit in the classroom."

"No," I insisted, then admitted, "Okay, I get a little woozy around blood."

"Take deep breaths. Blood freaks out a lot of people."

I was disgusted at my own weakness, but in my defense, it wasn't just the sight of blood that was making me light-headed. It was the fact that Layla's eyes were still open. It felt as though she were staring right at me. It made me wonder how the police could work around dead bodies when the victims' eyes were still open, staring at them as they did their jobs.

If I were to ask my cosmically attuned mother what it meant when someone died with their eyes open, she would have some explanation about the soul choosing to leave the body through the eyes. The eyes were considered one of the higher senses, so maybe when the soul left this way, it meant the person would reach Surya Loka, or the divine solar, the eternal light, sooner. There, the soul would be purified; then it took only another step or two to reach Chandraloka, or, literally, moon heaven.

Or maybe not. At least, not in Layla's case. Something told me heaven wouldn't be her ultimate destination.

But that wasn't nice of me, was it? As penance, I forced myself to turn and look at her again. Objectively speaking, in death Layla was even more beautiful than she'd been when alive. The muscles of her face were relaxed, now that she had no reason to spout vile threats or mercilessly ridicule anyone. I looked a little closer. The woman was literally wrinkle-free. She must've had some work done recently.

I took a breath to steady my whirling stomach. The last thing her eyes must've seen was her killer aiming a gun at her. I trembled at the thought. I'd stared down more than one killer with a gun. I would hate to think that would be the last thing I'd ever see.

Then I noticed the book splayed under her arm. She

must've dropped it when she fell. Or maybe the shooter dropped it. I reached down to take it, then stopped.

What was wrong with me? This was a crime scene. Still, my natural tendency was to rescue books, especially when they were in danger of being consumed by a puddle of blood. But there was no blood threatening to destroy the book.

I shivered again and turned to face the wall. *Think happy thoughts.*

"What happened?" someone called out.

"Stay back," Mitchell warned.

I turned and saw Gina standing with Whitney and my other students at the end of the hall.

"We're waiting for the police," I explained.

"Again?" Alice asked in disbelief.

Cynthia joined the group just then. I could see her shoving her phone into her pants pocket; then she craned her neck over the crowd and asked, "What's going on? Who is that?"

But Alice figured it out first. "Oh, my God, is that Layla? Oh, no. Brooklyn, is she breathing?"

"She looks dead," Whitney said flatly, and put her arm around Alice.

"She is," Mitchell murmured.

"Layla's dead?" somebody asked.

"If only," Cynthia muttered, then looked around and realized nobody was kidding. "Wait. Really?"

"Yeah," Mitchell said.

"Oh, my God." In a heartbeat, Cynthia switched hats. "Brooklyn, I'm a board member. I should supervise this activity."

Supervise this activity? What was she, a playground guard? And I noticed she still hadn't shown an ounce of sympathy for the dead woman. Not that I blamed her, really, but things were getting weird.

I gave Mitchell a pleading look. "They can't come down the hall. It's a crime scene."

"I'll keep them back." He started walking toward the group, then stopped and turned. "Don't touch anything."

"I know that," I muttered, watching him jog away. Maybe he didn't realize I was an old hand at murder scenes and knew all the rules. I even followed them, usually.

I leaned over to study the book on the floor by Layla and felt chills skitter down my spine. It was my *Oliver Twist*, the one I'd refurbished for her. The one I'd regretted giving her the first night of classes. The one she'd blatantly lied about. The one for which she'd given me so much grief.

I rubbed my hands together to warm up, but it wasn't working. I was freezing.

"Brooklyn, are you okay?" Alice called out from down the hall. I could tell she was crying, but despite her own sense of loss, she was worried about me.

I gave her a grateful smile. "Not really, but thanks."

"Do you want to sit down?"

"No, I'll stay here until the police come." I don't know why, but I felt an obligation of sorts. As the first person on the scene, I would protect the area until I could pass the duty on to the police.

"I feel so useless," Alice said, sniffling as she looked around. "Is there something we can do? Brooklyn, do you need a blanket or some water?"

"We could go outside and wait for the police," Gina said.

"It's too cold," Whitney whined.

"It's better than standing around." Gina grabbed her friend and they ran off.

Dale, one of my quietest students, appeared at the end of the hall. "Is somebody hurt?"

I looked up as Kylie said, "Where have you been?"

"I was working on my pages. What happened?"

"The center director's dead," Kylie whispered.

I was glad she hadn't said Layla's name. I kidded myself

that it sounded less personal, more clinical, to keep it semi-anonymous.

The students' conversation stopped as Naomi pushed through the crowd and headed down the hall toward me. I met her halfway and tried to stop her.

"Oh, not again," she said in dismay. "I leave the place for twenty minutes and somebody gets attacked again? It's not Minka, is it?"

"No, it's not Minka." She tried to brush past me and I grabbed her. "Naomi, stay back."

"Then who—" She screamed then, loud enough to pierce my eardrum. I guess she figured it out.

I pulled her close in a forced hug. She struggled to get away.

"Let me go. I need to—"

"No, you can't go near her."

"Let go of me, damn it. She's my aunt, my family. I don't—"

I shook her. "This is a crime scene. We've called the police."

"Why? She's not—"

"Naomi," I said bleakly.

"No!"

"I'm sorry." I wrapped my arms around her.

"No, no," she moaned. "It's not true."

"I'm sorry. Layla's dead."

She sagged against me. "You're lying."

"No, I'm not. I'm sorry. She's dead."

Hell, Layla Fontaine, artistic director, mover and shaker and bitch royale, wasn't just *dead*. She'd been murdered. Coldly, brutally, and audaciously. Someone had walked into BABA as bold as could be and shot her in the chest while at least twenty people worked in rooms nearby. Everyone in the building had to have heard the gunshot, so it wasn't like the killer was trying to be stealthy. No, he—or she—had used a gun, drawing almost instant attention to his deed.

Was her killer really so arrogant? Or just pissed off? Or desperate? Or insane? Did he really think he'd get away with it? Looking around and not finding any obvious killer types waving guns in the air, I saw clearly that, so far, someone was indeed getting away with it.

Had Layla and the assailant argued about the *Oliver Twist*? Was it a buyer who discovered Layla's lie about it being a first edition? Had he thrown the book at her, then shot her in cold blood when she laughed in his face?

My imagination had taken flight and I had to reel it back in. But as long as Layla had to die, that would be the motive I would want the killer to have.

I continued to hold Naomi in my arms as she cried and moaned. I understood what she was going through. Besides being her employer, Layla was her aunt. It wasn't easy to find a loved one lying dead in a pool of blood.

I'd been there, done that. It sucked.

"What the hell is going on out here?" Minka yelled from the door of her classroom. Her voice carried all the way across the building. And down the street and over the bridge and into Richmond County. Her clunky boots stomped across the gallery.

"Oh, God, don't let that cow come over here," Naomi whispered.

"I won't." Even in this grim circumstance, it made me smile to know I wasn't alone in my low opinion of Minka.

Over Naomi's shoulder, I watched Mitchell stop Minka from advancing down the hall. She stared daggers at me and I met her squinty gaze levelly. She started to say something; then her mouth slammed shut. And for that brief moment, I could see what she was thinking. She was thinking she'd gotten off easy with the gash across her head instead of a bullet hole in her chest. She was alive, not dead and lying in a pool of blood.

The sudden vulnerability I saw in her eyes made me look

away. I never ever, ever wanted to think of Minka as weak or helpless. It would take all the fun out of hating her.

"Stay back, please," Mitchell said, stretching his arm across the hall entrance to block her.

"Who the fuck are you?" she said, with a contemptuous curl of her lip.

Ah, there was the Minka we all loved to hate.

Mitchell simply waited her out, not taking his eyes off her for a second. After a long standoff, Minka huffed. "Fine, whatever. Jerk wad."

As she flounced back down the hall, I looked at Mitchell and sighed. "Sorry about that, but thanks."

"No problem. She's a peach. What else can I do to help?"

"Can you take Naomi to the lounge? She needs to sit down."

"No," Naomi protested. "I'm not leaving her."

"You've had a bad shock, Naomi," I said. "You need to sit down or you'll pass out. I promise I'll watch her until the police arrive."

"But she'd want me to stay with her."

"You're probably right." Layla had always loved bossing Naomi around. Still, she was a dead weight in my arms so I gave her an affectionate squeeze and said, "You're so thoughtful to consider what Layla would want, but I'm more concerned about you right now."

She sniffled, then began to sob. I traded glances with Mitchell, who immediately stepped forward and took hold of Naomi.

"You can come with me," he said gently, putting his arm around her shoulders. Before he led her away, he turned and said to me, "Police should be here any minute. I got Ned to stand guard at the other entrance to this hall."

"What other entrance?"

He pointed to Layla's office. "That office has a separate entrance leading to another hall that curves around to the back of the building. I had to run to the men's room the first night and got lost coming back. I followed the hall around and ended up in there."

I hadn't noticed a second doorway the other night when I brought Layla the book. Probably because I was so distracted by her sleazy scheme to pass the *Oliver Twist* off as a first edition.

I thought of Ned on the other side of the door. I didn't want to say it aloud, but even though I trusted Mitchell's instincts, I wondered if we could trust Ned.

Mitchell led Naomi away, and within seconds Tom Hardesty lumbered up, out of breath. "I was outside. It's cold. What's going on? Mitchell said you might need some help."

"He did? Well, maybe you could—"

"Wait. Who is that?" Tom peered around me to stare at the body. His eyes widened and his mouth dropped open. He shook his head. "No, it's not. No. No. No." His voice grew louder and more high-pitched and I scanned the hall looking for help.

Finally, I had to shout over him, "Tom, shut up."

"But she's . . . oh, God. She's dead."

"Yeah, we all got that," I said loudly. "Where were you when the memo went out?" I probably shouldn't have talked that way to a board member but he was such a twit. Seriously, Mitchell had sent this guy to help me and now he was having a panic attack? I'd lost any last drop of sympathy I might have had for him.

He didn't seem to notice my acerbic response, just shook his head and whispered, "I was outside making a phone call."

"Guess you missed all the excitement."

"She can't be dead," Tom whimpered, and tried to move closer.

I sidestepped to block him.

"Noooooo," Tom moaned.

I'd reached the end of my rope. "Tom, shut the hell up."

Without warning, he fell to his knees and tried to reach for Layla's hand.

"No!" I slapped his hand away just in time. "Crime scene. Get out of here."

He collapsed on the floor and curled up like a baby in a womb.

Stunned by his behavior, I yelled down the hall, "Where's Cynthia? I need her, now."

"I'll look for her," Alice cried, eager to be of service.

I stared at Tom. "Get a grip, man."

He began to weep as Cynthia stalked down the hall. "So this is where he disappeared to."

"Yeah," I said.

She dropped to her haunches and smacked Tom's head. "What the hell's wrong with you?"

"It's Layla," he sobbed. "She's . . . oh, my God, she's . . ."

"She's dead," Cynthia shot back. "And good riddance."

Whoa.

Tom didn't seem to notice his wife's antipathy as he rocked in agony.

"Jesus H," Cynthia muttered. She exhaled heavily, then took a deep breath and seemed to gather every last ounce of patience in her body. She patted his back and said in a soothing tone, "Come on, honey. The police will be here any minute. They can't find you like this."

That moved him to stand up. He wobbled once but she grabbed and steadied him.

He blinked, then gulped and said, "Thanks, honey."

She smacked his arm. "We'll talk about this later. Come on, let's go." Then she gripped his shirt to lead him away.

I had a feeling Tom would get an earful when he arrived home. Maybe that was a good thing. God knows, it seemed their relationship thrived on discipline. As they moved down the hall, I noticed that some of my other students had witnessed the entire scene.

Kylie grimaced. "This is all too surreal."

"Two attacks in one week is more than surreal," I said.

Whitney and Gina returned to the group, and Whitney rubbed her arms. "It's really freezing out there."

"Hey, I wonder if the local news will show up," Gina said.

"We should call them," Whitney whispered, and Gina nodded with excitement.

I rolled my eyes. Just what I needed, to be accosted by nosy reporters. All they had to do was link me to Abraham's murder and the Scotland murders and I'd be known forever more as Bloody Brooklyn—or some equally annoying nickname.

Brooklyn's Bloody Bodies "R" Us. Very catchy.

"Where are the cops?" I wondered aloud.

As if on cue, a siren screamed in the distance, growing louder and finally stopping right outside the front door.

"About damn time," I muttered, more than ready for a good stiff drink.

Chapter 8

As the sirens faded outside the building, I had a sudden realization. What was I doing here? Why was I the one protecting a crime scene as if it were my job? As if I were some officer of the court? I wasn't. I was just some poor schnook who'd seen too many dead bodies lately and knew the score. I realized the area needed to be as undisturbed as possible so that evidence could be saved and justice served. This time, I'd even left a fabulous old book on the floor, untouched. I wish I'd taken it, though. After all, it wasn't like the book had killed her, right?

I'd done my duty, but now I was starting to freak out over my recent proclivity for finding bodies. I couldn't blame my head for screaming, *Get away from the dead body! People are starting to talk!*

I heeded the message and signaled Mitchell over. "I need to return to the classroom."

He was taken aback. "You're starting up the class?"

"No, no. No more class tonight. I just need to get away from here. Can you watch her for me?"

Mitchell glanced over at "her," and said, "Sure. Go. I'll let the cops know where you are."

"Thanks, I think."

He chuckled as I scurried off, back to my empty classroom. I toed my shoes off and curled up in one of the cushioned high chairs stationed around the worktable. Now that it was quiet, I took a moment to wonder, again, what was up with my karma. Why me? Why dead bodies? Was the universe sending me a message? Whatever it was, I couldn't read it.

Layla was dead and I felt nothing. I mean, I was alarmed that a killer might be getting away with murder. But otherwise, I felt nothing except complete relief that I'd never have to deal with her crap again.

Maybe I would break into tears later, or struggle all night to get the picture of her dead body out of my head. But for now, I felt nothing. And that probably wouldn't help my karma situation much.

Since I planned to drive to Sonoma this weekend, maybe I would ask my mother for suggestions. She was dabbling in Wicca lately and could run a happy positivity spell on me. If not, I could always undergo some ojas replenishment. Or, what the heck, I might even get my chakras lubed. I was desperate.

And not that it was all about me, but did Layla have to die on a night when I was wearing my cutest outfit for my big night out with the hot British guy?

Yes, I was whining, but I'd gone to a lot of trouble earlier, calling up my best friend and fashion maven, Robin, and opening myself up to possible mockery by asking for her advice. So I deserved to whine for a minute in the privacy of my own brain.

Sure enough, Robin had enjoyed a few laughs at my expense. Then she'd gotten down to business, insisting that I wear the one dress I owned with my sexiest pair of black heels. She knew I owned them because she'd forced me to buy them a few weeks back for an art opening I'd attended that featured some of her newest sculptures.

I'd done exactly as she suggested. Why ask for expert advice if you're not going to take it? I'd even managed to fix my straight blond hair the way she'd instructed, using a touch of gel on my bangs for a chunky, punky look. Those were her words.

And it all seemed to work, if my students were any gauge. I was looking good. I was uncomfortable and my feet were killing me, but I looked good. And I felt good. Until Layla had to go and die.

So here I sat, feeling sorry for myself and guilty for it, plus worrying about my karma and my feet and Derek Stone and the future of BABA. Because even though I disapproved of some of Layla's methods, I couldn't see Naomi or Karalee or Alice running this place with the same skill and panache.

"Meow."

"Hey, Baba," I said, and leaned down to pick up the cat. He was large and unwieldy, but he seemed to need a comforting touch. I held him in my lap, stroking his soft fur, and wondered what he thought of this odd place he called home. Had he seen anything? Heard anything? Had he looked into the eyes of a killer tonight? If so, he would take his secrets to the grave.

"Meow."

"Yeah, I know, you'll never tell."

The door opened slowly and Alice poked her head in. "Oh, you're in here. I was worried. Are you okay? Do you mind if I come in?"

I smiled at her, glad to be distracted from my selfish woes. "Come in and sit down. I'm just hiding in here with the cat. We're feeling sorry for ourselves."

"Pretty kitty." Alice leaned over and scratched Baba's ears for a minute. The cat allowed it for a few seconds, then ran off. Alice straightened and pushed her long hair back off her shoulders. "Are you feeling sorry about Layla? Because I feel awful. And I'm so worried. I hate to even think these thoughts while Layla is . . . well. But I just don't know how we're going to go forward. Layla was everything to BABA."

She paced the floor, wringing her hands as she spoke a mile a minute.

"Naomi is a mess," she said, almost to herself. "The managers are both in a dither, and there's Ned. He's an odd Thomas, isn't he? Well, I just hope nobody expects me to pick up the slack. I'm one step removed from a basket case at the best of times."

"Alice," I interrupted, amused despite the fact that I had the same concerns, "things will work out. Nobody expects you to grab the helm. Everyone here needs time to grieve and regroup."

She pursed her lips in thought. "You know what, Brooklyn? I think I *should* grab the helm. Now is not the time to shrink back, but to move forward. Now is the time to hit the ground running, to ask ourselves, What would Layla do?"

She began to march back and forth, a little soldier now, shaking her fist with firm resolve. "I can't give in to the fear. We have a festival to get off the ground. And next month, the print arts program will be launching a new book. There's already publicity out on that and we've got a huge party at the end of the month. No, Layla would want us to proceed full steam ahead. There's no time for lollygagging, no time indeed."

Maybe she was channeling Layla, but whatever she was doing, I was glad to see she wasn't crying or rubbing her stomach anymore. Maybe her taking charge was a good thing, just the diversion she needed to take her mind off her friend's sudden death.

On impulse, I said, "Alice, I'm having a girls' night at my place tomorrow night. There's just a few of us, dinner, drinks, some laughs. Would you like to come?"

Her eyes went wide and her mouth opened, but no words came out.

"Is that a yes?" I said after a moment.

"You . . . you're inviting me over to your house? To meet your friends?"

"Yeah. You want to come?"

She sniffled. "I would be so honored. Thank you."

"We're just talking pizza and cheap wine here."

"It sounds wonderful," she whispered. "I've hardly met anyone since I moved here and I don't get out much, so you've got to excuse me if I'm overcome with emotion."

I laughed. "Okay, good. I'll write down the directions."

The door swung open and Inspector Nathan Jaglom walked in. I smiled, happy to see the homicide detective who had investigated the murder of Abraham Karastovsky less than two months before. Was it perverse to feel as if I were greeting an old friend?

"Inspector Jaglom, hello," I said, hopping down from the chair and walking over to shake his hand. "Do you remember me?"

"Ms. Wainwright," Jaglom said with a broad grin. "Of course, how could I forget you? Are you involved in this?"

"Only peripherally, I promise you." I waved my hands a little too frantically. "I was teaching a class when we heard the gunshot. I've got more than ten witnesses that will back me up."

"Good." He looked relieved, but not half as relieved as I was.

"Everyone in my class is a witness for each other, as well," I hastened to add. "We were all working when the gunshot was fired."

"Okay, that's good. We'll need a few minutes with each person, ask a few questions, check their IDs and contact info. Then you should all be free to go home."

"Okay, sounds fair." I noticed Alice then. "Inspector, this is one of my students, who's also the center's assistant director. Alice Fairchild."

He nodded. "Ms. Fairchild."

"How do you do?" she said, her voice barely registering. She gave me a questioning look.

"I met Inspector Jaglom recently," I explained, "when he worked on a case where a friend of mine was killed."

"Oh, I'm so sorry." She touched my shoulder in sympathy, then whispered, "I'm just going to wait in the gallery."

After she left the room, Jaglom browsed the front counter. Holding up one of my journals, he said, "Is this the kind of stuff you're teaching?"

"Yes. It's a bookbinding class."

"Looks good," he said, then smiled kindly. "So, how are you getting along these days?"

"I'm doing pretty well, thanks." I knew he was asking how I was dealing with Abraham's death. "Really, fine."

"Good." He turned as the door opened and Detective Inspector Janice Lee entered. "Hey, Lee."

"Sorry I'm late," Lee said, then saw me. "Brooklyn Wainwright. Why am I not surprised?"

"She's got witnesses this time," Jaglom said, and chuckled. I was so happy to provide amusement for local law enforcement.

"Listen," Lee said. "We've got two classrooms available for interviews. You want to take this room or the other one?"

He looked around, then shrugged. "Doesn't matter."

"Minka LaBoeuf is teaching in the other classroom," I said helpfully.

"I'll take this room," Lee said immediately.

Jaglom grimaced. "Great. See you later, Ms. Wainwright."

"You bet," I said, and waved in sympathy. They'd both had unpleasant run-ins with Minka during the investigation of Abraham's murder.

Lee took off her trench coat and draped it over one of the tall chairs. I couldn't help but notice she'd put on a few pounds. It looked good on her. And while it was none of my business, she could afford to gain another ten or twenty.

"What's up, Brooklyn?" she said, leaning back against the counter and folding her arms across her chest. She was Asian-American, tall and pretty, with a throaty voice some might consider sexy, but which I knew came from smoking too much. She had fabulous hair, thick, black, and shiny. And she intimidated the hell out of me.

"Not much," I lied, kneading my temple where another headache was brewing. "Although to tell you the truth, I'm a little tired of running into dead bodies everywhere I go. How are you doing, Inspector?"

"I'm a bitch on wheels since I gave up smoking," she said. "Otherwise, life is like a dream. I know what you mean about the bodies, though. I seem to have the same problem. Occupational hazard, I guess."

"I guess," I said, chuckling. "Hey, congratulations on the smoking thing." I guess that explained the weight gain.

"Yeah, whatever. Turns out, my mother was right. Guys don't like to kiss an ashtray."

"Really."

"Yeah, but who needs guys?" She shoved away from the counter and walked to the worktable, where she tested one of my student's glued pages for dryness. "This your class?"

"Yes, bookbinding." I glanced around the empty room. "My students are all hanging out in the gallery, soaking up the excitement."

"Excitement," she repeated, as she fiddled with the wing nuts on the press, flicking them back and forth a few times. "I hear there's been a lot of it around here lately."

"You could say that."

"Yeah, I could." She smirked, then seemed to remember she was there to do a job. "So, tell me about the victim."

I paused, unsure where to start, then figured I'd start at the top. "She was despicable."

"Hey, don't sugarcoat it. Tell me how you really feel."

"I kind of hated her."

She leaned back and crossed her ankles. "Guess it's a good thing you have a rock-solid alibi."

I blew out a breath. "It sure is."

She splayed her hands out. "So, tell all. Why was she so awful?"

I held up my hand and counted on my fingers. "She cheated, she lied, she came on to all the men, and she ruled this place through fear and intimidation."

"Sounds like a real piece of work."

"I had an argument with her two nights ago." I explained about the *Oliver Twist*, emphasizing the fact that I had left the book with Layla's body. "I'm ashamed to admit I went along with Layla's lie because I was afraid she'd ruin my reputation, maybe blackball me in the community and keep me from working here."

Lee nodded. "And how did that make you feel?"

"Like I wanted to kill her."

"Over a book?"

I shook my head. "It was the principle of the thing."

Lee cocked her head. "Boy, give the woman an alibi and she goes to town. You're sounding more and more like a suspect, you know."

"But I'm not," I said, smiling grimly.

She leaned her arms on the back of the high chair. "I heard some rumors about a situation in Edinburgh."

"I didn't do it."

She laughed. "They should've called me."

"So you could give me a character reference?"

"Of course," she said, then slapped her hands together. "Well, I should get back to kicking ass and taking names."

"Sounds like fun."

"It's what I live for," she said. "But first, tell me about the other people here. Did everyone hate this woman enough to kill her?"

I hedged. "Well, some were more enamored of her than others."

She eyed me sideways. "You giving me a little clue here?"

My lips twitched back and forth. "I hate to be a snitch."

"This isn't *Scarface*, Brooklyn. I need to find a killer. Throw me a bone."

I gave her a two-minute summation of everything that might relate to Layla's murder, including Tom and Cynthia's oddball behavior, Ned's general demeanor, Naomi's passive-aggressive ways, Minka's attack, and the Asian man who stormed out of Layla's office that first night.

"Sounds like a lot of strong emotions running rampant."

"You could say that."

"Are you thinking this angry Asian might've snuck back in here and knocked out Minka instead of Layla?"

"It's possible."

"Can you describe him?" she asked, writing in her notepad as fast as she could.

I gave it my best shot, then added, "I wish he was the only one she'd pissed off."

"That would make my job easier. But unfortunately, this seems to be a suspect-rich environment."

"I hate to think someone I know could've done this. Maybe there's a random psychopathic killer loose in the neighborhood."

"You know, there just aren't as many psychopathic killers running around as people think."

I took it philosophically. "Another myth busted."

She shrugged. "That's my job."

After I led her out to the gallery and pointed out the various players, Inspector Lee corralled most of my students back into the classroom. She isolated Cynthia and Tom, as well as the four staff members, Naomi, Ned, Marky, and Karalee, in separate offices, each with a cop taking preliminary information from them.

My students and I were dealt with quickly and told to go home. I walked back out to the gallery just as the front door opened. From across the wide space, I saw two men walk in with Gunther between them. Seconds later, Derek strolled into the foyer.

Without thinking, I gave a little cry and ran toward him. Derek saw me coming and opened his arms.

"I'm so glad you're here," I whispered, not even caring if I sounded like a wimpy girl.

"And I'm glad to be here," he said. "Especially now, with you wrapped around me."

My insides shuddered at his words. Could we just find a room somewhere and forget everything that had happened here tonight? He'd dressed up for our date, too, in a beautiful black suit, crisp white shirt, and dark crimson tie. I didn't know an Armani from an armadillo, but I knew his outfit had to cost a few thousand pounds. And it was worth every last penny, I thought, as I nuzzled up next to him and felt the soft wool against my cheek.

"What has you so upset, darling?" he said, his breath unsettling the fine hairs of my neck. "We saw the police cars. Was there another attack?"

"Yes. Oh, Derek."

"You're shaking, sweetheart. What's wrong?"

"It's Layla Fontaine."

"Beg your pardon?"

"She was murdered. A bullet in the chest. Blood." I shivered again.

He pushed back and held me at arm's length. "Layla Fontaine? Murdered?"

I gulped. "I didn't do it."

He opened his mouth to say something, but shut it quickly. He drew me close and I wrapped my arms around his waist. "Of course you didn't do it. For heaven's sake. I didn't for one minute think you were responsible."

"But I found her," I whispered. "And somebody's going to connect her death to Abraham's and, you know, what happened in Scotland. They'll just assume I had something to do with it."

He rubbed my back in a soothing, circular motion. "They'll answer to me if they do."

"Stone?"

Derek whipped around. "What is it?"

Gunther's face was pale. "Did you hear? Layla. My God, she's dead."

"Yes, I've just been told."

Gunther's Austrian accent seemed to grow thicker as he became more agitated. "Is this some kind of joke?"

I took a small step away from Derek. "No, it's not a joke."

Gunther's gaze homed in on me. "Who are you? What happened? A heart attack? Did she choke?"

I looked at Derek, then back at Gunther. "She was murdered."

"Commander Stone?" Inspector Jaglom approached. "I thought that was you. Welcome back to the States."

"Thank you, Inspector," Derek said, shaking the man's hand. They had worked together during Abraham's murder investigation. The first time I'd heard Jaglom greet Derek by the title of Commander, I realized the guy was actually a former commander in the Royal Navy. Before that, I was pretty sure he was a killer. Of course, he was convinced I was, too. Ah, the memories.

Derek continued, "Inspector, let me introduce you to Gunther Schnaubel."

There were somber murmurs of greeting; then Gunther said, "Inspector, I demand to know what happened here."

"That's what we intend to find out, Mr. Schnaubel."

Gunther rubbed tight knuckles across his jawline. "This is unacceptable. I spoke to Layla a mere hour ago. She sounded fine. We were to meet here and discuss certain arrangements."

"I'm sorry for your loss, Mr. Schnaubel," Jaglom said, studying the Austrian carefully as he pulled a notepad and pen from his pocket. "What sort of arrangements were you planning to talk about with the deceased?"

Gunther licked his lips. He had the grace to look flustered, as if he was just now realizing how big a bull's-eye he'd painted on himself.

I cleared my throat. "Inspector, Mr. Schnaubel is one of the honored guests Ms. Fontaine invited to the book festival running these next two weeks. He's a world-renowned artist and he's teaching several classes as well as donating some important pieces to the silent auction."

Gunther looked pleased by my words.

"I see," Jaglom said, as he wrote in his notepad. "What sort of artist are you, Mr. Schnaubel?"

"What does that matter?" Gunther said, angry now and posing with his fist on his hip and his nose in the air, as though he expected some underling to clean up the mess that was causing havoc in his well-ordered life.

"Let's talk some more in here, Mr. Schnaubel," Jaglom said, pointing down the hall to one of the rooms the police were using.

"I have nothing else to say," he said, his lips in a tight pout. Could he be more of a diva?

Derek leaned closer to Jaglom. "Inspector, could I have a word, please?"

"Certainly."

The two men walked slowly as they talked, down the ramp to the gallery, then up another ramp and into the east hall. What were they discussing? I wondered. What did Derek know that I didn't and how soon could I find out? And meanwhile, what was I supposed to do?

Gunther eyed me with suspicion but said nothing.

"I love your work," I said lamely.

He raised one imperious eyebrow. "Thank you."

"You're welcome."

Okay, enough small talk. I should've been nicer to him since he was a world-renowned artist and a guest here at BABA, but all the niceness had been drained out of me. I excused myself and walked away, wondering when this nightmare would be over.

Chapter 9

"You still haven't slept with the man?"

"Shh," I said in a frantic whisper. "I'd rather not broadcast it to the world."

"I don't blame you," Robin said in a loud whisper, as she arranged three kinds of cheese and crackers on a tray. "I'd be embarrassed, too."

"I'm not embarrassed," I hissed, then had to take a breath to calm down. I wasn't embarrassed, really. Just horribly disappointed that last night had been such a bust.

I'm not saying we would've ended up in bed together, but we didn't even go out. No dinner, no drinks, no nothing. It was a sad waste of a perfectly great dress and sexy shoes.

The whole evening had been consumed by Layla and the murder investigation. Even dead, the woman was ruining my life. By the time I got home, alone, I was exhausted. And once again, Layla had taken center stage. I winced at the unkind thought and waved it away. It was spiteful and stupid, and probably counted as another black mark on my karma scorecard. I just hoped the time I spent protecting the crime scene from the likes of the peculiar Tom Hardesty and the shrieking Naomi would weigh in my favor.

The police had questioned everyone. Gunther had been so flipped out after his interview with Inspector Jaglom, or his "grilling with the KGB," as Gunther so dramatically put it, that Derek and all of his men had to babysit him the rest of the night. Who knew a big guy like that could be such a little girl?

"So what happened?" Robin persisted.

"Nothing," I snapped, then took a calming breath and gave her the highlights: Derek's demanding client, a few screwy students and staff, murders, attacks, police all over the place.

"I'm sorry," she said. "I guess it'll happen when it's meant to."

"Now you sound like my mother," I said, smiling reluctantly.

"No, your mom would channel Romlar X, who would advise that the precise optimal moment for mating must be analyzed vis-à-vis your cosmic destiny." She smirked as she unscrewed the top off a bottle of New Zealand Sauvignon Blanc.

"Oh, dear God, you're right."

Robin and I were closer than two sisters, so she knew when I was upset or in trouble. I first met her when we were eight years old. My parents had moved my two brothers and three sisters and me up to the wilds of Sonoma County, to live on land they'd purchased with the other members of the Fellowship for Spiritual Enlightenment and Higher Artistic Consciousness. The first person I noticed when I stepped out of my parents' Volkswagen bus was Robin Tully, a short, fierce, dark-haired girl who clutched a baldheaded Barbie in her tight little fist. We clicked from day one.

Robin's mother was always traveling, searching for the miraculous all over the world. So Robin lived with us most of the time. That was fine with me.

Robin looked up from opening the second bottle of wine, a hearty Malbec my father had discovered and given to me to try. "So is Derek still as hot as ever?"

I laughed. "Does the sun still set in the west?"

"Yeah, that's what I thought," she said, fanning herself.

"Brooklyn, pizza is here," Vinnie trilled from the other room.

"Let the party begin," Robin said, and carried out the tray of goodies. I followed close behind with wineglasses and two bottles of wine.

As I set everything on the coffee table, I was happy to hear Suzie and Vinnie regaling Alice with horror stories of their chain-saw competitions. My friends and I had all agreed ahead of time not to bring up the subject of Layla. It would just upset Alice.

"It sounds so dangerous," Alice said, reaching for the white wine. "Chain saws are scary."

"It's nothing," Suzie said.

Vinnie beamed. "My Suzie is macho to the core."

Suzie rolled up one sleeve and popped her biceps.

"Whoa," Alice said, wide-eyed, and we all laughed.

Robin grabbed a cracker. "You guys should show Alice your work later on. It's impressive."

"Oh, I'd love to see it," Alice said, then pointed to one of the trays of cheese and crackers. "I don't mean to interrupt, but I wanted to let you all know that these are rice crackers. I was just diagnosed with celiac disease, so I'm trying to change my diet around."

"Oh, the gluten allergy?" Vinnic asked.

"That's right," Alice said. "No wheat, rye, barley, or oats. No pizza, which is sad, but I guess it's the gluten that was killing my stomach."

"That sounds very painful," Vinnie said.

"It was awful," Alice continued. "So now I'm determined to stay far away from anything resembling gluten. I had a simple blood test and they diagnosed it. And almost overnight, I feel so much better. No stomachaches, no leg cramps in the middle of the night."

"Ouch," Suzie said, wincing.

"That's good news, Alice," I said. "I'm really happy for you."

"Thanks." She grabbed a rice cracker and popped it into her mouth, then made a face. "Like I said, it'll take some getting used to."

There was a knock at the door; then I heard someone cry, "Yoo-hoo!"

"Is that my mother?" I said in alarm.

"No, it's Jeremy, one of our new neighbors," Vinnie said. "I left a note on their door that we were over here. I hope that's okay, Brooklyn. I believe we should all be good neighbors."

"It's fine," I said, and jogged down the short hall to my workroom, which was actually the front of my apartment. The door was open and a gorgeous man with bleached blond streaks in his hair was peeking inside.

"Hi, it's us," he said. "Your rude new neighbors."

"Come in," I said. "I'm Brooklyn."

"I'm Jeremy," he said, looking around. "What a great room."

A dark-haired Adonis followed him inside and stared at my walls of supplies and tools. "So this is where it all happens," he said. "I'm Sergio, by the way."

"I'm Brooklyn. Welcome to the neighborhood. Where what happens?"

Sergio pointed at the walls and cabinets. "Suzie told us what you do. All the book stuff. Fascinating."

Jeremy walked slowly around my central worktable, staring at the counters, where two large book presses were neatly arranged next to jars of brushes and filing tools and bone folders. Above the counters were wall-mounted shelves that held books and rolls of leather and heavy paper and threads of every color.

"Wow," Sergio said. "Cool stuff."

"Yeah, great energy," Jeremy said.

"Thanks, I like it, too," I said, smiling with pride. "Come on back. We're having wine."

"We didn't want to interrupt, but Vinnie left a note."

"No worries. We were hoping you'd come over." I ushered them through the hallway and into my living space.

"Hi, girls," Jeremy said, waving.

"Hi, boys," Suzie said with a grin.

"Ooh," Jeremy said, pulling Sergio into the room. "I like the way she's got this set up over here."

"Great chair," Sergio said, running his hand along the back of the big red Hawaiian-print chair that faced the green couch in the center of the room.

I couldn't help feeling a touch of satisfaction. I loved my place a lot. As the women moved everything over to the bar for easier access to the refrigerator, I gave the two men a minitour.

"My business called for a separate workroom office area," I explained, pointing out features as we walked around the wide-open space. "So I had the wall built between the office and the living area, then added a closet and powder room to accommodate my clients."

"Ooh, tax write-off," Jeremy said, wiggling his eyebrows at Sergio.

I laughed. "You betcha."

"It looks really nice." Sergio wandered over to the wall of windows with the eastern view. "I like the different seating areas you've arranged."

"Me, too." The windows on the east side of the room showed off a view of the bay that was worth the price I'd paid for the place. The view was pure luck. Two nearby buildings blocked the view from some of my neighbors' apartments, but my place was in the center of the top floor and I was able to see straight out to the bay.

I'd set two comfy leather Buster chairs, a shared ottoman, and a sturdy table in front of the windows. It was perfect for reading, which was one reason why I had a long, low bookcase running the length of the windows. Some mornings, I liked to sit there with a cup of coffee and a book on my lap, just staring out at the bay, feeling at peace with the world.

I hadn't felt that peaceful in a while.

I left Sergio and Jeremy sitting in the Buster chairs, plotting the redesign of their own space, took their wine requests, and joined the females in the kitchen area.

"I opened another bottle," Robin said.

"Thanks." I poured two glasses of red wine and took them to Sergio and Jeremy.

Sergio protested. "We shouldn't have barged in. Looks like you're having a girls' night."

Jeremy slapped his arm in good humor. "Oh, honey, we can do girls' night."

From across the room, Suzie said, "Hey, if they'll let me in, they'll definitely let you in."

Everyone laughed, and I said, "We're just hanging out and you're more than welcome to stay."

Sergio held up his glass. "We don't want to drink you out of house and home."

I smiled. "Then it's a happy coincidence that my dad owns a winery."

"I love this girl!" Jeremy said.

"Brooklyn, we need you in here," Robin said. "Alice needs consoling."

"I'm fine," Alice said, but I could hear her voice cracking.

I walked back to the kitchen and put my arm around her shoulders. "What's wrong, my friend?"

Alice burst into tears and ran to the bathroom.

Alarmed, I turned to Robin. "What did you do?"

She looked nonplussed. "Nothing. I swear. She was talking about all the cool people in your bookbinding class, and I thought she was going to burst into tears, so that's why I called you over. I thought I was kidding, but it turns out I was right."

"You called her your friend, Brooklyn," Vinnie said. "I believe that sent her over the edge. She seems a bit overwhelmed. Perhaps she does not have many friends."

"She just moved to town a month or two ago," I said.

"Well, that sucks," Suzie said. She drained her wineglass and held it out to me. "Please, sir, I want some more."

I blinked. "That's from *Oliver Twist*."

"Yeah, we watched it on TV the other night," she said with a cockeyed grin. "The Polanski version, which is very cool and dark, by the way." She slid off her barstool and went to the fridge to get her own wine. "But quite the downer. That kid couldn't get a break."

"I just finished rebinding a beautiful copy of the book," I said.

"Cool."

"Yeah, it was. Except it belonged to Layla."

"Ouch," Suzie said, hopping back up on her stool.

"Right. That was the book that caused all the trouble."

"Ooh." Suzie nodded. "Okay, that's weird."

Alice came back to the kitchen carrying a tissue and blotting her eyes. "I'm sorry to be such a twerp. You guys are just too nice. I don't have any girlfriends in town yet and my stomach gives me problems and so does my fiancé, and I'm under a lot of pressure at the center and Layla's dead now and I don't know how to do what I'm supposed to do. I'm floundering."

Vinnie patted her back. "I find I get flundery at times, too. It is good at these times to be with friends."

Alice nodded sincerely and sipped her wine.

There was a pause; then Robin said, "Flundery?"

Suzie snorted. "It's a Vinnie-ism. I figure it's a cross between fluttery and floundering and flucked up."

I pulled an apple out of the crisper and began to cut it up to go with the cheese. Glancing over my shoulder at Alice, I said, "I hope I didn't say anything to upset you."

"No, no," Alice insisted. "I'm a little emotional, but right now, it's because I'm so happy. I wish you were all my friends."

"We are your friends," Vinnie said.

Alice bit her lip. "Don't get me started again."

Sergio and Jeremy joined us then, and I refilled their wineglasses.

"All this wine reminds me," Robin said, nudging my arm. "Are you going to Annie's opening?"

"Are you kidding? My mom will kill me if I miss it."

"What's that?" Suzie asked.

I turned. "Remember I told you about Abraham's daughter, Annie, opening a kitchen store in Dharma? Well, the grand opening is tomorrow. You're all invited. All the free wine you can drink."

"What's Dharma?" Alice asked.

"Who's Abraham?" Sergio asked.

"Did somebody say free wine?" Jeremy said.

I laughed. "Abraham was my bookbinding teacher. He died a few months ago. Annie is his daughter. She's opened a kitchen shop in the village where my parents live, on the Lane."

"The Lane is Shakespeare Lane," Robin explained. "All the cool shops and restaurants in Dharma are there."

Sergio nodded in agreement. "I know the Lane. Very chic, not to be missed. I used to work with the chef who opened the newest restaurant up there."

"Cool," I said, excited to know we were all connected somehow.

"Dharma is where Brooklyn and I grew up," Robin said. "It's a small town in Sonoma County, in the wine country. Near Glen Ellen."

"It's charming, sort of chic and rustic all at the same time," I added, grabbing some chips. "Actually, most of Sonoma is that way."

"With heavy emphasis on the rustic," Robin said. "It's not quite up to Napa chic yet."

"Never will be," I admitted.

"Nope," she agreed. "We should probably just go ahead and call it redneck."

"But with money," I said. "Lots of big-city money. Lots of old wine money."

"And new wine money," she added, and we both laughed.

Over twenty years ago, our families, along with a few hundred other ex-hippies and Deadheads, had followed their mystic teacher, Robson Benedict, to Sonoma County. We had lived communally on several thousand acres of land, and over the years the members planted vineyards as they built their spiritual and artistic community. Today, Dharma was incorporated and everyone in the commune was wealthy, thanks to the grapes we'd grown when we first moved there.

"It's going to be a big, fun scene," Robin said. "I'm driving up for the weekend and staying through Tuesday."

"I'm just staying for the day," I said. "Anyone want to join me?"

"Suzie and I would love to go," Vinnie said. "But we have plans. We're setting up a new installation in Marin."

"You're having an art show?" I asked.

"In San Rafael," Suzie said. "It's part of their annual Big Art show."

"It's a play on words," Vinnie added. "All the art is very big in size. Do you get it?"

"They get it," Suzie said.

"Your art is definitely big," Robin said.

"Thank you," Vinnie said, bowing her head.

Everyone smiled.

"I would like to go to Sonoma," Alice said abruptly. "I mean, if it's okay. I wouldn't want to—"

"Yes, Alice," Vinnie piped up before I could answer. "You must go to Dharma. I suggest that you take advantage of Brooklyn's mother's knowledge of Ayurvedic massage. It is possible that your chakras are weakened and you might need rebalancing."

Alice's eyes widened in alarm.

"Vinnie, don't scare her with that mumbo jumbo," Suzie said, and turned to Alice. "Here's the deal. You spend the day drinking good wine and eating great food. You get a massage, relax, chill out. Brooklyn's family is wild. You'll have a good time and come back ready to kick some ass."

"That pretty much describes the experience," Robin said.

"It sounds wonderful," Alice said. "I would love to go."

"Is Stuart in town yet?" I asked. "He's welcome to come, too."

"Oh, no." Alice frowned. "He would probably love it, but he's still in Atlanta."

"Okay," I said. "We'll leave around eleven tomorrow morning."

"I'll be here."

Saturday morning was a classically gorgeous San Francisco day, cold and sunny with a sky as blue as a Boucher painting. I took Van Ness north through the Civic Center, past car dealerships and supermarkets, skirting both the dicey Tenderloin and exclusive Nob Hill before reaching Lombard, where I turned left toward the Presidio. I would've avoided this route on a weekday but today we zipped along at a smooth pace.

I stayed on Lombard and entered the Presidio, preferring the winding turns and hairpin curves to the straightforward smoothness of Highway 101. As I drove through the park, past the rows of stately, historic wood-framed and brick homes formerly assigned to army officers but now leased to the public, I glanced over at Alice. I had to hide my smile because while I wore jeans, boots, and a bulky sweater, she wore a prim white blouse with a rounded collar tucked into black trousers. She carried a thin black cashmere sweater and a small black shoulder bag. Her trademark velvet headband held her hair away from her face, and there were tiny pearl dot earrings in her ears.

No matter what the occasion, she was petite, demure, and sweet. I was none of the above.

We emerged from the wooded Presidio, passed the bridge toll plaza, and drove onto the Golden Gate Bridge. Alice glanced around in wonder. "It's so beautiful." She seemed less tense than I'd ever seen her before. That had to be a good thing.

"I love this view," I said as I took in the green rolling hills of Marin ahead and the blue Pacific Ocean to my left.

"It's so amazing," Alice said, sitting up in her seat to try and see over the bridge railing. After thirty seconds, she sat back down and stared at the hills. "I just can't get over it."

"You've driven across the bridge before, haven't you?"

"No. I've done my share of wandering around the city, but I haven't ventured much farther yet. There just hasn't been enough time."

"Oh, my God. I'm suddenly feeling the weight of responsibility."

"You hold yourself responsible for me having a good time outside the city?"

"That's right, and I take it very seriously."

"Okay then," she said, laughing. "I expect to be shown a good time."

"Yes, ma'am." I saluted and laughed with her. Within a minute or so, we were off the bridge and zooming through Marin County. Somewhere around Corte Madera, I asked Alice where she was from. She started talking in her speedy run-on style and didn't let up until we passed the old wagon on the hill with the sign that read WELCOME TO SONOMA COUNTY.

Alice had attended a Catholic boarding school while growing up in Georgia. Catholic school would be bad enough, but a boarding school? I told her I couldn't imagine anything more strict than Catholic nuns in a boarding school. She regaled me with story after story of the bad girls she grew up with and where they were now. Clearly, it was true what they said about Catholic girls.

"They" being my two brothers and their dodgy friends, Eric and Zorro (his real name). Both boys had been forced to attend Catholic school in Glen Ellen when we were kids. They'd railed against the nuns and the rules and the uniforms, but they'd spoken in hushed, reverential tones about those Catholic school girls.

As we passed the town of Glen Ellen and headed toward the Valley of the Moon, I realized I now knew more about Alice Fairchild and her life as a Catholic school girl than I knew about some members of my own family.

She'd met Layla when they both attended a fund-raising conference in Atlanta. She admitted that Layla could be abrasive, but Alice knew that behind Layla's tough exterior was a sensitive soul. She had challenged herself to get to know Layla better and found out that the woman didn't have many girlfriends. No wonder she didn't know how to treat other women.

I thought it was a little naive of Alice to think Layla had an ounce of goodness underneath that mean-girl outer shell, but Alice certainly seemed to have found a friend.

"I really admire what she built at BABA," Alice said. "I'd like to stay for a few years, then once Stuart and I start a family, we might move back to Georgia. If we do, I've always dreamed of opening a small arts center. I know I could put everything I've learned about fund-raising to good use. I'd love to pick your brain sometime about how I could set up some bookbinding classes for grown-ups. I've already talked to Karalee about her Saturday classes for kids. They're amazing."

"She's great with the kids," I said.

"Yes, she is. But now that Layla's gone, I'm not sure what to do."

"I'm sure the board would love it if you'd stay. But you don't have to decide anything right now. Just take your time."

I left Highway 12 at Montana Ridge Road and we wound

our way toward Dharma. I was giving Alice some pointers on setting up book craft classes as we turned onto Shakespeare Lane, the two-block-long stretch of shops and restaurants that constituted the epicenter of downtown Dharma.

"You were right," she whispered, looking from side to side as we drove past the pretty shops and tree-lined sidewalks. "It's beautiful. You're so lucky you grew up here."

"I think so," I said, smiling as I glanced around. "It cleans up pretty well, I must say."

And I was willing to bet it beat a nun-infested Catholic boarding school by a mile.

I found a parking space a block from the main drag and we walked to Annie's store. On the way, I pointed out the tasting room our winery operated, along with two good restaurants and a couple of high-end clothing shops. There were other stores in the area as well, a small luxury hotel and spa, and numerous B and Bs.

We passed Umbria, the town's newest restaurant, and I reminded Alice that this was the place Sergio had mentioned last night. Next door to that was the Good Book, the independent bookstore where I occasionally gave crafty bookbinding classes. And next door to the bookstore was Warped, my sister China's yarn and weaving shop.

I looked through the window and saw China teaching a knitting class to a small group. I caught her eye and waved, and she beckoned me inside.

If it wasn't obvious, my siblings and I were all named for places my parents visited back in the days when they followed the Grateful Dead. There's my oldest brother, Jackson, named for Jackson Hole, Wyoming, where the Dead never played but where my parents' best friends lived and where Jackson was born. Then came Austin, named for Austin, Texas, where the Dead performed with Willie Nelson and Bob Dylan. The story on Savannah was that Mom and Dad attended a raucous show in Atlanta with the Dead and Lynyrd Skynyrd, then drove to the coast and stopped overnight in Savannah, Georgia. Our little Savannah was conceived that night.

My baby sister, London, was named for London, Ontario, Canada, where Mom went into labor while visiting friends after a Toronto Dead show. China's name came from the China Lake Naval Air Weapons Center, where my parents got arrested for protesting against nuclear weapons. They had some great memories of that place. And I was named after the New York borough, having been conceived in the balcony during intermission of a Grateful Dead show at the now defunct Beacon Theatre.

"Come on, Alice," I said. "I'll introduce you to my wacky sister."

"Is that Annie?"

"No, Annie's not actually a member of my family, though you'd never know it if you saw her with my mom."

"Hey, girl," China cried, running to greet me. "You come for the opening?"

"Yeah." I gave her a hug, then turned. "This is my friend Alice."

"Hi, Alice, nice to meet you." They shook hands.

"Your shop is beautiful," Alice said, looking around in awe. "So many colors."

"Thanks. Have a look around."

"I will."

I watched Alice whip around, trying to check out all the displays. China's shop was so intriguing, it was hard to decide what to look at first.

One whole wall was covered in square cubbyholes, each one stuffed with a different color and weight of yarn. There were wire baskets hanging at different levels from the ceiling, some piled high with luxurious yarns, others with bunches of colorful embroidery threads. Several tables showed off knitted and crocheted blankets, adult and baby sweaters, booties, gloves, and more. In one corner was a massive loom with a half-completed multicolored blanket,

China's latest work in progress. It would eventually sell for thousands of dollars.

China was a talented weaver with a fantastic sense of design. She was the one who helped me get my loft pulled together when I first moved in. While I loved all my sisters, she was my favorite, the one I could most relate to. This was probably because she ate red meat and made a point of sinning on a regular basis.

"Have you seen Mom today?" I asked.

"She's at Annie's right now, and she's all wigged out of proportion about London and the boys coming to visit."

"That's so unfair," I said.

"I know," China said. "Everything stops when London shows up."

We laughed, but it was true. London was our youngest sister, and though I would never say it to her face, the prettiest. Growing up, she'd always tried to keep up with me and China and our other sister, Savannah. And she usually succeeded. Even now that we were all grown up, she was still doing it. For instance, two months after China gave birth to her beautiful baby girl, Hannah, London had to go and have twins. One boy and one girl.

She'd also married the perfect man. Trevor was a handsome doctor who happened to own a popular winery up in Calistoga. I mean, really, a doctor *and* a winemaker? She was such a show-off! I loved London and Trevor and the boys, but she could never be my favorite sister. She was too perfect. Not that I would ever tell her that.

My mom insisted she didn't play favorites, but she got all google-eyed whenever London and her babies came to visit.

"Is Trevor coming, too?" I asked.

"Of course. He'll be by later this afternoon."

"And what about Savannah?"

"She's still a freak," China said, crossing her eyes and sticking out her tongue.

"Ah, feel the love," I said, giving her a one-armed hug. "I've missed you so."

"I've missed you, too. You're my favorite. Don't tell the others. By the way, you realize we've inherited another sister, right?"

"I know," I said. "And I blame myself. Mom is insane about Annie, don't you think? I guess it's because of Abraham."

China agreed. "I admit I'm a little protective of her myself."

"Me, too, but don't tell her I said so. She's really fun to tease."

Annie, or Anandalla, as her mother had named her, was Abraham Karastovsky's daughter. A daughter he'd never met until the week before he died. That's when Annie showed up, giving Abraham the shock of his life. In a good way, of course. They'd made plans and were looking forward to getting to know each other. Then he was killed and my mother took Annie under her wing.

Since Abraham hadn't known about Annie, and hadn't had a chance to change his will, he'd left his entire estate to me, his lifelong pupil and apprentice. I'd made some changes and now Annie had a small trust fund, and she and I were co-owners of Abraham's palatial home in the hills overlooking Dharma. Those changes had assuaged a small part of the boatload of guilt I'd been dealing with ever since Abraham died.

Annie's mom died shortly after that, and she moved to Dharma. The entire community had adopted her, especially my mother, who considered Annie the fifth daughter I'd never known she needed.

"We've got to go," I said, hugging China. I told her we'd meet up with her at Annie's store later. Then I grabbed Alice and we continued walking the Lane.

There was already a crowd gathered in front of Annie's

place. I was delighted when I saw what she'd named her store.

Anandalla!

It was perfect. It sounded so *Dharma*. Alice followed as I pushed my way into the packed store, stopping every few feet to greet old friends and introduce them to Alice. I spotted Robin on the other side of the spacious shop and we waved at each other. But I couldn't get there from here, not through this crowd.

I couldn't see Annie anywhere, and before I could track her down, Mom found me and wrapped me up in a major mama-bear hug.

"Blessed be, sweetie," she said in greeting, and I was reminded of her recent Wicca training. "Let's walk outside. It's crazy in here." She led the way, worming around the crowds to the door, then out to the sidewalk.

"Good job, Mom," I said when we hit the fresh air.

She closed her eyes and raised her face to the sunshine. "It's so nice out here."

"It's a beautiful day in the neighborhood," I sang.

She smiled at me. "Now, sweetie, I want you to have a good time today, but also, Robson needs to talk to you sometime while you're here."

Robson, also known as Guru Bob to us kids, was the spiritual leader of the pack.

"Okay, I'll stop by his place a little later." I turned and gestured to Alice. "Mom, this is my friend Alice I was telling you about. She's the one who wants to get a massage today."

"Blessed be, Alice," Mom said. "The spa is expecting you."

"Thank you, Mrs. Wainwright," Alice said. "It's so nice of you to make the arrangements for me."

"Can you take Alice with you, Mom?"

Mom turned to me. "Sweetie, I had to cancel my usual

massage to help Annie today, but I called Savannah. She's going to the spa, so I thought she could take Alice with her."

"Oh." I looked at Alice. "Do you mind going with my sister? Savannah's much nicer than I am, anyway."

Mom frowned. "Don't be silly. You girls are all wonderful and kind."

"Of course we are," I said, laughing. "Veritable paragons."

Mom touched Alice's arm. "Did you have a specific type of massage in mind, Alice?"

Alice shook her head. "I have no idea what—"

Mom whipped her hand away. "Oh, dear."

"Mom, what's wrong?"

She studied Alice's face for a few seconds, then reached out and placed two fingers in the center of Alice's forehead.

Alice flinched.

"Don't be afraid," I murmured. "She's touching your third eye. It'll tell her everything she needs to know."

"Whoa," Mom muttered, and moved her fingers away.

"Mom?"

Ignoring me, she pulled out her touch-screen phone and pressed a number. "I'm calling the spa back. Alice needs immediate attention."

I grinned at Alice. "Mom'll take care of you, see?"

"She's wonderful," Alice whispered, and looked around. "I feel so safe here."

Mom hung up the phone and gripped Alice's arm. "You're to see Tantra Pangalongie. She's a specialist. A true healer."

"A specialist in what, Mom?" I asked. I'd heard about Tantra. The woman was fierce.

Mom took a deep breath. "Panchakarma."

"Wait," I said. "Are you sure that's necessary?"

"Absolutely," she snapped. "She needs it."

"Why?" Alice asked, glancing back and forth. "What is it?"

The look on Mom's face was more serious than I'd ever seen, even when we were children and behaving badly. But the look quickly disappeared and she patted Alice's arm. "Your aura tells me you need an extraspecial treatment today."

Alice frowned. "Really? You can see my aura?"

"Mom sees all, knows all," I said lightly. Then I gave my mother a warning glance as Alice fished in her purse for a tissue. "Mom, Alice is a little sensitive."

"No, no, I'm fine," Alice insisted. "It's just a massage, right? It'll be fun."

"Absolutely fun," Mom said, smiling her Sunny Bunny smile, God help us all. When Sunny Bunny appeared, there was no room for arguments. "Here comes Savannah. You girls will have a great time getting pampered."

I turned to greet Savannah and burst out laughing.

She'd shaved her head.

"I knew you'd love it," she said wryly.

"God, you're weird." I gave her a big hug, then rubbed her smooth head. "Strangely enough, it looks good on you."

I introduced her to Alice. "You two play nice."

"We will," Savannah said, and grabbed Alice's hand. "Come on, Alice, let's go get pampered."

Alice turned back with a tremulous smile. "I'm excited. See you in a while."

I waved. Once they were halfway down the block, I turned to Mom. "Are you sure the panchakarma is the way to go?"

Mom frowned as she stared off at Alice and Savannah. "Only if she wants to live."

Chapter 10

"Okay, Mom," I said, after catching my breath. "You've succeeded in scaring the bejeezus out of me, so spill."

"Oh, sweetie." Mom linked arms with me and we strolled slowly down the sidewalk. "I know what your feelings are when you hear me rattle on about auras and such."

"None of us can pass up the opportunity to tease you, Mom," I said, squeezing her arm. "But you've been right about these things more often than not."

"Then you must trust me. That girl has problems. She has a gray aura. And it's absolutely opaque."

Gray aura? I'd never heard of it. "So what does that mean?"

"Well, depending on the shade of gray, it might simply indicate that Alice feels trapped in her life. Or, it could point toward depression."

"She doesn't seem depressed," I mused.

"There's another possibility." Mom paused, then sighed. "She could be terminally ill."

"What?"

"I'm sorry, dear," she said, patting my hand. "I'm just the messenger. The good thing is that the gray wasn't dark enough to call it black."

"There are black auras?"

"They're very rare." Mom's shoulders shook and she rubbed her arms. "Gives me chills just to think about it.

Black aura is often seen in abused children, torture victims, and occasionally, heavy drug addicts."

I thought about that. "I don't think she does drugs."

"No, of course not."

"But she was raised by nuns in a Catholic boarding school. I hate to think there might've been some abuse going on."

"Oh, dear, I hope not."

"She seems ridiculously grateful for every little scrap of friendship anyone shows."

"Maybe she was deprived of such things growing up."

"Maybe." Talk about depressing. I'd just met her and already considered her a friend. I didn't want to find out she was dying.

If I could have laughed off Mom's aura thing as a big joke, I might have been able to ignore her dire calculations. But as I'd told her, I'd seen her land right on the money too many times to blow it off.

The problem with Mom being right was that Alice was now undergoing a radical Ayurvedic treatment known as panchakarma, or *cleansing*, which was a really nice way of describing the purging, bloodletting, and high colonics used by practitioners of the regime. They looked for every way possible to draw out poisons and toxins in the system, basically cleaning out every bodily orifice they could find. It was a lengthy procedure normally done for terminally ill patients who'd tried everything else.

Alice wasn't going to thank me for this.

"Keep good thoughts, sweetie," Mom had said. "Today is a day for positive thinking. You won't help your friend if you act depressed over her state."

I was pretty sure she wouldn't be grateful either way, but no point in saying that. "Don't worry. I'll be perky as a petunia."

"That's my good girl. Tell you what. I'll crochet a healing sachet for Alice to wear."

"Sounds attractive," I mumbled.

"My Wicca skills improve every day," she said. "Your father thinks I make one hell of a witch."

"Uh, Mom, I'm not sure he meant—"

"Don't say it." She laughed and slapped my arm. "Let's go help our Annie."

I glanced around and realized we'd walked down the block, turned around, and now were back at Annie's store. We stared through the wide plate-glass window. "Is she inside?"

"I don't see her," Mom said, "but she's been swamped all morning. She might be in the back, placing orders. I'd better go help out. Are you coming in or heading to Robson's?"

"I'll head over to his house now and be back to help out in a little while."

"Blessed be," she said, and gave me another hug before I took off down the street.

Nothing was a very far walk in Dharma. Guru Bob's lovely home was just up the hill on a piece of land that jutted out to provide magnificent views in three directions. I'd always considered it the catbird seat as far as property in Dharma went.

I approached his two-story Edwardian mansion with some trepidation. It's not that I didn't like him; I did, very much. But he was a man of higher consciousness, and even if you didn't drink the commune Kool-Aid, there was something solemn about being in his presence that made you want to talk in quiet tones and behave respectfully. It was a little disconcerting.

I knocked on the front door and waited less than ten seconds before he opened the door himself.

"Brooklyn," he said jovially. "How are you?"

"I'm fine, Robson." I'd never dared to call him Guru Bob to his face, but he probably knew we'd nicknamed him that years ago. He seemed to know everything that went on when it came to his town and his people.

He ushered me into his well-appointed, art-filled home and led the way to a small elegant sitting room. A tea service was set up on the coffee table. Or did that make it a *tea* table?

A door off the tea room led to Guru Bob's small library. I'd helped him acquire a number of rare books over the years and knew how wonderful and extensive his collection was. I could hear papers being shuffled and footsteps moving around the room. Someone was working in there.

"Please sit, gracious," Guru Bob said, indicating the beautifully restored Regency-style sofa. He called most people *gracious* on the supposition that we were all filled with varying amounts of grace. I'd heard him say that when he called you gracious, he could watch you become more present to the moment.

He sat in a comfortable side chair and began to pour the tea. "How was your trip to Edinburgh?"

"Very nice," I said politely, then added, "Well, there was an unfortunate incident or two while I was there. An old friend was killed."

"Ah, yes. Kyle McVee."

"You heard about Kyle? How . . . Never mind." Why bother asking? The man knew everything.

"I have my sources." He smiled mysteriously.

I laughed. "Right. Mom, Dad, Robin, and the forty-four conscious beings that astral travel with you wherever you go." I gasped and slapped my hand over my mouth. I couldn't believe I'd just said that.

But Guru Bob fell back in his chair and laughed out loud. It was a rare sound and I was inordinately pleased to be the cause of it.

"Oh, Brooklyn," he said when he'd caught his breath. "I have missed you here in Dharma." He took a quick sip of tea, then added, "I know your work demands that you stay in the city, but perhaps you could make it up here more often. I know your mother would enjoy seeing you."

I frowned. "Did my mom ask you to say that?"

He laughed again. "No, of course not. I just know her well enough to tell you so."

"I guess you do."

We both sipped our tea for a moment. I took a petite tea cake and popped it into my mouth. The silence was not uncomfortable, but I was starting to wonder what he wanted to discuss with me.

As if he could read my mind—and he probably could—he put down his teacup. "Now, I have some business to discuss with you."

In the past, my siblings and I had devoted hours to trying to figure out if Guru Bob could read minds. Now I wondered if maybe he was just an expert at body language. It probably didn't take a highly evolved conscious being to figure out mine. Derek did it all the time, too. Not that Derek wasn't a highly evolved guy. It's just that . . . well, you'd have to meet Guru Bob to know what I was talking about.

"I have a book I would like you to work on," he said.

I sat forward on the couch. "Oh, that's great."

"Yes, it is," he said, grinning at my reaction. He stood and walked to the door of the library. "Gabriel, do you have the book for Brooklyn?"

"It's on the desk," Gabriel called.

Gabriel?

Guru Bob strolled to an antique escritoire on the opposite wall. He opened the desk panel and picked up a small wrapped package.

"It is Marcus Aurelius," he said as he unwrapped it and handed it to me.

Uh, hello? *Gabriel?*

I stared at the book, then back at the doorway. No one was there. Maybe I'd misunderstood what Guru Bob had said. I glanced back at the book and started to turn it over, but the front cover fell off in my hands, leaving bits of thin thread dangling from its severed edge.

"Oh, dear," I murmured.

He frowned. "As you see, it is in terrible condition. But it is a rare volume and I do not wish to give up on it just yet. The paper is excellent quality. I am confident you can bring it back to life."

"Of course." I carefully turned it over to see how the back had fared. Normally, the back cover would be in slightly better condition than the front because the hinges weren't worked as much. That was the case with this book. Though faded, the original leather had been a light golden brown, with gilded borders and a raised spine. The gilding was badly rubbed.

The book was printed on pages of thick vellum. The first letter of each chapter was illuminated in red, blue, and gold, with gilt ornamentation.

"Gorgeous," I whispered, and looked up at Guru Bob. "I'll take good care of it."

"I know you will, dear."

"Would you like the cover to be similar in color to the original?"

"I think that would be the best choice."

I was distracted by a movement at the door to the library and looked over, then blinked in disbelief.

"Gabriel?"

"Hey, babe." He stood leaning against the doorjamb, looking as cocky and handsome as ever in a tight black T-shirt and worn black denims. God help all womankind, but the man was devastatingly handsome. Not to be trusted, ever, but devilishly good-looking, nonetheless.

I glanced at Guru Bob, then back at Gabriel, who couldn't stop smirking. I looked at Guru Bob again, this time with purpose. "Robson, what is he doing here?"

"Gabriel needed to keep himself busy," Guru Bob explained. "And I agree, so I have hired him to alphabetize my books and set up a computerized card catalog."

"Keeps me off the streets," Gabriel said.

Alarmed, I turned to Guru Bob. "Robson, can we talk privately?"

He laughed. "Gracious, I am well aware of Gabriel's penchant for the finer things. If anything turns up missing, I know where to find him."

"Really?" I said intently. "Because I haven't been able to find him at all. But then he turns up when you least expect it. And in the strangest places."

Like, for instance, in my hotel room in Edinburgh a few weeks ago. But that was a long story and I was much too sober to relive it at that moment.

"You will find him here for the foreseeable future," Guru Bob assured me. "He is doing an excellent job."

"Good to know." I gave Gabriel a stern, narrow look that sent a clear warning: *Don't pull anything here. I'll be watching you.*

He winked at me, then went back to work.

Discombobulated, I picked up my teacup and finished my drink. Then I stood and slipped the book into my purse. "I'd better get back to Annie's. Are you going to stop by today?"

"Most certainly," Robson said. "I am so pleased that Anandalla found a home here and I am indebted to you for bringing her here."

"I may have discovered her, but it was Mom's influence that kept her here."

"Your mother is a gift from the gods."

I smiled. "Yes, and she's probably wondering why I'm not there helping out. So I should be going."

"See you around, babe," Gabriel said from the doorway.

"Yeah, okay. Bye." I was flustered. I couldn't help it. He was a gorgeous bad boy. Who could resist that?

Guru Bob accompanied me to the front door and gave me a light hug. "You are not to worry about Gabriel, gracious. At his core, he is a good man and knows I am not someone to be taken advantage of."

"Of course you're not. And I don't mean to tell you your own business, but are you sure you know him as well as you think? Don't get me wrong. He's helped me out of a few jams. But he's also . . . well, I'm concerned that he might . . ."

"Your concern touches me, gracious," he said, "but let me allay your fears." He placed his hand on my shoulder, and instantly, waves of calm radiated from my shoulder into every muscle of my body. I took several deep breaths and leaned against the door as he told me a story.

"When I was a younger man," he said, "I traveled to the Middle East, starting in Turkey and journeying northeastward to the Hindu Kush. My plan was to spend a year following in the footsteps of Mr. Gurdjieff, in search of the miraculous. I found it everywhere."

George Gurdjieff was a Russian mystic whose teachings were among the many that Guru Bob encouraged the members of his fellowship to study. Gurdjieff's idea of self-remembering was said to be a cornerstone of esoteric study.

"Then, five years ago," he continued, "a number of my own fellowship men decided to make the same trip through the Hindu Kush. They were determined to go with or without me, so I agreed to accompany them. One of my goals for this trip was to track down my old friend Mushaf, a Yezidi holy man I had met on that earlier journey. He, too, had been in search of higher wisdom and had left his home in Kurdistan to traverse the Kush."

"Did you find him?"

Guru Bob sighed. "We hired a reputable guide, but when we arrived in the village where I had last seen Mushaf, our guide asked too many questions and was thrown in jail.

Within a day, an armed skirmish broke out among several tribes and we were trapped in the cross fire."

"What did you do?"

He smiled ruefully. "I prayed. Several days before we arrived, there had been an American drone attack within a few miles of our location. I believe that the air strike, quickly followed by our presence in the area, is what stirred up the tribesmen."

"I would've been scared silly."

"It was a dangerous time. One of our group spoke French and a few words of Dari, and made some garbled attempts to bribe our guide out of jail."

"Did it work?"

"No," he said darkly, lost in the memory. "Things were about to come to a head and I was concerned for my men, as well as our jailed guide. On the third day, with gunshots ringing all around the small hut we inhabited, a light-skinned man appeared at the door. He wore the typical garb of the region and his head was wrapped in a keffi-yeh, but he was different from the other men in the village. Tall. Brash. When he began to speak American English, I thought I was hallucinating."

My eyes grew wide. "No way," I whispered.

Guru Bob gave me one of his beatific smiles. "Yes. It was Gabriel. He had heard a rumor that there were Americans in trouble in the area and had traveled up the mountain to help us."

"But what was he doing there?"

Guru Bob's lips twisted in mild vexation. "I thought at the time that it was better not to ask."

"Yeah, probably so." But my mind was reeling with pos-sibilities. Had Gabriel been a spy? A mercenary? A smug-gler? It was all too coincidental that he happened to be in the same place as Guru Bob.

Guru Bob went on to explain that Gabriel spoke perfect Farsi as well as the various Pashto dialects. He was able to broker a deal to return their guide to them and quell the tribesmen long enough for Guru Bob and the men to escape down the mountain and find the nearest train station.

Guru Bob shook his head in wonder. “He saved our lives—of that, I have no doubt.”

“Wow, I guess so.”

“Perhaps it had been naive of me to assume we could pass through the region safely after so many years of war,” Guru Bob added with a sad sigh. “But people have done it for centuries and still do, today. And there are many trustworthy guides in the area. Added to that, the fellowship men are a stubborn lot and were determined to make the journey. I could not let them go by themselves.”

I frowned as something disturbing occurred to me. “Did my father go on that trip with you?”

“He did.”

“So he knows Gabriel?”

“He does.”

So Gabriel had saved not only Guru Bob’s life; he had also saved my dad’s life. I didn’t know how to react, except to feel grateful.

“Gabriel’s heroics do not end there,” he assured me. “Recently, once again, he saved the life of someone extremely dear to me. I owe him a great deal.”

“He’s got a strange habit of . . . Oh, you mean . . . ?”

“Yes, gracious,” he said softly. “I speak of you.”

I tried to swallow around the lump in my throat. The first time I met Gabriel was right after Abraham died. I was in a noodle shop on Fillmore Street when a lunatic kid with a gun threatened to kill me. Gabriel walked in and kicked the gun out of the kid’s hand. I’d thought at the time that he just happened to be in the neighborhood, but I’d found out later that he’d been following me.

“You knew he saved me that day?” I said.

Guru Bob tilted his head and stared at me. What was I thinking? Of course he knew. He knew everything.

"For these reasons," Guru Bob said, "when Gabriel shows up at my door and requests sanctuary, I welcome him."

As I walked back to the Lane, I considered, not for the first time, how very lucky I was to have grown up in Dharma. Most people laugh or look with suspicion when they hear someone was raised in a commune. Hippies, drugs, raggedy clothes, and marijuana-covered hillsides are just some of the images that come to mind. But my childhood was blissful. That's the only word for it.

And if ever there was a place that could be considered sanctuary, Dharma was it. But why did Gabriel need sanctuary? I didn't feel comfortable grilling Guru Bob about it, but I would be sure to ask Gabriel the next time I saw him.

I'd been gone for over an hour, so I wondered if Alice was finished with her treatment. Probably not. I wouldn't be surprised if Tantra the healer kept her there all day.

I reached Annie's shop and was amazed to see people out on the sidewalk, waiting to get inside. I greeted more old friends and eased my way through the door in search of Annie.

She found me first. "Brooklyn! You made it."

She hugged me. I could tell she was thrilled with the way the day was going.

"Annie, the store's beautiful."

She looked around, taking in everything at once. "I know. I love it. I love this town. Your mom has been so great. And Austin and Jackson and your dad helped hang the racks and the shelves. Everybody's been amazing."

I was glad to hear that my brothers had warmed up to Annie. When my family first met her, they were concerned that she was lying about her connection to Abraham. My brothers had insisted she take a paternity test before I could write her into Abraham's trust.

I looked around. They'd all done a great job setting up

the place. The room was ultramodern in design with a high ceiling, industrial lighting, and exposed ducts that gave it an urban feel. Chrome wire shelving along the perimeter added to the clean, open feel of the space. In and among the shelves and rows of stock, round tables were decorated with place settings for dining, except every setting was different. It was a creative way to display all the different flatware, dishware, and accessories available in the store. Near the back, one full counter was a cooking station, and the chef in charge was handing out samples of the goodies he cooked using Annie's pots and pans.

"This is so clever," I said, marveling at the setup. "Who knew you were so talented?"

She laughed. "Don't think I don't know that's a major compliment, coming from you. My day is officially complete."

"Sounds like you're happy."

She looked at me in surprise. "I am. I really am. I'm so happy. Thank you." Then she shocked me by hugging me again.

I had to blink back tears. "Okay. Good."

"Okay." She sniffled. "That's enough of that crap."

"No kidding. Now what can I do to help?"

She sent me back to the stockroom to help Mom, who sat at the computer checking what was selling. She would tell me what to look for, I would find the items and take them out to the store to restock the shelves. After a while, Dad joined me and I lost track of time as we ran around adding more spatulas and baskets and canisters and dishware and linens to the shelves.

I must've been working for over an hour and my arms were aching from stretching up to reach the higher shelves and carrying thirty-pound Dutch ovens and cappuccino machines back and forth from the stockroom. "Mom, will you tell Dad I'm just going to step outside for a quick break?"

"Okay, sweetie."

I made my way through the store, which was still crowded but maneuverable, and stepped outside to enjoy the beautiful day. The temperature was mild and people were out taking advantage of it, strolling the wide sidewalks, chatting and window-shopping. I waved to a few of the locals and felt a wave of nostalgia sweep over me. Guru Bob was right. I really did need to get back here more often.

I glanced up the road and saw Gabriel walking into town. From two blocks away, he saw me and grinned. I could see his stunning smile from here. I had to laugh. Damn, but the man was tall, gorgeous, and incorrigible. He was wearing the black leather duster he'd been wearing the first time I saw him in that noodle shop on Fillmore Street.

I'd thought of him as the man in black that day. A mysterious stranger. My hero. And that's what he looked like now as he moved forward inexorably, like a force of nature, the duster brushing his strong calves as he approached.

I waved and his grin broadened.

A car backfired and I jolted in surprise, then chuckled at my own foolishness. I looked at the passing cars, wondering which one was to blame for making me look silly. I gazed back at Gabriel, expecting to see his sexy eyes trained on me, but he was gone.

No. He wasn't gone. He wasn't grinning. Instead, he lay sprawled on the sidewalk.

I screamed and ran. As I got closer and saw the blood streaming from his head, I knew it wasn't a car backfiring I'd heard a moment ago.

Gabriel had been shot.

Chapter 11

"Call nine-one-one!" I shouted.

"What the hell's going on?" Joey Turturino asked as he pushed open the door of his dad's fishmonger's shop.

"Somebody's been shot!" I cried. "Call nine-one-one."

"I'm calling right now."

The shop door slammed and I turned back to Gabriel.

"Don't you dare die," I said fiercely. My hands shook too much as I felt his neck for a pulse, so I laid my head on his chest to listen for a heartbeat. I had another quick flash of déjà vu and realized I'd been checking for signs of life a lot lately.

Gabriel groaned.

I raised my head. "You stay alive, damn it. I'm sick of people dying on me. And yeah, that's right. It's all about me." Tears sprang to my eyes and I brushed them away. I'd get emotional later.

He moaned softly.

"My feelings exactly," I whispered, trying to keep it light. It wasn't easy. I finally risked a glance at his head. I could see where the bullet had grazed his temple, taking a big chunk of skin off the side of his head. Blood was everywhere. Dear God, how close had he come to having his head blown off?

My stomach reeled and I had to sit back on my ankles, staring at the sky, gulping in air.

Sirens screamed, and within seconds a fire engine and a paramedic truck blocked the Lane.

One of the firemen helped me stand up. He walked me over to Joey's shop, where I sat on the brick ledge under the store window. I stared in mute disbelief at the paramedics scampering around. Seconds later, my mother and Robin ran over.

"Somebody said you were hurt," Mom cried and grabbed me in her arms.

"Not me," I whispered. "Gabriel."

"Gabriel?" Robin asked. "The same Gabriel from—"

"Yeah," I said quickly, stopping her. She'd been in Edinburgh and knew the whole story.

"That nice young man who works for Robson?" Mom said, baffled. "What happened?"

"I don't know for sure. I thought I heard a car backfire, but when I turned, Gabriel was on the ground. It was a gunshot. His head is all bloody. There's so much blood."

"Okay, sweetie, calm down."

Robin walked around, looked at the ground. "If a bullet grazed his head, I bet we can find it."

"Good idea." I started to jump up, but Mom held me down by my shoulders.

"No. Just wait until your equilibrium returns. You've had a shock and your dosha balance is skewed."

"But if there's evidence, we should—"

"No," she said fiercely.

"Mom?"

Her whole body shuddered and she squeezed me tight again. "Maybe it's my own balance that's skewed, but I need you to just sit still for a minute, please, sweetie?"

"Sure," I said, holding on to her. "Mom, you're shaking."

"They said you were hurt," she whispered.

"I'm fine," I said, resting my head against her shoulder. "It's okay."

"You may be fine, but I just aged ten years."

We stood on the walkway, holding each other and watching as the paramedics worked on Gabriel.

"Don't let him die, Mama," I whispered.

Mom began to rock slightly and I knew she was chanting. She tended to blend Buddhist chants with Grateful Dead lyrics when she prayed. Maybe she was adding a little witchcraft this time. Whatever worked. I just wanted Gabriel to stand up, dust himself off, and flash me a wink and a grin.

It was wrong, seeing him laid out on the ground like that. He was too big, too strong. Too invincible. I began making deals with the gods, if only they would keep him alive.

Two paramedics wheeled a collapsible gurney over, and four men lifted Gabriel onto the pad. They'd attached a thick brace to his neck and wrapped a bunch of gauze around his head.

All good, right? It meant they were taking him to a hospital, not a morgue.

"Come on," I said, pulling Mom with me. "I want to make sure he's going to be okay."

A female EMT turned and looked at me. "Are you a relative?"

"Yes," I said immediately. Lying for a good cause didn't count against karma, did it? And even if it did, I was beyond caring. "He's my brother."

She nodded. "He's unconscious. We'll know more when we get him to the hospital."

"His head . . ."

"Yeah, he took a blow, but he's alive, and he's strong."

"Right," I said, nodding. "Yes, he is."

As they rolled Gabriel to the truck, Dad ran up to us, followed by Annie, Savannah, China, and Alice.

Dad grabbed me in a hug. "You're all right?"

"I'm fine, Dad. It's Gabriel."

He looked at me, stroked my head as if to make sure it

was all in one piece, then turned and jogged over to talk to the paramedics and check on Gabriel.

"What happened?" Annie asked.

"Who was hurt?" Savannah demanded.

"Are you okay?" Alice asked, taking my hand and squeezing it.

"Thanks," I said, answering Alice first. "I'm fine."

Mom pulled Annie and Savannah aside to explain what had happened while I talked to Alice.

"Did you have a good massage?" I asked, to distract myself.

"Oh, my goodness," she said, her eyes staring off at the horizon. "It was like no other massage I've ever had."

"Yeah, I'll bet."

"But I feel so . . . clean." She sounded dazed, but happy.

"Really? Wow. That's great." Unbelievable, but great. It took a small load of guilt off me to know that she'd survived the panchakarma treatment so well. I searched around for the EMTs and saw that they had Gabriel in the ambulance now.

Alice continued to squeeze my hand as she stared at the ambulance. "Is your friend going to be okay?"

"He's alive but unconscious." It felt good to say it aloud. I couldn't begin to think how relieved I was that they hadn't zipped him into a body bag.

China clutched my arm. "Honey, you have blood on your hands."

I gasped.

Alice released my hand and stared at her own, which was now spotted with blood. She wobbled and her head began to lob.

"Grab her," I said.

China reached under Alice's arms and hoisted her up before she could collapse.

"Jeez, I thought you were the wimp," China said to me.

I grabbed Alice's left arm. "Oh, this one is light-years beyond me in wimpiness."

China grimaced as we both struggled to keep Alice standing. "Lucky for me, she weighs a lot less than you."

"Thanks for that."

Savannah helped us move Alice to the same ledge by the fish shop that I'd sat on minutes ago. China pulled a packet of moist towelettes from her pocket and handed me some. "Here, I carry these around in case Hannah gets messy. You need to get rid of that blood."

"Oh, God, thanks," I said, still in a daze. It took me four wipes to clean the blood off my hands.

My sisters agreed to watch Alice while I ran back to talk to the paramedic. She told us they were taking Gabriel down to Sonoma Valley Hospital, less than ten miles away.

"I'm going by Robson's to tell him what happened," Mom said. "I know he'll want to drive over there with me. Do you want to come with us?"

"I'll go with you," Annie said instantly. She had tears in her eyes and her breathing was shallow. Was she going to pass out, too?

"Annie, honey," Mom said gently. "You have a new store to run."

"But I want to be there."

Mom rubbed her shoulder. "I promise we'll call you as soon as we hear anything."

Mom gave me a pointed look, so I grabbed Annie's other arm and we led her back to where Savannah was still standing with Alice.

Clearly, Gabriel had managed to worm his way into the hearts and minds of the good citizens of Dharma. Well, Annie's heart and mind anyway. I couldn't blame her. The man was a walking, talking bad boy heartthrob.

Mom and I jogged back to the ambulance. The EMT said they were ready to go.

"Your father's going to take care of Annie and the shop," Mom said. "Do you want to ride with Robson and me?"

"No, I'll get my car and meet you there." Turning to Savannah, I shouted, "Keep Alice with you, okay?"

"No problem. Go."

Whether you're sick or healthy, hospitals are horrible places to be. This one was only a few years old, so the walls were still clean and white. Cheerful paintings and colorful chairs brightened the waiting area. The large-screen television actually worked, although the volume was kept down. Picture windows revealed views of the parklike grounds and a rushing creek and the nearby Sonoma Mountains. But it still sucked to be here.

Guru Bob, Mom, and I alternately paced, sat, drank coffee, laughed nervously, or teared up, depending on the moment and the mood.

Once we got to the hospital, I was really glad Guru Bob had come along. He took care of filling out Gabriel's admittance forms, a good thing since I didn't even know the man's last name. The first time we'd spoken after the Fillmore Street noodle shop fiasco, Gabriel had given me his business card. It read, simply, "Gabriel."

If Guru Bob knew Gabriel's last name, more power to him. He did have a way of knowing things about people. He also seemed to have a direct line to heaven. For that reason and others, I was glad he was here. Gabriel would need all the help he could get.

The double glass doors of the waiting room opened and Alice and China walked in. I felt immediately guilt-ridden for leaving Alice on her own, so I was glad to see her.

She ran over and gave me a hug.

"What are you doing here?" I asked.

"I figured you could use some support while your friend is being looked at."

"Thanks. I guess you're right."

"Any word on how he's doing?" China asked.

"Not yet," I said listlessly. I'd had a tough week and the body count was rising. I wanted to sleep for two days straight.

Alice patted my back and walked away. A few minutes later, she handed me a foam cup. "It's hot tea with sugar. You need to keep up your strength."

"Thanks."

"Let's sit for a minute," she said, pulling me toward a row of chairs.

"I'm so sorry I dragged you into this," I said, blowing on my tea. "I can try to find you a ride back to the city."

"Don't be silly," she said. "My life is so much more exciting when you're around. Besides, I already feel so close to everyone here. I want to stay, if it's okay."

"Absolutely. I appreciate it."

I watched Guru Bob put his arm around Mom. She leaned her head on his shoulder and sighed.

Alice turned to me, her eyes bright with unshed tears. "How wonderful to live in a place where everyone cares for each other so much."

"It's a good place to live," I said.

"Gabriel's lucky to have such great old friends," she said wistfully.

I smiled. "I've only known him a month or so, but Robson has known him a lot longer."

"Well, he's a lucky guy to have friends in Dharma. It's a wonderful place."

"It really is."

Heavy footsteps echoed in the hall and a shiver tickled my shoulders and spine.

Derek Stone walked into the waiting room.

It took me a few seconds to register that it wasn't a mirage. Then I set my cup of tea on the floor and rushed to greet him. "What are you doing here?"

He hugged me tight enough to cut off my breathing.

"I've been trying to track you down all day," he said in a furious whisper. "Finally made it to Annie's store and she told me where you were."

I eased back to catch my breath. He put his arm around my shoulder to keep me close as we walked down the hall, away from the group.

"Were you already in Dharma when all this happened?"

"I have to assume so." He raked his fingers through his hair. "I dropped Gunther and one of my men off at the tasting room around two fifteen, then drove back toward Glen Ellen to fill the gas tank. By the time I got back to Annie's shop and spent almost fifteen minutes trying to find you, you must've already been on your way to the hospital."

"Gunther came up with you?"

"Yes, he got wind that I was driving up here and insisted on tagging along to go wine tasting."

"Why were you coming to Dharma?"

"For Annie's grand opening. Your mother e-mailed me with the news."

My mother e-mailed him? He corresponded with my mother but not me? Okay, I needed to let that go.

"I'm just glad you're here," I said.

He gritted his teeth, then said, "Yes, well, I must say, it gave me a bit of a shock."

"What?"

He shook his head. I'd never seen him look quite so nonplussed.

"You see," he began, "I spoke to Annie, asking where you were. She seemed rather distraught and said there had been a shooting and you were on your way to the hospital." He chuckled without humor. "Naturally, I thought she meant you were the one . . . well, I can see plain as day that you're fine."

"You thought it was me who'd been . . ."

"Yes." He smiled, or tried to, then had to clear his throat

before adding, "I believe I broke the land-speed record getting here."

"I'm so sorry." I wrapped my arms around him. He buried his face in my hair.

"Scared the living daylights out of me." He gave me one last squeeze, then pulled away. "I'm sorry for your friend, but I can't tell you how happy I am that it's not you."

"Thank you, Derek." I felt my eyes water as I took hold of both his hands. "I'm so sorry you had to worry."

"Worry? Oh, I wouldn't call it that," he said ruefully. "Anguish, perhaps. Or torture. Don't ever do that to me again."

I stretched up to kiss him lightly on the lips. "I promise."

"Good." We turned and walked back down the hall.

"Oh, Derek," Mom said, running over. "It's good of you to have come."

He and I broke apart and Mom moved in for a hug. She and Derek had bonded awhile back when a gun-toting killer invaded my home and tried to make me the next victim.

"Hello, Rebecca," he said. Then he shook hands with Guru Bob.

Somehow it was right that Derek had shown up. Maybe I'd wished for it. I seemed to draw strength from his presence. Warm happiness flowed from my heart into every part of me.

Could I be more sappy? I didn't see how. But it didn't matter. I was all bubbly inside and felt destined to live sappily ever after.

"Now, how do you know Gabriel?" Derek asked.

I blinked. Oh, dear. I wasn't about to bring up a certain kiss in a certain hotel room in Edinburgh. And why was I even thinking about that when Derek was this close?

"Gabriel works with Guru Bob," I said carefully. "He knows books and so do I. So we've had a few business dealings together."

If you called Gabriel sneaking into my house and stealing a priceless fifteenth-century edition of Plutarch "business dealings." But at least he'd done it for Guru Bob. The Plutarch theft was one reason why I didn't trust Gabriel. But he clearly had Guru Bob's seal of approval. And my father's, I guessed. I was anxious to look more deeply into the whole Gabriel connection, but that would have to wait until he was out of the hospital.

"And what happened today?" Derek asked.

"It's still not clear," I said, and explained what I thought had happened.

"And you were first on the scene?"

"Yes." I looked at him. "Again."

Sensing my unease, he gripped my hand. "And the blood?"

"Was really bad," I said, then added quickly, "But I didn't pass out."

"Good girl," he said, and kissed my cheek.

He knew me too well. I'd passed out the first time I met him, when he found me kneeling over Abraham's body, my hands covered in blood. It was sweet of him to be concerned.

"Do we know if Gabriel is out of danger?" Derek asked.

I waved my hand toward the nurses' station. "They won't tell us anything."

He flashed the nurses a determined look. "Why don't you go sit and let me give it a try."

I frowned. "Sure."

Derek walked over to the nurses' station and struck up a conversation with the big scary nurse supervisor. Within seconds, she was giggling and touching Derek's arm. He leaned in and whispered conspiratorially and she laughed out loud. Good grief.

He turned and walked back to me, smirking all the way.

I smirked, too, as I watched Nurse Ratched staring fondly at his ass the whole way.

"They're getting him settled in a room," he reported as we all gathered around him. "He's had a CT scan. There's no brain damage, but he's been slipping in and out of consciousness for the last hour, so they're keeping him overnight, at least. He may have a concussion, so they've given him a very light painkiller and are monitoring him constantly. Depending on how he does overnight, they'll probably discharge him in the morning."

"Oh, Derek, thank you," Mom said.

"There's more," he said. "Apparently, he wrenched his neck when he fell. When he leaves the hospital, he's to remain in bed, keeping very still for several days. He'll need a caregiver. Is there someone in Dharma who can stay with him?"

"Mom will find someone," I said.

"He'll stay with us," Mom said immediately. She glanced at Guru Bob, who nodded in agreement.

"I'd like to see him before we leave," Guru Bob declared.

Derek nodded. "Let me speak with Sandy."

Sandy. Didn't it just figure that he and Nurse Ratched were on a first-name basis. But I couldn't blame the poor woman for rolling over in the face of all that British hotness.

Guru Bob tapped his fingers on the side table, making me realize how upset he was. He rarely expended useless energy like that, rarely showed so much emotion. He always said that negative emotions pulled us out of the moment. Gabriel's injury had shaken him badly. I wondered if he knew something we didn't know.

Well, of course he knew things. He was all-knowing. But my mind immediately went to some worst-case scenarios. What if Gabriel was more badly injured than we were being told? Or what if he was hiding out in Dharma? Maybe killers were after him. He wasn't exactly a paragon of virtue, after all. Let's face it, he stole things from people. Had he taken the wrong possession from the wrong person?

Was Guru Bob in danger as well? Were we all in danger? Was my imagination running wild?

Derek jogged back from the nurses' station less than a minute later. "They'll allow two of you in to see Gabriel today, and for a very brief time. Sandy will let us know when he's settled."

Once again, Derek Stone had worked his magic.

The group decided that Guru Bob and I should be the two people to visit with Gabriel. Guru Bob went in first, and after three minutes he came out and it was my turn.

I walked into the room and saw Gabriel in bed, hooked up to an IV. His eyes were closed, his head heavily bandaged, and his skin more pale than I'd ever seen it. I almost whimpered. I didn't even know the man that well, but I knew that he was too strong, too full of life to be brought down like this.

I wanted to know what he was doing in Dharma. Why was he seeking sanctuary? Who was after him? But I knew this wasn't the time or place to ask.

I approached, took his hand in mine and whispered, "Gabriel."

His eyes flickered open and he gave me a tired smile. "Hey, babe. You look hot."

My eyes swam with tears. "Yeah, so do you."

He tried to laugh but it took too much effort. "I look like shit. But I'll be okay. I heard you took care of everything."

"I just did what I could to keep you from bleeding all over the clean streets of Dharma."

"Good little citizen," he whispered.

"That's me." I fiddled with his sheets, pulled them a bit tighter. "You're going to be okay."

"Yeah." He closed his eyes, exhausted by the brief exchange. A few seconds later, his eyes still closed, he whispered, "Babe, do me a favor."

"Of course," I said, leaning closer.

"Get me the hell out of here."

"I'll do my best." I hesitated, then said, "Gabriel, did you see anything? Do you have any idea what happened out there?"

He shook his head back and forth slowly, his forehead wrinkled in pain. "Don't remember much. They told me I was shot, but I don't remember being hit. Don't remember falling."

"Do you remember me waving at you?"

"No," he whispered. "Did you wave to me?"

"Yes."

He closed his eyes. "I should've remembered that."

"That's okay, don't worry," I said, squeezing his hand lightly. "We'll find out what happened."

"Babe," he whispered, opening his eyes as much as he could manage. "Be careful out there."

"I will. You sleep for a while and we'll have you out soon."

I got to the door and turned around to wave good-bye, but he was already asleep. I walked out and saw Derek talking to a Sonoma County deputy sheriff. Another uniformed officer was speaking with Guru Bob.

Mom pulled me aside. "The police are interviewing all of us. They've confirmed that Gabriel was hit by a bullet."

My stomach sank. I mean, I'd already concluded it was a bullet, not some stray flying pebble. But having it confirmed didn't make me feel any better.

Mom continued, "Derek says they'll leave a guard here tonight."

"Good," I said, even though it was awful to think Gabriel might still be a target. On the other hand, I was relieved to know that the police were taking his safety seriously.

When it was my turn to talk to them, they jotted down

my information and promised to do everything they could to find out what had happened. As we spoke, it occurred to me that some of the stores on Shakespeare Lane had security cameras, so I mentioned it. I was happy to hear them say they'd already begun collecting the tapes and might be able to piece together a likely scenario from the evidence.

I wanted Gabriel's assailant found.

I stared at my hands, where no trace of Gabriel's blood remained. It was disturbing, to say the least, that within the span of one week, three people I knew had been attacked. One was dead. Did anything connect them? Layla and Minka, definitely. Both of those attacks had taken place at BABA. But now, some fifty miles away in Dharma, Gabriel had been hurt. He could've died. Was there anything linking the three? Besides me?

I brushed the thought aside. There was no way they were connected, especially because if they were, it meant that I might be the only common denominator.

One way or another, I was determined to find out why the people I knew were being targeted for murder.

Chapter 12

Outside the hospital, I said good-bye to Derek. He had heard from Gunther, who was insisting on exploring more wineries. Derek muttered something about conducting a more thorough vetting of clients next time; then he took off to join the demanding Gunther and head to points north.

Alice and I followed Mom back to Dharma for dinner. Because of Gabriel's situation, the meal was a somber affair. I wanted to ask my dad about his trip to the Hindu Kush and find out how well he knew Gabriel, but again, it wasn't the time or place. The rest of the family didn't know Gabriel well, but the very thought of such a violent attack occurring in our peaceful little town was upsetting to all of us.

Sunday morning back in the city, I threw on jeans, a turtleneck, tennies, and a peacoat and walked three blocks to South Park, one of San Francisco's hidden neighborhood treasures and my favorite place for a leisurely breakfast.

The park was a block-long patch of green grass with picnic tables and a small playground at one end. The green was an island surrounded by small storefront businesses, shops, restaurants, and Victorian-style apartments. Like many San Francisco neighborhoods, South Park was a mix of chic and charm with a hint of scruffiness around the edges. During the day, people strolled the sidewalks and parents pushed their kids on the swings. At night, the homeless skulked in with their bags and blankets and took over the park for their sleeping quarters.

My personal choice for best Sunday brunch was a little French bistro at the far end of the green, where I always ordered French toast with a slice of succulent Niman Ranch ham, lots of syrup and butter, and café au lait.

I sat outside, where the air was cold but the sun was shining. The *Chronicle* was spread across my table so I could read the latest news as I ate my breakfast and zoned out on the background hum of political discussions, French jazz, and children screaming for joy on the nearby swings.

Back home, the rest of the day passed in a quiet blur except for one highlight: a long Sunday-afternoon phone conversation with Derek. At times I felt like a teenager, smiling and sighing at what he said. Despite having seen him the day before, we had a lot to catch up on.

When I was young and received a phone call from a boy, there would always be those long lapses while we both searched desperately for something to say. There was none of that with Derek. It seemed as though we'd never run out of things to talk about. When we finally ended the call, I felt as though I'd spent an hour on a quiet tropical island of calm. Well, calm except for that little spark of sexual tension that ran through the conversation and caused my nerves to quiver nonstop.

Monday morning, I was pouring my first cup of coffee when I remembered I had a funeral to attend. Dismayed, I raced to get ready, dressed in my best black suit, grabbed my coat and headed out for Colma.

I didn't berate myself too badly for forgetting Layla's funeral. I'd had plenty of distractions over the weekend. I pumped up KFOG and drove onto the freeway. The drive was relatively painless since I was going against all the traffic streaming into the city.

Colma is a suburb south of San Francisco, located just beyond Daly City, and is where most San Franciscans go to be buried. It's a pretty little town, but is known far and wide as the necropolis of San Francisco.

Essentially, a necropolis was exactly what Colma was established as. It all started back in 1900, when the geographically minuscule city of San Francisco began running out of space to bury its dead. Cemeteries were banned because the city needed room to house the living.

Nowadays, there are so many cemeteries in Colma that even the Chamber of Commerce admits that the dead outnumber the living. The citizens seem to take their reputation in stride since their official town motto is "It's good to be alive in Colma."

I followed directions to Holy Cross Mortuary and found the chapel where they were holding Layla's memorial service. It was a good turnout, with close to three hundred people gathered in the modern glass-walled hall. Layla would be pleased at the turnout, I thought.

The sun poured in, lending the proceedings a natural lightness that Layla might not have earned were she still alive. I didn't mean that to be harsh. It's just that there were a lot more grins and handshakes and business being attended to than any tearful mourning of the dead.

Derek saw me drive up and park, so he left his men to deal with Gunther and he and I walked in together. I was grateful for that. As we took our seats, I glanced around and saw Inspectors Lee and Jaglom standing on the sidelines.

The service was blessedly short, with no sniffling, no sad moans emitted in moments of remembrance. Layla had no family except her niece, so other than Naomi, I didn't see one person raise a tissue to wipe away a tear. Even the singing, which usually got to me no matter who was being memorialized, didn't elicit any outward signs of grief. That is, until the small choir began to sing "You Are So Beautiful." That's when Tom Hardesty choked up audibly and had to pull the handkerchief from his pocket. He was sitting two rows in front of me, and I saw his wife, Cynthia, elbow him. He flinched and straightened up immediately.

There was no graveside service, thanks be to Buddha.

Naomi had arranged for the after-service gathering to be held at BABA. By the time I got there it was two o'clock and the bar had a line three deep, snaking across the upper gallery. I noticed (because I notice these things) that the vigilant bartenders had set up several large trays of glasses already filled with white or red wine for the masses to grab as they passed. Grateful for their attention to detail, I obliged, taking a glass of red that turned out to be surprisingly good.

When I saw Naomi near the north hall entrance, deep in conversation with fellow staffers Karalee and Marky, I couldn't help raising an eyebrow. She had changed her outfit in between the service and the wake and was now dressed to kill. She should pardon the expression.

It was a little creepy, seeing her in a spandex top and skintight black pants with stiletto heels. She looked like the Mini-Me version of Layla, right down—or up—to her hairdo, which was piled high on top of her head and spilled over in a sexy cascade.

Despite Naomi's eerie similarity to her aunt, I had to give her kudos. She'd pulled this party together and the place was jumping with two open bars and rows of tables filled with hearty appetizers, finger foods, and desserts. The BABA board members seemed to be impressed and I'm sure that made Naomi happy.

There were current and former BABA students, teachers, artists, and book people from all over the Bay Area. Losing a luminary like Layla was a big deal to this community. Even if you didn't like her, you had to acknowledge her power and influence on the business of books and fine art.

I greeted my friend Ian McCullough and his significant other, Jake, who were talking to Doris and Teddy Bondurant. I stopped to chat about books and Layla for a few minutes, then moved on to schmooze with others in the room.

Naomi was working it as she'd never done when Layla was alive. I figured she wanted the board to recognize that she was the one person capable of taking Layla's place.

I scanned the room and finally picked Alice out of the crowd. A number of board members surrounded her by the south hall and they carried on an animated conversation. Alice was a real asset to BABA and I wondered if the board would consider her more capable than Naomi of filling Layla's shoes.

Looking from one side of the room to the other, from Naomi to Alice, reminded me that the board of directors would have to make a decision soon. Who would run BABA in Layla's absence? Taking in the current scenario, Naomi on one side, working the bar and hanging with her peeps, and Alice on the other, talking like a grown-up to the board members, I was beginning to realize where the power in the room lay. Despite the wardrobe change and the party planning, Naomi didn't stand a chance. But that was just my opinion.

As I sipped my wine and soaked up the party atmosphere, I had another thought. Even though BABA was run as a nonprofit, that didn't mean Layla hadn't been paid handsomely, or that she didn't have other income. Because of the way she had hobnobbed, the way she had dressed, the quality of her accessories—yes, even I could tell they were pricey—I'd always assumed she was somewhat wealthy in her own right. Would Naomi inherit everything, or did she have other relatives waiting in the woodwork?

Chances were, Naomi stood to inherit it all. And suddenly I smelled a motive. Not that she didn't already have one, but it would have been nice to find out Naomi had killed her aunt Layla for good old-fashioned greed, rather than the simple fact that auntie had been an infuriating bitch.

Speaking of infuriating bitches, I spotted Minka at the buffet table, scarfing up the guacamole as she talked to Karalee, who gazed around the room, seeking a safe place to hide. I wanted to look away, but seeing Minka in her black cabbie hat that didn't quite cover her still-bandaged head, I was reminded that Gabriel had been injured, as well. And I'd vowed to discover any possible connection between Gabriel, Minka, and Layla.

I drained my wineglass, because if I was going to have to talk to Minka, I needed fortification. On the way across the room I gave myself a pep talk to remind myself that if Minka could shed the slimmest ray of light on recent events, we—I mean, the police—might be able to track down the killer.

I straightened my shoulders and gritted my teeth. I could do this. I approached the buffet table. Karalee saw me first and her eyes lit up. I grabbed hold of her arm in a show of fondness, sure, but really I just wanted to keep her from running away. It wasn't easy. She was ready to escape Minka, but I was even more determined to keep her here. I needed a shield.

"Hey, Minka," I said jovially, like a complete fraud. "How's your head feeling?"

She whipped around and her mouth gaped. Not a pretty sight. I would never eat guacamole again.

Her upper lip twisted in a snarl. "You're joking, right? Am I supposed to believe you care?"

Today, in honor of the dearly departed, she wore her favorite clothing mash-up: pleather, spandex, and animal prints. Her pants were black and brown cougar spots and her short shiny jacket was a bold zebra print. But the most disturbing part of her outfit was what it didn't cover up. Two wide inches of pale belly fat were exposed between the jacket and the pants.

"Of course I care," I said, swallowing my distaste. "I saved your life, remember?"

"No, you didn't. You're so full of shit."

What could I say? She was right. "But I just hate the idea that anyone might be attacked here at BABA. And then poor Layla was killed two days later. I mean, don't you think that's scary? That could've been you."

"Whatever." She glanced at Karalee and rolled her eyes.

"I've got to go," Karalee said quickly, and tried to break away.

"No," I said, jerking her back to my side. I exhaled from the exertion. "So, Minka, here's what I was wondering about the other night. Do you remember hearing anything right before you were hit? Like heavy footsteps, maybe. Or somebody humming or whistling. Were there any sounds coming from any of the offices?"

Did I sound as big an idiot as I felt? Probably.

She wrinkled her nose. "Not that it's any of your business, but no, I didn't hear anything besides the usual crap-ass chamber music coming from Layla's office."

Crap-ass? Layla had played pretty classical music. Figures Minka would hate that.

"What about odors?" I persisted. "Do you remember smelling anything unusual? You know, like perfume? Men's cologne? Minty fresh breath? Sweat, maybe? Garlic?"

"God, you're so bizarre."

"Is that a yes or a no?" I said.

"That's a go-fuck-yourself."

"Minka, that's rude," Karalee said.

"Yeah, well, fuck you, too."

I gave up on the niceties. "What the hell were you doing in the hall, anyway? Weren't you supposed to be teaching a class?"

"Screw you," she said with a sneer. "I've had it with the third degree. I might owe you my life, but that doesn't mean I have to put up with your crap."

"Look, I just—"

She flipped me the finger and stomped off.

So, maybe it was a little bizarre, asking her about sounds and odors. After all, she probably couldn't get past her own overwhelming sulfur scent. Or was that brimstone? Whatever it was, she reeked like the spawn of Beelzebub that she was.

"Hey, I remember smelling something that night," Karalee said, her forehead creased in thought. "It was like, I don't know, incense or something. Huh. I didn't think about it until you asked that question. Huh."

She was starting to sound like Ned with the huh and the huh. She shrugged and walked away.

"That seemed to go well," Derek said, approaching me on my blind side. He handed me another glass of red wine.

"Thanks," I said and took a big sip. The perfect remedy for a Minka-induced headache. "I didn't realize you were watching. I'm so glad I had a witness."

"I thought I was hallucinating when I saw you walk over and talk to her."

"Were you hoping to break up a catfight?"

"I only dreamed," he said sardonically.

I shook my head and took another sip of wine. "She's so stupid. What was I thinking?"

His eyes narrowed in on me. "Yes, what were you thinking?"

"I don't like that look you're giving me," I said, and tried to stare him down. But his gaze was unyielding. He was, after all, a professional. "Okay, fine. I thought she might have some clue about the night she was attacked."

"Have we not had this conversation before?"

My shoulders slumped, but I snapped back to attention. "Look, I just want to make sure that BABA is safe. You can't blame me. First Minka, then Layla. And then Gabriel over the weekend, not that he had anything to do with the attacks here. But it just makes me worry that I'm—oh, I don't know—something like a murder magnet."

There, I'd said it.

He shook his head. "Darling Brooklyn, you can't tell a lie to save your life. But I must hand it to you. You never give up trying."

My jaw dropped. "You think I'm lying?"

"Yes, I think you're lying," he said easily, and sipped his wine. "Because you are."

"I'm not—"

"My love, I'll say it again: You're the world's worst liar." He took hold of my arm and led me away to a quieter spot. "The fact is, you simply can't help sticking your pretty little nose into places it doesn't belong. I understand the appeal of investigating a murder, but you could get yourself hurt. So I'm inclined to advise you against it."

"But—"

"You appear to have a short-term memory problem, so let me remind you of a certain psychopathic killer who had you trapped in St. Margaret's Chapel in Edinburgh not so very long ago."

I shuddered, then glanced around to make sure we weren't being overheard. "Of course I remember that."

"I'm glad."

"But that was a completely different situation. This time I'm not involved. I'm not a suspect. I'm just concerned about being the common factor among three attacks in less than a week."

"You?" He shook his head as if to rearrange his brain cells. "You think you're the cause of these attacks?"

"No, not the cause. But don't you think it's strange that I'm the one who found all three victims?"

"Strange, yes. Connected, no." He pointed toward the small cluster of cops who'd just walked into the party. "There's Inspector Lee. Let's go see if she can be charmed into sharing her latest findings with us."

"That's why I keep you around, sport," I said.

"Music to my ears, my dear."

I stared at him. "Music."

"Beg pardon?"

"Yes, let's go see the inspector," I said. I placed my empty glass on a nearby tray and took off across the room.

He caught up with me in two strides. "You're in a hurry all of a sudden."

"I just put something together."

"So you did get something out of Minka."

"Maybe."

Taking hold of my arm, he took a detour, pulling me down the hall and into an empty classroom. "What is it?" he demanded.

"Minka said she heard music coming from Layla's office just before she was attacked. But I just remembered that by the time I came down the hall and found her, there was no music playing. So someone turned off Layla's stereo in the interim."

"The person who attacked Minka."

"It's a long shot, but if the power button is a smooth surface, they might've left a fingerprint."

He gave me a mind-blowing kiss. "That's why I keep you around, sport."

I laughed and took his hand. "Let's go talk to the police."

After Inspector Lee assured us that the fingerprint crew would be here shortly, Derek went off to make a phone call and I joined the party, entering the upper gallery as Naomi, at the central podium, introduced Gunther to the crowd.

He took the microphone and in his thick Austrian accent told everyone that he intended to keep his word and conduct the lithograph classes Layla had announced last week. He added, "Layla would insist. She would probably haunt me if I did not stay."

That got a big laugh, but Gunther looked disgruntled. I wondered if Naomi had threatened him with her aunt's poltergeist. More than likely, he'd signed a contract and she'd threatened him with a lawsuit.

I was happy he was staying because I planned to sit in on one of his classes and learn his techniques. And more important, if Gunther stayed, then Derek would stay.

Naomi took her place back at the podium. After several calming breaths, the room hushed and she spoke. "My aunt was a woman to be reckoned with."

There was respectful applause.

"If there's one thing Aunt Layla would've insisted on, it was that the Twisted festival must carry on as scheduled."

This was met by thunderous cheers. It seemed to feed her as she continued, "And if there's one thing *I* insist on, it's that the gala culminating the Twisted festival be even bigger than Layla planned. And Charles Dickens is going to have to share the evening's honors with Layla Fontaine."

Now along with the enthusiastic clapping, I could see tears glistening in the eyes of many. Who knew Naomi could rock a crowd like this? Maybe she was channeling her aunt Layla. Minus the sexual innuendo, thank God.

"Now, please enjoy yourselves as we celebrate the life of a wonderful woman and the work she did for the Bay Area Book Arts." Naomi wore a satisfied grin as she took in the cheers and applause. She signaled the crowd to settle down so she could add, "I've been told that the bartenders just opened a case of 2007 Kosta Browne pinot noir. For all you wine snobs in the room, this is your moment."

"That's all of us," somebody shouted.

True enough. This was San Francisco, where nine out of ten of us were inveterate wine snobs. There were laughs and cheers as the thundering hordes raced to one of the two bars in the gallery.

"That was a smart move," Alice said from inches away.

I jumped a little, then laughed at myself. "You snuck up on me."

"Sorry." She linked arms with me. "I was just saying it was smart of Naomi to order all that great wine. It'll endear her to everyone."

I looked around, then murmured, "Everyone but the board of directors. They seem firmly in your camp."

"So you noticed the two camps?"

I nodded and she sighed. "I hate the idea, but Naomi is determined to turn this into a competition. I just want to work together to keep things going at a professional level."

"That speaks to your higher level of experience and understanding of business. The board will surely recognize that in you."

"Thank you, Brooklyn." She squeezed my arm. "That means a lot, coming from you."

Like Naomi, Alice was dressed completely in black, though her look was more sedate. A simple long-sleeved black knit dress skimmed her calves. Black boots and her usual black velvet headband completed the look.

Alice shivered as she glanced around. "I can't help wondering if Layla's killer is here in this crowd."

I followed her gaze and saw Cynthia and Tom Hardesty with their heads close together. They looked as though they were arguing about something, which was not unusual. Tom looked shaken but Cynthia appeared resolute. Then Tom peeked timidly around the room.

Alice and I both looked away.

I glanced back in time to see Tom give Cynthia a peck on the cheek, almost like a son would kiss his mother. It was a little peculiar, but that pretty much described their relationship.

"Do you think he was having an affair with Layla?" Alice whispered.

I stared at Tom, considering, then shook my head. "He might've wanted to, but do you really think Layla would stoop that low?"

"Oh, never. But I wonder if she spurned him and . . ." She covered her mouth, unable to finish the alarming thought.

A spurned man might be more than capable of murder, I thought, watching the Hardestys for a few more seconds. Then I shook my head. "Tom wouldn't have the guts. But Cynthia is a different story."

Alice gasped. "She's just ballsy enough to do it. She seems so contemptuous of people."

I nodded. "You don't miss much, do you?"

"I'm going to confess something," Alice said, and took a deep breath. "Cynthia scares me more than anyone else in this room."

"She is awfully big-boned," I allowed.

"I know. She could smash me like a bug."

I chuckled, then sobered as Naomi walked past, followed by three board members, one of whom signaled Tom and Cynthia to join them. The group walked down the hall into Naomi's office and closed the door.

"What was that all about?" I wondered, then exchanged looks with Alice. "Do you know what's going on?"

"Not a clue. But I'm going to find out."

I followed Alice as she threaded her way through the crowd. She could be determined when she wanted to be. We made it to the closed office door in record time. But it wasn't necessary to get that close. Through the door we could hear Naomi from halfway down the hall.

"I deserve that position," Naomi cried. "I do everything around here. She means nothing to this place—do you hear me? Nothing."

"But Layla had confidence in her." That was Cynthia's voice. "I'm sorry, Naomi, but she didn't feel the same way about you."

"Well, Layla's dead now," Naomi said pointedly. "And I'm the only one who knows how to run this place."

"And we agree, dear," Tom said gently, trying to placate

her. "That's why we're giving you a raise and a more prestigious position. What more do you want?"

"I want the executive director position," she snapped.

"Naomi, don't make this harder than it already is."

"I'm not the one making it harder. You are. Why shouldn't I fight for what I want?"

"Because we've made our decision."

"But it's not the right decision," she said, her voice rising. "I'm the one who does all the work and some newcomer gets the job? Not fair!"

"Naomi, please," said Cynthia. "We're only doing what we think Layla would want us to do."

"For God's sake, stop kowtowing to Layla," she cried. "I know what you thought of her. How can I be sure you didn't kill her?"

There was silence.

"Whoa," Alice whispered.

I had to agree—that was harsh. Even if I'd had the same thought five minutes ago.

"I'm sorry, dear, but the board has made its decision."

"You'll be sorry, all right. You'll all be sorry."

The door flew open and Naomi ran out, then stopped when she saw Alice.

"You!" she cried, pointing. "You knew all along. Are you happy now?"

"I didn't. Naomi, I—"

"Stay out of my way, you troublemaker."

"You're upset," Alice said softly, "so I'm going to let that go. Maybe we can talk later and work things out between us."

"Oh, buzz off, all of you." Then Naomi marched down the hall and disappeared into the crowd.

I turned and looked at Alice, who was holding her stomach and swaying back and forth.

"Are you going to be sick?"

She nodded her head vigorously.

"Go." I pointed and she raced off down the hall.

So, I thought. *The formerly dowdy young Naomi has inherited a spine after all. Along with her aunt's temper.*

Cynthia walked over, looking shell-shocked. "Did you hear any of that?"

"Some of it," I confessed. "She was pretty upset."

"It was worse up close. I'm worried she'll quit because, unfortunately, she's right. She knows how this place runs."

"She won't quit," I said with certainty. "This job is her life. Give her a few days to calm down."

"I feel so bad," Cynthia said. "Her aunt just died and now this."

"You had to make a decision quickly," I said, touching her shoulder in understanding. "They'll just have to learn to work together."

"I don't know about that," Cynthia said, shaking her head in apprehension. "Naomi looked like she wanted to kill us all."

Chapter 13

Any thoughts of spending time with Derek after the party were squelched once again when Gunther the Troll announced that he wanted Derek and his men to go to dinner with him. At first, Derek had refused to indulge him, exasperated with the man's capricious changes to his well-ordered operation. He took Gunther aside and told him he would pull his men off the assignment if the Austrian didn't start taking the death threats against him more seriously. Interpol had already reported that several operatives of the European prime minister whose daughter Gunther had compromised had entered the United States.

But Gunther had insisted the fancy dinner was something he'd planned weeks ago and he wondered aloud why it wasn't on Derek's schedule.

Derek wondered as well. Knowing him as well as I thought I did, I knew his own calendar would be accurate and up-to-the-minute. So that meant Gunther was lying. In the end, though, Derek relented for the sake of client goodwill. I was outwardly gracious in defeat but privately irate. Did Gunther know that Derek and I had made plans? Did he care? And how fancy could a dinner with a bunch of guys be?

"Oh." How stupid was I? There would be women there, of course. Gunther was a good-looking guy, an internationally known artist. He could drum up a wild party with one phone call.

"Ugh." I so didn't need the image of Derek surrounded by wild, eager party girls. I took a deep breath and shoved those thoughts right off the bridge, into the bay where they belonged.

As he said good night to me, Derek whispered that his original plan had been to spend the evening with me. It was clear what he meant and it tickled my heart, though I would've preferred that other parts of me be tickled instead. But enough about my sorry excuse for a love life.

I was grabbing my coat from the deserted back cloakroom when someone tapped my shoulder, effectively scaring the living daylights out of me.

"Huh. Brooklyn."

My chest stuttered in fear. But it was just Ned. No worries. He'd caught me off guard, that's all. "Hey, hi, Ned. How're you holding up?"

" 'Kay," he said, his gaze darting every which way. "Weird stuff."

Those three words were the most Ned had said to me in all the years I'd been coming here. "That's to be expected, I guess. But you still have a job, right? Everything will work out, right?"

"Huh. Me and my printing press." As he spoke, he chewed the skin around the nail of his ring finger. "We're a team."

"You sure are," I said casually, though inside I was starting to wonder why Ned had chosen tonight and me to demonstrate his nascent social skills. "Well, I'd better be going now. Good night."

"You're smart."

I shifted back, surprised. "Thanks."

"Huh." His lips thinned and his forehead furled sullenly. "She was bad."

I frowned. "I'm sorry, Ned. Was Layla mean to you?"

"Huh." He looked around furtively, then whispered, "I see things."

"Huh." Now I sounded like him. "What sort of things?"

"You watch out," he muttered, then added, "Okay, g'night." And he shuffled out of the room.

I opened my mouth to call him back, then shut it. What things had he seen? Flummoxed, I glanced around again, then shook off the chills I felt from his last statement.

I see things.

Right now, I couldn't think about the things Ned had seen. My life was already weird enough.

I see things.

Was Ned watching me? I buttoned up my coat and headed for the front door, where I turned and stared back at the room. I didn't see Ned but I knew he was in there somewhere, watching. I just couldn't figure out if that was a good thing or a bad thing.

As I passed through the gallery, I noticed Naomi swilling wine and holding court by the bar. Seconds later, Inspector Lee walked back inside the gallery with two uniformed cops.

She skirted the crowd and moved directly toward Naomi. I saw the moment Naomi grasped what was happening. Her eyes widened and she turned and walked away quickly. Lee signaled for the cops to go after her, down the hall that led to the bathrooms.

Poor Naomi. She was not having a good night.

Monday's class had been canceled due to Layla's memorial service and wake, so Tuesday evening I was back in my classroom laying out supplies at each student's place for the traditional journal they would create over the next three nights. Heavy cardboard matte, already cut to size, for the boards. Signature pages cut to fit. A thin piece of spine stiffener. I'd also laid out more pieces of cloth on the side counter for them to choose from. There was every conceivable pattern and color for the covers and heavy construction paper for the pastedowns, the decorative paper glued to the inside covers to hide the dull boards and ragged turnings.

Alice arrived a few minutes early and helped me assemble the tools we would need this week. After expressing confusion and concern about last night's confrontation with Naomi, she changed the subject and raved about our weekend visit to Sonoma. Then she asked about Gabriel.

"He's okay," I said. "I talked to my mom this afternoon. He's still in the hospital, but he'll be coming home tomorrow. He was having some problems sleeping, but I guess they've worked those out. I'm still kind of freaked out that it happened."

"It's so frightening."

"I know. But he's really strong. Mom will take him to her place and spoil him so much, he'll run shrieking out of there eventually."

"Your mother is wonderful," Alice said.

"Thanks. I think so, too. She should've had ten kids because now that we've all moved out, she's started adopting people. First there was Annie, now Gabriel."

"You're so lucky. She has such a big heart."

"Yeah." I frowned. "I already feel like Annie's my sister, but I don't really like to think of Gabriel as my brother."

She smiled. "I see what you mean. He's awfully cute."

I opened the Ziploc bag of glue sticks. "Oh, he's beyond cute."

"Yes, even with his head wrapped in gauze and lying on a gurney, I could tell how handsome he was."

As she walked around the table, placing bone folders at everyone's place, I observed her. I didn't know how my faux sister Annie would feel about it, but I wondered if it would be crazy to fix Gabriel up with Alice. She was a beautiful girl, smart, funny, compassionate, and spirited. But despite those qualities, she had a touch of fragility. I had a feeling Gabriel would chew her up and spit her out, and I would lose one or both of them as a friend.

Then again, was Gabriel really a friend? I exhaled slowly. No, he was more like an extremely attractive nuisance. I'd only known him a short while, only seen him a few times. He showed up at the strangest moments and he'd saved my life on more than one occasion. Now I knew he'd also saved the lives of both my father and Guru Bob. So he was definitely hero material, but what if he was a spy or some kind of a mercenary? He'd been known to skirt the law when the situation called for it. All in all, he probably wasn't the best choice for Alice.

Not that she needed me to set her up. She had a fiancé, for goodness' sake! In my excitement to change careers from crime investigator to matchmaker, I'd forgotten all about Stuart.

Laughing at myself, I finished passing out glue brushes as the rest of my students arrived for class.

Since we'd missed Monday night's class as well as half of last Thursday's class when Layla's body was discovered, I had to cancel the construction of this week's miniature book and go directly to the larger journal. I did a quick recap of the basic nineteenth-century bookbinding techniques we'd covered last week. I promised my students that next week we'd move to the twenty-first century and have some fun.

"Tonight I'll give you a quick background of eighteenth-century binding, but we won't be doing any hands-on work in that style."

"Why not?" Jennifer asked.

"A few reasons," I said. "First and foremost, eighteenth-century bookbinding was all about the tools. You sort of had to wrestle a book into shape. This was the age of gilding, and the French predominated."

I passed around some photographs showing different

styles of gilding on book covers. "Some would say that if you're studying eighteenth-century bookbinding, you're essentially studying the work of Pierre-Paul Dubuisson, the French master bookbinder and royal gilder to Louis the Fifteenth. These are his works as compared to his students' work. You can see who the master is."

Without warning, Mitchell broke in with a tacky and slightly lewd Maurice Chevalier imitation. Something about an invitation to come up to his place to see his gilding.

The class burst into laughter.

"Thank you," I said, laughing along with everyone. "Best offer I've had in weeks." Sadly, that was true.

"I've done some academic presentations of Dubuisson's work along with some comparative studies of his gilding designs vis-à-vis his students'. But I'll spare you the details."

"You don't have to," Alice said loyally.

"Thank you, Alice," I said, and laughed again. "But I'll just move on to our next book."

Since I was leading them through the same steps we'd taken to make last week's book, the students moved smoothly through the process with only a few reminders from me. It was just as well, because I was having a hard time staying focused. I was burning with curiosity about Naomi. Had the police arrested her last night?

The dinner break finally arrived and I dashed out to find out what had happened. I knocked on Naomi's door and was almost surprised when she called out, "Come in."

"You *are* here," I said as I opened the door. "I was a little worried."

"Oh, it's you, Brooklyn," she said with some disappointment. "What is it?"

Ooh, feel the warmth. Had she been expecting someone else to come knocking? I was amazed to see her sitting there as though nothing had happened in the last few days to change her life. But I was even more shocked to see her looking like such a fashion plate. She wore a peach jacket that suited her skin tone and fitted her small frame to perfection, giving her the look of a true professional. Her makeup was subtle and her hair curled softly around her face. The mouse had come out of her shell, to mix a metaphor.

"You look great," I said.

"Thanks," she said, and her expression softened a little. "What's up?"

I stepped inside and closed the door. "This is sort of a sensitive issue, but Layla had a book with her the night she died. It was the *Oliver Twist* I restored for her. I'd like to buy it from you once the police return it."

Naomi's eyes widened—in fear? Or was that speculation? But her face calmed instantly and I was no longer sure what I'd seen. "I'm sorry. I don't know what book you're talking about."

"Layla talked about it the night of the Twisted opening party, remember?"

"Sorry, can't help you."

My eyes narrowed. She flinched. What game was she playing? She'd had a bad week, so I gave her the benefit of the doubt and explained the book again. "Since the police took it in for evidence, you probably won't get it back in time for the silent auction, so I'd like to buy it whenever you do get it back."

She carefully exhaled. "Oh, yeah, I think I know the book you're talking about." She pushed her hair away from her face and set her jaw. "No. Sorry, it's not for sale."

I couldn't tell what was going on in that brain of hers, but she was carrying the mini-Layla bit too far. My gloves were off now.

"Naomi, I did the restoration work on that book. I know it from cover to cover, and I can assure you, it's not what you think it is."

"What are you talking about?"

"I'm talking about its market worth. It's a truly beautiful book and worth a lot of money, but it's not the rare first edition Layla pretended it was the other night."

"Layla wouldn't lie."

I almost laughed. "Oh, please. Layla lied plenty. And this time she lied to a room full of wealthy BABA contributors and supporters. And she did it knowingly and willfully."

"Stop it. I don't believe you."

I had to think for a moment. Naomi did wield some power at BABA, but I didn't think she was capable of sabotaging my career like her aunt was. So I decided to plunge ahead with the truth. "I'm sorry, Naomi, but Layla was not being honest about the book. And if you continue her lie and try to pass it off as a first edition, you'll get caught. Whoever buys it will find out soon enough what the book was really worth. Do you know how fast your funding would be cut off if your corporate sponsors found out about it?"

Naomi's face was a sickly gray. She blinked rapidly and shook her head. "I can't . . . it's not . . ." She mumbled something incoherent, pushed away from her desk, and ran from the room.

"Well, that went well." I blew out a breath and wandered back to the gallery, looking for someone else to browbeat.

"Hello, darling."

Shock and pleasure overcame me. Derek was loitering by the bookshelf in the north alcove, thumbing through one of the many other copies of *Oliver Twist* on exhibit.

I slipped my arms around his waist and rested my head against his rock-solid chest.

"Ah, that's lovely." He wrapped his arms around me.

"What are you doing here?" I asked.

"Hoping to see you, of course."

"That's so sweet."

"I'm a sweet guy."

"But isn't Gunther giving a class tonight?"

"Is he?"

"Very funny. That's why you're here."

"Yes, well, I'd still rather see you." He seemed reluctant to let me go and I was perfectly happy to stay right where I was. After another minute or so, he said, "No matter what happens, I'm taking you out tonight."

"Are you?"

"I am." He leaned his head back and frowned at me. "You're not otherwise engaged, are you?"

"Do you care?" I asked.

His mouth twisted into a sexy grin. "Of course I care."

I patted the lapel of his bazillion-dollar Savile Row suit. "Then I'm available."

"I'm glad."

We continued to smile at each other and I tried to put a name to the emotion running through me. I felt . . . happy. No, more than happy. Blissful. Complete.

There was that sappiness again. Really, I didn't need anyone to complete me, for God's sake. I was complete all on my own.

And how complete could someone else make me feel when I'd never even been on a date with him? Crime scenes, yes. But unless crime scenes counted as dates, I barely knew him.

And just how happy and blissful would I be when he left? Did I really want to open myself to the pain I would suffer then? Because he *would* leave. His home was six thousand miles away. He'd only been to San Francisco a few times on business.

But none of that mattered to my heart right now. Or any other parts of me, either. I didn't know what was going on between Derek and me, didn't know where we would end up, but I was tired of fighting against the tide. I just wanted to be with him.

I rested my head on his custom-suited shoulder.

"Don't ever play poker," he said, brushing back my hair to nuzzle my neck.

"Why not?"

"Your face is an open book."

I lifted my head and studied his face for a moment, then frowned. "I can't read one word on yours."

"That's because I'm a highly trained operative," he said, bending his head to graze his lips along my jaw.

I laughed. "Oh, Commander, does that line really work?"

"I believe it's working right now," he murmured, and kissed my neck.

After that exhilarating dinner break, I found myself racing through the second half of the class. There was more laughter and lots of questions. I tried to slow down, tried to be attentive to everyone's needs, but I just wanted to get out of there.

I'd already given myself the lecture about appearing too eager, but let's face it, that ship had sailed. Apparently, my heart was on my sleeve. Go ahead and call me an idiot. It couldn't be worse than the names I'd already called myself, including fifty-seven kinds of stupid.

Somehow I managed to get through the class. I made sure everyone had someone to accompany them to their cars. For once, Mitchell wasn't paying attention as he strolled off with the other two librarians, deep in conversation.

I straightened the room and walked out to the gallery. Derek wasn't in the immediate vicinity so I checked the alcoves and the hallways, then wandered into Gunther's classroom. It was empty. I could see lights on in the office wing so I ambled down the hall, thinking Derek might've struck up a conversation with one of the managers.

Naomi was the only one still around. She sat at her desk, pounding on a calculator and writing numbers on a sheet of paper. A single lamp illuminated the desk surface, leaving her face in shadow.

"Hi, Naomi," I said.

Her hand jerked and the pencil slid across the page, leaving a dark mark. "Damn it."

"Sorry to startle you," I said.

She exhaled and I could see a frown appear on her face. "It's okay. I thought everyone had left. Look, about the book," she said, erasing the pencil smudge.

"Oh, we can talk about that later," I said, glancing down the hall. I had bigger things on my mind than the *Oliver Twist*. "I'm looking for Derek Stone. I was supposed to meet him after my class."

"Really?" Her eyes gleamed with intent. "He left awhile ago."

I frowned. Maybe she misunderstood. "Derek Stone? The British guy? He left?"

"I know who he is." Thump-thump-thump went the eraser. "He left with the police."

I froze, unsure if I'd heard her right. Her thumping eraser was getting on my nerves. "The police were here?"

"Yeah. Oh, you must've been in class."

"Right. So he left at the same time the police did?"

She chuckled scornfully. "Not exactly."

I had to hold myself back from strangling her as my voice rose. "Then what, exactly?"

She stared up at me and I could see how much she loathed me at that moment. I guess maybe I'd laid it on a little heavy earlier, when I accused her dearly departed aunt of lying.

"The police took him in for questioning," she said.

In shock, I had to force the word out. "Why?"

She made an exasperated sound and waved the pencil around. "Oh, come on, Brooklyn. You know, about his thing with Layla."

My ears were starting to buzz and I felt dizzy. "What thing with Layla?"

She pulled a face. "What rock have you been hiding under?"

"I'm not sure." My knees were wobbling and I grabbed the doorjamb. "Spell it out for me."

Her smile was gloating. "Derek and Layla?"

"What about them?"

"They were having an affair, Brooklyn. Layla broke up with him. He carries a gun. You do the math."

Chapter 14

Derek? Layla? *Affair?*

No, it wasn't true. I staggered out of her office, then stopped and stared at the wall, trying to focus. But I couldn't. I felt nauseous and my throat was so dry I couldn't swallow.

I swung around and stepped back into Naomi's office. She looked up and I caught a glimmer of triumph in her eyes. And in that moment, I knew she was fabricating the entire story. Evidently, the bitch strain ran deep in Layla's family. I braced myself, sucked in a few deep breaths, and struggled to gain back some of the strength that had drained away a minute ago.

"You're lying," I said, taking another step into her office.

Naomi's lips curved into a smirk. "Uh-oh, looks like Brooklyn's jealous. So you didn't know about the two of them?"

"No," I said, more easily now. "Because there's no such thing as the 'two of them.'"

She licked her lips, an obvious clue that she was making it up as she went along. "Yes, there is."

"I'm not sure why you're lying to me, Naomi. Maybe because I threatened you earlier about the book. But right now I don't care about that. I just want you to know that if you lied to the police about Derek, that book will be the least of your worries."

"I'm not lying and it has nothing to do with the book." She stood and walked around the desk, then sat on the edge. It was an imitation of her aunt, and even knowing she was lying, I wanted to smack that fake sympathetic smile off her face. "I'm sorry, hon. I guess you didn't know. But it shouldn't be such a big surprise. You know Layla would screw anything that moved. Of course, in Derek's case, I couldn't really blame her. He's totally cute."

"Cute," I murmured, and wanted more than anything else to throttle her. All of a sudden, pictures flashed in my head of Layla gripping Derek's arm that first night. Of Layla rubbing her leg up against Derek's. Of Layla patting his backside.

And right then, I was immensely glad she was dead. I hated her. There, I'd said it. To myself, anyway.

Meanwhile, Naomi sighed dreamily. "Actually, cute doesn't really describe Derek, does it? He's more hot and sexy than just cute. And dangerous, you know? Wouldn't mind getting some of that myself."

The crass words were so incongruous coming from her mousy little mouth, I just shook my head. "You know, *hon*, I have no idea why Layla thought so little of you, because you're so much like her."

She gasped and her cheeks began to blotch. Guess I had struck a nerve.

I continued. "I'm sure if we call the police right now and tell them that you made a mistake, they'll understand."

"It's no mistake," she cried, and her lower lip popped out in a pout.

"Okay, you stick with that story, but I suggest you start looking over your shoulder, because something's going to come back and bite you on the ass."

With that, I walked out, grabbed my coat from the gallery rail where I'd draped it earlier, and ran all the way to my car.

The drive home was touch and go, emotionally speaking. I knew Naomi was full of crap, but my mind kept drifting into possible scenarios that could very well be true.

I thought back to the first night I'd met Derek at the Covington Library, the night Abraham died. Derek had been stalking the crowded main hall, an outsider observing the goings-on of the wealthy and influential people who filled the space. More than once I'd caught him frowning at me from across the wide room. Later, in Abraham's workroom, he'd found me covered in blood and accused me of murder. It was a strange beginning to what had become a lovely friendship—and more.

But now I recalled that Layla Fontaine had been there that night. Had she and Derek met there? Maybe they'd attended Abraham's show as a couple.

"Oh, shut up," I muttered. Then something else occurred to me and I pounded the steering wheel in disgust.

Layla had been in Edinburgh for the book fair. Now I recalled several nights when Derek had been unable to see me. I hadn't given it a second thought at the time. Why would I? I thought he had obligations at Holyroodhouse Palace. Now, I couldn't be sure. Maybe he and Layla had been frolicking all over Edinburgh while I . . .

Oh, God, at this rate I would be insane before I got home. So I didn't go home. Instead, I drove through the city, to Pacific Heights. I was feeling just perverse enough that driving up and down astoundingly steep hills might actually soothe my jumbled brain. Or at least give me something else to obsess over.

When I first moved to San Francisco, I considered it my civic duty to practice my hill driving. I realized after doing it a few times that it was actually fun in a strange and crazy way, and always provided a nice distraction.

Tonight, I had a breathless moment going up a treacherous hill on Filbert Street where I stalled out and had to alternate between the emergency brake and my fancy foot-pedal work. And prayer. It wasn't pretty, but it was exhilarating and I made it to the top of the grade.

Because of all the one-way streets, I had to circle around, taking Leavenworth to Chestnut to Larkin before I was able to drive down beautiful, touristy Lombard Street with its absurdly winding turns, vivid pink hydrangea bushes, neat green hedges, and incongruous palm trees. The night was clear, and as I took the first turn, a carpet of city lights undulated toward the shining pillar that was Coit Tower standing sentinel at the top of Telegraph Hill.

With the next turn, I could make out the ebony surface of the bay. Many miles beyond the water, the vague outline of the Berkeley hills was silhouetted against the night sky.

At this time of night, there were only a few other cars making the descent, so I eased off the brake pedal and drove briskly around the two remaining sharp, twisting curves for which the redbrick-paved street was justifiably famous.

Years ago, when my parents had first brought us kids here, we piled out of the car and clambered down the stairs that lined both sides of Lombard. I'm sure we were shouting and pushing and laughing all the way. When we got to the bottom, we crossed and climbed up the other side of the street, stopping every few steps to turn and gaze out at the incredible view of the city, with the blue waters of the bay and Alcatraz Island beyond. I remembered thinking how cool it would have been to live in one of the houses that lined the crookedest street in the world. Now, as I drove down, I thought how awful it had to be to deal with the daily onslaught of tourists and the constant line of cars, the photographers, the screaming kids.

Despite the ubiquitous tourists and the cars and the kids, I loved San Francisco. Who wouldn't fall a tiny bit in love with a town where you could walk into a bar and sit down between a Trotskyite and a drag queen and wind up three hours later at a Giants game with both of them? For a place that was remarkable for its lack of pretension, San Francisco was unashamedly self-indulgent. San Franciscans adored their town. One of the first things a new resident learned was that San Francisco dwellers capitalized the *t* and the *c* when referring to the city of San Francisco. This was *The City*. And while most cities didn't require full participation, San Francisco did.

I smiled as I coasted down Filbert again, feeling much better than I had earlier. The hills had done their job.

I headed for home, and less than fifteen minutes later drove into my parking garage. I found my space, turned off the engine, and rested my forehead on the cool plastic hardness of the steering wheel.

Unfortunately, the reeling thoughts of Derek and Layla were back in full force and I knew I wouldn't survive the night if I didn't find another distraction. So I pulled out my cell and called Robin.

The next morning, I woke up puffy and so exhausted I didn't want to get out of bed. I felt hot and wondered if maybe I had a fever. Everything hurt and I was certain I was coming down with a cold or the flu.

I lay in bed, pondering the night before. I'd been an embarrassing mess. And good friend that she was, Robin had rushed over to keep me company. She poured wine and listened to me rant. Occasionally, she would remind me that Layla and Derek together was all a big fat lie, and I would agree and thank her. Then I'd go off on another tirade. I think we laughed a lot. I hope so.

I guess I didn't have the flu, after all. I had a bit of a hangover. We'd finished a full bottle of wine. Or rather, I'd finished it. I think Robin had nursed one glass, just to keep me company. She really was the best kind of friend.

I climbed out of bed and trudged to the kitchen, where

I downed two ibuprofen, then started the coffeemaker and stumbled off to the shower. I let the water pour over me for a long time, trying not to think. But it was impossible; all sorts of errant thoughts kept filtering through.

I examined every word Derek had ever said to me, picking them apart, searching for ulterior meanings.

I stared at myself in the mirror. The truly pathetic thing was that I was doing all this to myself, clear in the knowledge that Naomi was lying. What kinds of torture would I be going through if I'd actually believed she was telling the truth?

It was a sickness and I hated it.

I buried myself in work, dragging Guru Bob's book out of my bag to begin the restoration. It was a beautiful little gem and I was happy and honored that he trusted me to do the job, but my heart wasn't in my work today.

Nevertheless, hours later I'd photographed every inch of the book and taken it apart, piece by piece. I saved every bit of sinew and thread I could salvage, spreading the pieces out across my worktable, mapping it on wide strips of white construction paper. I loved my work, but I was tired and cranky and wanted to take a nap in the worst way.

But it was already three o'clock and I knew if I lay down now, I'd sleep right through my class. So I made a small pot of Peet's coffee, hoping it would get me revved up enough to go teach my class. I felt marginally better after two cups. As I washed my cup in the sink, the phone rang. I ran across the room to grab it.

"It's not true," Derek said flatly.

My heart stuttered at the sound of his voice and I had to clutch the edge of the bar stool to keep myself steady. My hands were shaking. When had I turned into such a weenie?

"Why should I believe you?" I said, hating the vulnerable tone of my voice. Even though I believed him, I still wanted to hear him deny it twenty different ways.

"It's not true," he said again, enunciating every word. "I don't know why Naomi lied to the police, but I'm going to find out."

"How did you know it was Naomi?"

He paused. "You know it, too."

"Yes."

"What else do you know?"

"I think she did it to get back at me."

"Why would she use me to get back at you?"

I gritted my teeth and said, "I might've threatened her a little."

I heard him sigh; then he said, "What time is your class?"

"It starts at six."

"I'll be by in ten minutes."

"Okay. You can—" But there was only a dial tone in my ear. I was going to let him park in the building but I guessed he could manage on his own.

Glancing around, I saw more dishes in the sink and the couch pillows thrown about. I bustled about the loft, straightening and cleaning, polishing the coffee table and mentally preparing myself to see Derek again. Cleaning always helped distract me from my problems. It was a wonder my place wasn't sparkling from floor to ceiling.

And yet, despite the fun diversion of scrubbing the sink, little thoughts began to sneak in. Had Derek spent the night in a jail cell? Or had the police let him go and he'd come back to BABA, looking for me? Probably not, and it was just as well. I'd spent the entire evening gibbering like a nincompoop. Poor Robin! She'd listened to me blather on and on, babbling about Derek, wondering what he'd been doing and when he'd been doing it. And why did it matter?

I'd managed to let my fears get the best of me, even though I'd seen right through Naomi's lies. I'd been enveloped in a nasty, miserable red haze of jealousy. Or is jealousy a green haze? Either way, it wasn't pretty.

I guess one could conclude that my feelings for Derek were even stronger than I'd realized. And that was so freaking scary, I wanted more than anything to grab the mop and clean my kitchen floor. But I couldn't. I had five minutes to pull myself together, so I rushed to my room and gave it my best shot.

The doorbell rang. I ran down the hall, then skidded to a stop. It wouldn't do for him to hear me racing to the door. And since when had I ever played games like this?

I blew my bangs off my forehead and walked the rest of way.

"Oh, hi." There, that didn't sound awkward. Not at all. Much.

"About time," he murmured and took one step into the house, but it was more like he stepped into *me*, fitted his mouth to mine and took.

And nothing else mattered.

Out on the sidewalk an hour later, after we'd had a nice conversation and some tea . . . no, really. After that long, lovely kiss at the door, Derek had pulled me into the living room, where he insisted we sit down and talk. He proceeded to assuage any fears I might've had about him and Layla. Of course, I assured him that I hadn't given it a second thought, but he persisted in telling me the whole story.

He'd never met Layla before, but a mutual friend had told him to look her up when he got to the city. This was weeks ago, and they'd planned to meet over cocktails the night of the Covington Library event, when Abraham died. Derek found me with blood on my hands, and the rest was history. He never contacted Layla again. So I had spoiled their big date. I did not regret it.

Then, when Derek showed up at BABA with Gunther,

Layla thought they ought to pick up where they'd left off and go for cocktails after the party. Derek quickly disabused her of that possibility.

He wasn't as sure of Naomi's motives as I was. He suspected Layla had lied to her niece about him to save face. He had a point, I thought. After all, how would it look to her underlings if the great and powerful Layla couldn't lure a man into her bed?

I stood on the sidewalk as Derek opened the passenger door of his Bentley.

"I can drive my own car," I said in protest.

"Why bother?" he asked. "I'll drive you to your class, and afterward we'll go out to dinner. Do you like Italian?"

I gazed at him across my shoulder. "Is the pope Catholic?"

"Italian it is," he said, patting my butt. "Now get in the car."

I laughed lightly and climbed into the butter-soft leather seat of the Bentley and buckled my seat belt. The car smelled new. And sexy. Or maybe that was just the mood I was in.

Derek hopped in and started the engine. "I need to make one stop. Do you mind?"

"No, we have time."

"Good." Within minutes, he'd driven over the bumpy streetcar tracks running down Market Street and continued up Kearny to Pine. We talked of normal things, the weather, my family, Gunther's brilliant lithographs. He drove two more narrow blocks to Stockton, then pulled into the elegant porte cochere of the Ritz-Carlton.

"We're stopping at your hotel?" I said, a tad incredulous, though I shouldn't have been. He was, after all, just a man. "We don't really have time for this."

Although, if pressed, I would be more than willing to comply. I was learning quickly that I was that kind of girl.

He checked his watch, then pierced me with a look. "You're right. You have to be at work in one hour, and I intend to take a lot more time than that."

I broke out in a sweat and started to whistle.

He laughed. "I simply forgot my wallet, darling. We'll only be a moment."

"Okay." Because really, how often did I get a chance to go to the Ritz?

"It's not like you to forget your wallet," I said as we entered the hushed lobby.

"I was in a rush to see you."

I smiled at him. As excuses went, that was a good one.

We rode the elevator up to the penthouse. I thought about it. The penthouse suite at the Ritz-Carlton went for what, ten thousand a night? The guy had an expense account that didn't quit.

Derek stopped at room 919, slipped his key card into the slot, and opened the door. "You can look at the view while I find my—"

He halted abruptly and I almost slammed into him. "Find your what?"

"Shit."

Derek rarely swore.

"What's wrong?"

"Stay here," he said, reaching behind his back to grip my arm.

"What is it, Derek?"

He turned and put a finger to his lips "Shh. Somebody's been in here."

I whispered, "Maybe just the maid?"

"No."

"How do you know?"

He looked at me over his shoulder. "A man knows when his fortress has been breached."

My heart stammered. Now, why did I find his words

so sexy when they should've been just plain ridiculous? Maybe it was something in the British accent that gave them gravitas.

It was my turn to grab his arm as I glanced around anxiously. "They might still be here."

"You're to stay right here," he said with an urgency that I'd rarely heard from him.

I nodded briskly. "All right."

He didn't have to tell me again. I'd been accosted in a hotel room recently and didn't relish a repeat experience. I watched from the safety of the elegant foyer as he conducted a swift but professional sweep of the room.

After shifting all the pillows and checking under the couch, he moved to the dining table and chairs and on to the coffee table. Finally, he approached the small Regency-style desk next to the wall of windows. He checked the drawers, pulling each one out completely and turning it over to see if anything was attached underneath. He ran his hands smoothly over the top surface, then squatted down and felt under the desk.

"Ah," he whispered, and crouched on his hands and knees to get a good look at whatever it was he'd felt. After prying it from beneath the desk, he stood.

"Is it a bomb?" I asked, cowering closer to the wall of the entryway.

"No," he said, bemused. "It's a book." He ripped duct tape off a Ziploc freezer-strength Baggie as he walked toward me. I ventured into the room and met him halfway, watching as he undid the plastic zipper and pulled a book out of the Baggie. He appeared lost in thought as he studied it. Then he looked up.

"I suppose this is your bailiwick," he said, handing the book to me. "Any thoughts?"

I frowned. "My first thought is that this is really weird."

The book was crimson morocco leather, in near perfect condition. The spine was elaborately gilded with *The Leg-*

end of Sleepy Hollow written in gold between the raised bands. The paper was heavily gilded on all three edges. I opened it to check the date of publication: 1905.

On the inside flyleaf, facing the title page, was a full-color Arthur Rackham illustration of Ichabod Crane and a pretty woman dressed in pink frills, walking under a gnarly tree. Hiding among the branches of the tree were a band of evil-looking pixies, grinning maniacally.

"Oh, it's charming," I whispered, turning it over to check out the back joint along the spine. It was strong, in mint condition.

"Yes, it's lovely, I suppose," Derek said grudgingly. "Why it was left here, hidden, I have no idea."

"No." It was indeed lovely and extremely rare; of that, I had no doubt. I imagined a collector would be willing to pay twenty or thirty thousand dollars, if not more.

"What in the world was this doing in a Baggie under your desk?"

He bristled. "I didn't put it there."

"Of course you didn't," I said. "I'm just wondering who did. And why."

I could feel the tension radiating off him. While I studied the book, he paced back and forth in front of me, visibly furious. It made me wonder how someone like him, with his legendary self-control and fervent belief in the order of law, could stand to be put in a position of having to defend himself to the police.

He probably felt upside down and discombobulated, although he might describe it in less whimsical terms. Whatever you called it, I knew the feeling. I felt his pain.

"If I knew who did it," he said tersely, "they'd be in jail by now."

Baffled, I shook my head. "What were they trying to prove?"

"Isn't it obvious?" He took the book from me and studied it for a few seconds, then handed it back. "I wouldn't be surprised to find that it's one of Layla's books. Clearly, someone put it here to frame me."

"How would they get in?" I waved away the question. "Never mind. Housekeeping." I had intimate knowledge of the ease of slipping a key off the housekeeping trolley.

"Exactly."

"But who? Naomi again?"

"I don't know." His fists clenched as he paced. "Is she smart enough to carry out such an elaborate scheme?"

"She's smart enough, but this would take more than mere smarts. It's so brazen, it's almost . . . diabolical."

"Yes, it is." He gritted his teeth. "And I'm determined to find out who did it."

"I'll help," I said immediately.

He tilted his head to study me.

"What?" I demanded finally. "I'm going to help. I don't care what—"

"Yes, I can use your help."

"—you think, I'm . . . what? I mean, it's not like you can stop me, but . . . really?"

He flashed me a sexy, lopsided grin. I wondered if he could hear my little heart pitter-patter as I returned his smile.

"Yes, really." His grin faded and he reached out to touch my cheek. "Because whoever tried to frame me has also hurt you, darling. And that is one thing I cannot forgive."

Chapter 15

En route to BABA to confront Naomi, I called the police to report the break-in of Derek's hotel suite. They transferred me to Inspector Lee's voice mail, where I gave her the rundown on Derek's hotel room, the book, and where we were headed now.

As Derek brought the Bentley to a stop directly in front of BABA's doors, Inspector Lee returned my call. I put her on speaker.

"Don't even think about walking inside until I get there," Lee shouted. "I'm calling a unit to meet you. They should be there in two minutes. Two minutes. Do you hear me?"

"I hear you," I said. "But I have a class to teach and Derek's just hanging out here with me."

"Do not walk inside that building," she shouted.

"No need for hysterics, Inspector," Derek said calmly. "We'll wait right here for you."

"Hysterics?" she said softly, venom dripping off the word. "You ain't seen hysterics, pal. I'll slap both your asses in jail if you're not outside when I get there."

"Harsh," I said, meeting Derek's amused glance.

"You ain't seen harsh, either," Lee groused.

"Now I'm intrigued," Derek said.

She just growled, then hung up.

I stuck my cell in my jacket pocket. "I think she likes us."

"What's not to like?" He leaned over, unlocked the glove box, and pulled out a really scary-looking gun. "By the way, I think you should wait in the car."

"No. Whoa. A gun?" I waved my hand at him. "There are people in there. My students. That's not necessary, is it? It's just Naomi. She's hardly a . . ."

"A what?" he said. "A *killer*? We don't know that, do we?"

"But—"

"Sweetheart, believe it or not, I'm a highly trained professional. I'm not going to shoot up the place."

"I know, I know," I said, as fear and nerves set up shop in my heart. "But that gun is really big."

"Thank you, darling."

I snorted a laugh, ladylike to the end.

He reached for the door handle and I grabbed his arm. "Let's just give it a minute, please? I'd rather have the police confront her than us."

"You're about to get your way," he said, as police lights flashed behind us. "They're prompt anyway. I'll give them that."

"I'll say." I had a feeling Inspector Lee had threatened her fellow officers with the wrath of God if they didn't get here before we went inside. Good to know she could pull strings like that.

We climbed out of the car. It was dusk and the air was chilling. I pulled my jacket tightly around me as we met the two officers on the sidewalk. One was a woman with blond hair pulled back in a ponytail. The other was Officer Ortiz.

"Hello, Officer," I said, and smiled at him.

He looked at me with suspicion. That hurt. I hadn't done anything to him. Yet.

"Officers," Derek said jovially. "It's good of you to join us. Shall we?" He swept his arm up as if we were about to enter a grand ballroom.

"You're not going anywhere, Jack," Ponytail said.

"And you are . . . ?" he asked in his most upper-crust snooty British butler accent.

"Norris. SFPD."

He inclined his head and switched to his smooth-as-silk James Bond license-to-kill voice. "Derek Stone, at your service, Officer Norris."

Ortiz ignored them both and jerked his chin toward me. "What's going on here?"

"Naomi Fontaine," I said. "We believe she planted evidence in Mr. Stone's hotel suite. We want to ask her some questions so we called Inspector Lee to join us. Just wanted to keep everything aboveboard."

Derek added, "There won't be any trouble, but we're happy you're here. Shall we go in?"

"Hold it, pal," Ponytail said.

"It's okay, Norris," Ortiz said to her. To Derek he said, "I go first. You stay back."

Derek shrugged, but complied.

Norris flexed her shoulder muscles, making her ponytail bob. "Let's roll."

The only thing rolling were my eyes as she manfully adjusted her weapons belt. Then she moved and we followed close behind them, all the way to Naomi's office. The door was open but Officer Ortiz knocked anyway.

She looked up and gasped. "What in the world?"

"Hi, Naomi," I said, waving from behind the cops.

"What's wrong?"

I bent to catch Ortiz's gaze. "Do you mind?" Then I slipped in front of him and held up the *Sleepy Hollow* book.

"Derek found this book in his hotel suite. Are you familiar with it?"

She lost all color in her face and her mouth did that trout-caught-by-a-fishhook thing again. Open, close, open, close. Finally, she said, "I—I . . . Where did you get that?"

"I just told you. Weren't you listening?"

She shook her head back and forth. "I didn't . . . I don't . . ." She grabbed her purse. "I'm calling my lawyer."

Norris yelled, "Put the bag down." Both cops drew their guns.

Naomi screamed, dropped the bag, and held up her hands.

Inspector Lee came running down the hall, gun drawn.

"I want my lawyer," Naomi wailed.

I turned to Derek. "I guess that answers the question of guilt."

Derek stared at Naomi. "Before they haul you off to jail, I want to know why you were so intent on framing me."

Her eyes widened. "It . . . it wasn't me."

"And yet, you want to lawyer up," I said, and jabbed my finger at her. "Not a good-faith gesture, Naomi." I turned to Inspector Lee. "You're arresting her, right?"

"For what?" Lee asked. "Being an idiot?"

"If only," Norris muttered, reluctantly slipping her gun back into the holster at her hip.

"Breaking and entering?" I suggested, then pointed at the book. "Or stealing a priceless art object?"

"Where'd she steal it from?"

I frowned at Derek. "From Layla, I guess."

Lee pushed back her jacket and holstered her gun. "So she basically stole the book from herself. Come on, let's get out of here."

"Brooklyn!" Naomi cried. "I didn't do it."

I glared at her. "I'm having a real hard time believing anything you say, Naomi." I turned down the hall in time to see Karalee jump back into her office and slam the door. Great. Everyone in the building would know all about it within minutes.

Naomi ran into the hall. "Wait. Can I have my book back?"

"Civilians," Norris muttered, hand resting on her gun.

Lee laughed without humor. "That's a joke, right, Ms. Fontaine?"

"No," she said earnestly. "I need that book for . . ."

I cocked my head. "For what?"

"It's evidence," Lee said, ending the discussion.

I slipped the book back into the Baggie and handed it to the inspector.

Naomi's eyes widened; then her shoulders slumped and she walked back to her office and closed the door.

Derek and I followed the cop back to the gallery.

Lee turned and held up her hand to stop Derek. "We're going to have to search your hotel room, Commander."

"Didn't you already do that?" I asked.

Lee looked at me as though I'd been smoking lettuce or something.

I glanced from her to Derek and back. "But you arrested him," I said haltingly. "Why didn't you . . ."

Derek put his hand on my shoulder. "I wasn't arrested, darling, just questioned."

"Oh, good." I turned to Lee. "You should fingerprint his hotel room."

"Wow, good idea," she said.

I shook my head and sighed. "Go ahead and mock me, but I've had a bad day."

"Yeah, me too," she said, her tone friendly again.

"You won't find any fingerprints," Derek said tightly.

Lee gave a philosophical shrug. "Let's give it a shot anyway."

As predicted, the police didn't find any fingerprints in Derek's hotel room, so Naomi was safe from imprisonment. For now.

After my class, Derek and I went out to a marvelous Italian restaurant near Nob Hill. Over tender short ribs in a Barolo reduction with sweet potato ravioli, accompanied by a stunning Bartolo Mascarello, Derek shared what he'd learned during his evening at the police station. He'd spent half the night there with Inspector Lee. Suspect or not, he still had that British commander vibe going for him and the San Francisco cops loved him. Hell, who didn't?

On the night of Layla's death, the police had confiscated her computer. What they found among her personal and business records were several bank accounts to which large deposits were made on a regular basis. A separate ledger with three different entries noted down payments of twenty thousand dollars each, for the books listed, with the merchandise scheduled to be turned over that very week.

"*Down* payments? Of twenty thousand dollars? For each book?" I mentally picked my jaw up off the floor. "Was there a list of the books being sold?"

"Yes," Derek said, then tasted the deep red wine.

"Well?" I waited, but he was intent on torturing me as he swirled the wineglass, then took another sip. "Derek, swallow the damn wine and tell me what books they were."

"Patience, darling. Your father wouldn't approve of my drinking something this exquisite any other way."

"You're right," I grumbled, and slumped back against the booth. "Just tell me if one of the books was an *Oliver Twist*?"

His eyes sparkled as he set down his glass. "I think you've already guessed."

"It was," I whispered, then tried to put the pieces together. "I thought it was being saved for the silent auction, but the real reason Naomi didn't want to sell me the book was because it was already promised to another buyer."

The wine steward poured more lovely red liquid into my glass. When he left, I looked at Derek. "There's no way that *Oliver Twist* is worth twenty thousand dollars, and that's just the down payment. I mean, I did a damn good job of restoring it, but how much did Layla expect to get paid? Whatever it was, it's a completely fraudulent deal."

"Yes," he said, and bit into a succulent piece of beef. "And where does Naomi fit in?"

"I don't know." I cut into a pillowy ravioli square.

"Well, I can tell you that the police went by to speak with Naomi Monday night."

"I saw them come in." I swallowed the bite and almost swooned. The buttery ravioli sauce was extraordinary. "Oh, my, I need a moment."

"It's rather good, isn't it?"

"It's heaven." I took a sip of wine, then exhaled softly. "Ah. Where was I? Oh, yes, the police showed up during the wake, just as the crowd was thinning out. Inspector Lee had Naomi in her sights and it looked as if they were going to arrest her. But she was back at work last night, free as a bird."

"They merely confiscated her computer," Derek revealed. "They've combed through it. It appears she knew nothing about these prepayments."

"Oh, she knew," I said, absently pointing my fork at him. "She's hiding something. Why else would she be so nervous when I asked her about the *Oliver Twist*?"

"And this was the same *Oliver Twist* that Layla mentioned she was auctioning off at the Twisted festival?"

I considered the answer as I munched on a perfectly prepared haricot vert. "I thought so, but now I'm not sure. If it's listed as a presale, how can they be auctioning it off?"

"Are there two *Oliver Twists*, perhaps?"

"I have no idea," I said, grabbing my wineglass.

"I believe we should pay another visit to Naomi."

As we drove away from the restaurant, I called Inspector Lee to explain the situation. I described Naomi's reaction when I'd mentioned I wanted to buy the *Oliver Twist*.

"I'm willing to swear she knew about Layla's prepayments," I said. "I'm going to confront her, with or without a police presence."

"With," Inspector Lee barked into the phone. "You'll wait for me."

"Gladly," I said, and winked at Derek. He'd already bet she wouldn't miss it for the world.

"And just so you know," Lee said. "We gave her back that *Oliver Twist* book a few days ago."

I stared at Derek.

"The plot thickens," he murmured.

"Yes, doesn't it just?" So last night when I'd asked Naomi if I could buy the *Oliver Twist*, she'd already obtained it from the police. She had to have known exactly what book I was talking about. And judging from the dull pallor of her skin when I told her it wasn't a first edition, I was willing to bet she'd already sold it.

It was midnight when we parked the Bentley in front of the building, so I doubted we would find Naomi at work. Inspector Lee was already there, waiting with two other cops. BABA was locked up for the night, but low lights shined through the textured glass section of the door.

Sure enough, after Inspector Lee hammered her fist on the door for almost a minute, Ned lumbered over to let us in.

"Huh," he said. "Late."

"Yeah, go back to sleep," Lee said.

" 'Kay."

Ned trundled off and Lee led the way to Naomi's office and pushed the door open. "You're working late, Ms. Fontaine."

Naomi jerked and shrieked at the same time. "You scared the hell out of me! What do you want? I'm not doing anything wrong."

"Then you won't mind showing me what you're working on," Lee said. She rounded the desk and grabbed the mini-computer. I was pretty sure it was a move that wouldn't hold up in court, but I liked it.

"You already took my work computer!" Naomi cried, trying to grab it back. "This one's mine!"

"Looks like an Excel spreadsheet," Lee said, and made eye contact with me as she began to read off the screen. "It's a list of books and prices. What's this column?" She squinted at the small screen. "Date acquired. Date purchased. Date completed."

"We often sell our books," Naomi whined. "It's not a crime. The books belong to Layla. I mean, me."

"But passing a book off as more rare or better than it really is to gain a higher price is a crime," I said. "It's called fraud. It's like theft, only really worse." Okay, I was blathering. I silently beseeched Inspector Lee to pick up the ball.

Her gaze narrowed in on Naomi. "Are you defrauding your clients, Ms. Fontaine?"

Naomi took a deep, shuddering breath. "I didn't know it was fraud! Layla has all these people she sells books to, and they were calling me. They wanted their money. Or . . . or they wanted their books. One man came by and he was not kidding around. He threatened me, told me I'd be sorry if I didn't comply, so I gave him the book he wanted."

"The *Oliver Twist*?" I asked.

Her face was a mask of shock and pain. "He said Layla promised it to him. He said he already paid her part of the money, so I gave him the book and he gave me the rest of the money."

She gasped. It was clear she wished she hadn't brought up the money. But she had, and I believed her admission signified that she wasn't cut out to be as wicked as her auntie Layla.

"What did this man look like?" Lee asked. "The one who gave you the money?"

"He was . . ." Naomi winced and looked away.

"Go ahead," Lee coaxed.

She took a deep breath. "He was Asian."

"Ah, my people," Lee muttered. "So? Tall? Fat? Short? Bald?"

"Tall. Normal build." She gazed up at Lee with a sycophantic smile. "He was really nice-looking."

"Swell. Did you get a name?"

Eager to please now, Naomi nodded. "Mr. Soo."

"And how much money did he give you?"

Naomi chewed her lower lip. Now I could see her brain calculating how much to tell us.

"How much money, Ms. Fontaine?" Lee repeated, softly this time, but with more deadly intent.

Naomi's shoulders shook nervously. "Ten thousand dollars."

"In cash?"

She nodded, clearly miserable at having to disclose the true amount.

"No wonder you could afford a new wardrobe," I marveled.

"It's my money," she said defiantly. "I'm Layla's next of kin, so her book business comes to me."

"Book *business*," I said in disgust. "Sounds more like a ring of book *thieves*."

"I'm not a thief. The book belonged to me."

"Did it?" I asked. "Or did it belong to BABA?"

"We should probably finish this up downtown," Lee said. She signaled to the cop watching from just outside the office door and he came forward instantly.

"No," Naomi cried, and burst into tears.

I couldn't blame her. I was ninety-nine percent positive she was innocent, because as much as she'd attempted to channel Aunt Layla, trying to dress like a hooker and conduct business like a shark, Naomi just couldn't pull it off. She'd given it her best shot, but she was missing the key ingredient, the true bitch gene.

So if Naomi was innocent, who killed Layla Fontaine?

Chapter 16

Defeated, Naomi stood and the cop walked her out the door. They didn't handcuff her because she wasn't being arrested. She was just being taken in for questioning.

Inspector Lee followed them out the door and down the hall. I was about to tag along when I realized they'd walked out without Naomi's notebook computer.

I hesitated for a nanosecond, then picked it up to check the screen. Hey, I couldn't help myself. The spreadsheet wasn't extensive, but it did list at least twenty books. I located both *Oliver Twist* and *The Legend of Sleepy Hollow*.

No wonder Naomi had blanched when she saw me with the *Sleepy Hollow*. Somebody—Mr. Soo, maybe?—might've threatened her over that book, as well.

I noticed the second page tab at the bottom of the spreadsheet and clicked on it. It took me to a list of mostly foreign-sounding names. That made a strange sort of sense. There was a huge market for fine art and antiquarian books in Asia and the Middle East, and buyers there were willing to pay top prices for the highest-quality books.

In a separate column, Mr. Soo's name was listed in most of the cells, while the name of a Mr. Tangorand filled the remaining spaces. The columns weren't identified. Were they the buyers? Or brokers, maybe?

"Still investigating, my dear?"

I twitched at the sound of Derek's voice. "Stop sneaking up on me."

"Better me than Inspector Lee," he whispered loudly. "Who has not left the building, by the way."

"Okay, okay." As I set the notebook back on the desk, I noticed the corner of a business card sticking out from under Naomi's desk blotter.

I pulled it out, read it, and waved it in the air. "It's Mr. Soo's."

Derek shook his head. "You're impossible. Come on, let's get out of here."

We got into the Bentley, and instead of starting the motor, Derek watched me. I wasn't sure why. Then he reached over and smoothed my hair back from my face, one finger skimming my cheek slowly. And I knew.

He leaned in and I met him halfway. The kiss was warm, soft, purposeful. Wonderful.

"Where would you like to go?"

I knew what he was asking. It was the moment of truth. Did I have a choice? On a semantic plane, of course I had a choice. But if you could listen to the butterflies in my stomach, they were shouting—as loudly as butterflies could shout—Yes. The jackhammers in my heart pounded out Go-Go-Go. Desire flooded my brain and my face felt flushed. So I guessed I had my answer.

"Let's go back to your hotel."

His eyes narrowed, then relaxed, and he smiled and kissed me again. "Thank you."

He was thanking me? I wanted to thank him, too, but I sat silently, simply trying to breathe as he put the car in gear and drove off slowly. Was he as nervous as I was? Maybe. He was driving slower than usual.

As we pulled into the porte cochere in front of the Ritz-Carlton, two valets rushed over to open the car doors.

We walked through the lobby, hand in hand, and I felt as

though every eye in the place was watching us. Could they tell what we were about to do? My throat began to dry up. I had to lick my lips and take several slow, deep breaths.

As we waited for the elevator, Derek's cell phone rang. I wanted to scream, *Don't answer that!* But I behaved myself. He pulled the phone out, clutched my hand, and walked away from the elevator doors.

"Stone," he said into the phone.

As someone spoke to him, he wrapped his arm around me so that I was pressed against him.

He groaned, then uttered a quiet expletive. "You've got to be kidding me." We made eye contact and I watched him say, "Fine, I'll be there shortly."

He ended the call, then pulled me closer so he could bury his face in my hair. I heard him whisper another expletive. It was so unnatural to hear it coming from him, I pushed myself away.

"What is it?" I asked. "What happened? Who was that?"

"Inspector Lee," he said, his voice muffled against my neck. "Naomi just gave up Gunther to the police."

As we waited for the valet to bring Derek's car around, Gunther called him as well, demanding that Derek post his bail. Derek explained to his client that since he hadn't been arrested yet, he might be jumping the gun just a bit.

But Gunther wasn't in the mood to quibble. The police had taken over his hotel room and were conducting a search. We headed over there, and as he drove, Derek filled me in on what Inspector Lee had told him.

It happened while Lee was questioning Naomi. She'd asked why Naomi had tried to implicate Derek in the murder by insinuating he'd had an affair with her aunt Layla.

Naomi had nattered on about how Layla was always bragging about her conquests. Derek was supposed to have been one of them. Naomi said her aunt tried to hit on any man who showed up at BABA. She named names. Lee wrote all of them down. Then Naomi dropped the Gunther bomb. According to her, Layla and Gunther had jumped each other the first night Gunther arrived in town. They'd been having hot sex regularly after that. The night Layla died, Gunther showed up to have sex with Layla in her office.

Ew. I'd been in that office. Good thing I hadn't touched anything.

Lee tried to call Naomi's bluff, but the girl insisted she wasn't lying about this one. The police had no choice but to track Gunther down at his hotel and question him. They'd quickly obtained a search warrant, and after a preliminary investigation of his room, the cops found another rare antiquarian book hidden in the armoire behind his clothes.

Inspector Lee wanted me to examine the book.

Gunther wanted Derek to be there while he was questioned.

I wanted to be left alone with Derek.

Was I cursed? I was definitely sensing a pattern here. Everyone was getting what they wanted but me, and possibly Derek. Through half-closed eyes, I checked him out while he drove. His lips were tight with irritation and pent-up emotion as he took the next corner more sharply than necessary. I couldn't blame him. I was frustrated beyond belief. And there was nothing I could do about it for the foreseeable future.

So I concentrated on other questions. What did the books in the hotel rooms mean? Who had put them there? If Naomi had planted them, why? Was she angry at the men in Layla's life? Why Derek? As it turned out, he had little connection to Layla, but Naomi seemed to believe otherwise.

I wondered if there were other books planted in other hotel rooms still left to be discovered. It was an odd way to distract everyone from the real crime.

Derek was completely innocent, of course, but I didn't

know Gunther from a gopher. What little I did know included the facts that he liked to party and he craved attention. I guess he craved Layla, too. That alone made him a suspect in my book.

We arrived at the Clift Hotel and took the elevator to the sixth floor. The police were milling outside a room halfway down the hall and we walked toward them.

"They're here," one of cops shouted into the room. Then he jerked his head toward the door. "Go on in."

We entered the suite, a large, pleasant space that featured ultramodern Philippe Starck furnishings of blond wood covered in cool fabrics of white, lavender, and coral. Gunther was pacing furiously in the area next to the dining table. He was a mess. His clothing was rumpled and his hair stood on end, probably from his own fingers grabbing and scratching in aggravation. His shoes were kicked under the table. Derek strolled over to join him while I searched out Inspector Lee. She found me first.

"There you are," she said, emerging from the bedroom. She held the book out for me. "It's already been checked for fingerprints."

I must've looked as horrified as I felt, because she quickly added, "We didn't mess it up."

"I hope not," I muttered. The book was still in its Ziploc bag, so I popped it open and eased the book out. I scrutinized it for a few minutes, turning it over in my hands, studying the joints, the gilding, the leather, the paper.

"This is a real beauty," I said. I had no doubt that it was a first edition of *Treasure Island*, dated 1883, which made it very rare and fine indeed. The brown buck leather cover showed only the slightest rubbing in a few spots. The frontispiece, a superb color illustration of three pirates gloating over a chest filled with gold, had an inlaid page of tissue covering it. This was often done in books with fine engravings, in order to guard against the picture rubbing off on the title page opposite.

"Be careful with this," I said, handing it back to Inspector Lee. "It's probably worth thirty or forty thousand dollars."

Lee bobbled the book in stunned disbelief. "You're shitting me."

"I'm not," I said. "You really don't want to drop it."

"Why in the world?" she muttered under her breath as she turned the book over and thumbed through the pages. "Nice pictures, but still, it's just a book. What some people will waste their money on."

"It's a small piece of fine art," I said. "People who love books and are fascinated by the art that goes into making them are willing to pay the price."

"Yeah, whatever."

I remembered seeing *Treasure Island* listed on Naomi's computer screen. I squeezed my eyes closed to try and picture the spreadsheet in my mind. I think the price might've been close to one hundred thousand dollars.

I wanted another look at that spreadsheet. Who was the buyer for this book? Had he already made the down payment? Was he scheduled to pick up the book sometime soon?

"Can we talk somewhere privately?" I said.

Inspector Lee gave me a suspicious look, then said, "Come into my office." She walked through the bedroom, into the luxurious bathroom. "So what's up, Wainwright?"

I glanced around at the rubbed marble walls and walk-in rain-forest shower. "Nice place."

"I like it," she said with a shrug. "What's on your mind?"

"You saw Naomi's spreadsheet, right?"

"Gee, let me guess. You saw it, too."

"Well, it was right there, so . . ."

"Yeah, I know. So cut to the chase."

"I was thinking that if you want to trap these book scammers, I can help. We set up a sting." Revved up, I began to pace. "There's no way Naomi is the ringleader. That was probably Layla. So someone new has taken over. We can find out who. I know books, so I'll be your contact. I'm sure they're scalping the buyers. I remember the *Treasure Island* was listed for six figures. It's not worth that much, but they're jacking up the price, promising more than what's really in the book. Like the *Oliver Twist*. It's not really a first edition but someone will believe it is, and they'll pay the price. I can call and set up a meeting. Then we can—"

"Whoa, whoa, easy, girl," Lee said, waving her hands at me.

"Come on, this'll work."

"We're not running a sting operation," she said sarcastically. "This isn't TV, Brooklyn, and you're not Angie Dickinson."

I frowned at her. "Angie Dickinson?"

"*Police Woman*?" she said. "Sergeant Pepper Anderson? Come on. What are you, anti-American or something?"

"Hey, it's a little before my time."

"Mine, too," she said, grinning. "But my dad loved that show."

I smiled reluctantly. "Okay, so I guess that's a big N-O on the sting operation?"

"Good guess," Inspector Lee said dryly. "But thanks for the offer."

I shrugged. "Fine. When you change your mind, you know where to find me."

"Yeah, right." Her phone rang and I left her to it, walking back into the living room, where Derek was waiting for me.

"I apologize, but I'm going to stay for a while," he said, stroking my back. "Shall I arrange for a driver to take you home?"

"Will you be stuck here all night?"

"It's beginning to look that way."

"Then I guess I . . ."

At that moment, Inspector Jaglom walked into the suite, followed by the two cops who'd been standing in the hall earlier. They were all joined by Inspector Lee, who came out of the bedroom and approached Derek's client.

"Gunther Schnaubel," she said, "you're under arrest for the murder of Layla Fontaine."

I woke up the next morning and grabbed a cup of coffee, then called Derek. He answered immediately, sounding tired.

"Did you make it home last night?" I asked.

"No, I'm still at police headquarters."

I expressed my sympathy, then asked, "Did you find out what happened? Why did they arrest Gunther?"

"They obtained an Interpol report. Gunther was arrested several times for breaking and entering back in Austria. It was years ago, but that didn't matter."

"Oh. That sucks."

"Yes, doesn't it? So he not only had the skills to break into my hotel room—he was also having an affair with the murder victim. It's circumstantial, but they can hold him for forty-eight hours while they try to drum up more evidence."

"But why would he break into your hotel room and hide a book there?"

"To divert the police from himself to me."

"But then, why would he hide a book in his own room?"

"Exactly," he said in a withering tone. "That's the point I keep bringing up to the police. They say it could be a ruse to divert suspicion away from himself, so they're going to hold him for the next day or so."

"Are you stuck there?"

"No, I was just leaving as you called."

"Good," I said. "You should get some sleep."

"Unfortunately, that's all I'm good for right now. But I'd like to see you later. Have you any plans for this afternoon?"

I hesitated, then came clean. "I thought I might drive over to Chinatown."

"Ah, that's my girl."

* * *

We parked in the Union Square garage and walked a block up Grant Avenue to the steps of Chinatown. Derek had insisted on coming along and I was glad of it. Even though I'd walked the colorful streets of Chinatown dozens of times in the past, I'd never before been there on a mission to roust a possible extortionist.

I suppose it was harsh to call Mr. Soo an extortionist until we heard his side of the story, but I was happy for Derek's company, anyway.

We walked along the narrow sidewalk, past electronics stores and teahouses and jewelry shops filled with ivory, jade, and amber and thousands of rainbow-colored strands of beads. Souvenir shops hawked every conceivable tchotchke known to man, from ornately beaded silk slippers and wallets in every color to wooden back scratchers, articulated wooden snakes, kites of every shape and size, willowy bird cages, Chinoiserie teapots, jewelry boxes, and delicate eggs on wooden pedestals.

Butcher shops displayed rows of cooked ducks hanging from metal racks, drying in the breeze. Baby bok choy, snow peas, and ruffle-leafed Chinese cabbage filled the vegetable stands in front of the markets. I breathed in the scents of fried wontons and sweet sausage buns and wanted to eat everything I could smell.

Two blocks into the heart of Chinatown, we found the address on Mr. Soo's business card.

"It's a take-out joint," I said, casting a disappointed look inside the seedy café. The cashier sat on a high stool, daintily dangling her shoe while she read a magazine and twirled her thick hair around her fingers. It wasn't the most appetizing way to attract customers.

I checked Soo's business card. "Suite 317."

We walked past the restaurant storefront to a door just beyond it. A clouded porthole window allowed a view inside, and Derek held his hand up to block the sun's glare as he stared through.

"If you'd rather wait out here, I wouldn't think any less of you," he said.

"But I would," I replied with determination. No way was I going to chicken out now. "Let's go."

He pushed the door open and we walked inside. The door slammed shut behind us, instantly casting the enclosed space into darkness. The narrow hall led to a set of stairs and we started climbing. I tried not to breathe in too much. The place was dank, gloomy, and redolent of sesame oil and sweet and sour pork.

"Guess he's on the third floor," I whispered.

Derek led the way to the third-floor landing and pushed open another door to a long hall. There was more light here, with doors on either side leading to offices or apartments. We got to number 317 and knocked.

I wasn't surprised when no one answered, but I was taken aback when Derek tried the doorknob and it opened easily.

"Should we go in?" I asked, unsure of walking into someone's private dwelling. Although, truth be told, it wouldn't be the first time I'd done so.

"It's an office," he said, moving ahead into the room.

"Oh, good." I followed him into Mr. Soo's office, where a glass block wall separated the small dingy waiting area from an interior room. Dark, scarred wainscoting ran halfway up the walls, met by peeling flowery wallpaper in faded shades of green and pink. Two rickety folding chairs were set against one wall with a small plastic table between them. Despite the shabby surroundings, it was oddly comforting to see two well-thumbed back issues of *Fine Books & Collections* magazine lying on the table.

I had my own subscription to the well-respected industry magazine, so I took it as a good sign that whoever worked here was serious about books.

Derek knocked on the door leading into the next room. Once again, there was no answer.

"Is it locked?" I asked.

"No." He pushed the door open and walked in. I followed him and skidded to a stop.

The room was in a shambles. Two padded chairs were upturned and torn open. The cottony stuffing was scattered around and bits of it fluttered in the air, stirred by our movements. One wall of bookshelves had been completely overturned. Books lay everywhere, jumbled in piles, covers splayed, pages bent. It was a mess.

"Oh, this is horrible," I said, picking up the volume on top. "These are expensive books. How could anyone—"

Footsteps echoed down the hall. Derek put his finger to his lips, then grabbed my hand and ran over to another door. I hoped it led to a way out of there, but it didn't. Derek swung the door open and we pushed our way into a tiny, cramped bathroom, barely big enough for one person, with a stained toilet and a sink that wouldn't fit my two hands. The fixtures were rusted and water dripped intermittently from the faucet.

Derek shut the door and locked it just as footsteps sounded in the outer room. The thudding steps moved closer, coming into the torn-up room just outside the bathroom door.

I swallowed nervously and rested my head against Derek's back, slipping my arms around his waist. I could feel his muscles flex, feel the tension in his body as we waited anxiously.

"What the hell?" a man said, his voice raspy.

Another set of footsteps joined the first man and that person swore ripely.

"What do we do now?"

"Find that book, damn it."

"Oh, man, there's no way. There's gotta be a thousand books here."

"Then get started. I'm not leaving without it."

"Shit," the other man whined. But he began moving things, searching for something.

I winced as I heard them throwing books around. Derek squeezed my hand in understanding and I could've kissed him. The tiny room was tight and uncomfortable and not much bigger than an airplane bathroom, but if I had to be shoved up against another human being in close quarters, I was perfectly happy to have it be him.

I had a sudden memory of another tight space I'd hidden in recently. I'd been shocked to learn Derek was hiding in there, as well. Those were some good times.

One of the men must've tried to pick up the fallen bookcase because I heard the screech of heavy wood against wood.

Then one of them began to scream.

"Oh, my God!" Then more screams.

"What?" his partner said. "Shut up! Whoa, holy shit, let's get the hell out of here."

Two sets of footsteps scrambled and someone fell; then both of them tore out of the room, fleeing down the hall.

There was silence. I realized I was holding my breath, so tense I thought I might crack in two.

Derek quietly unlocked the door, then pushed back against me until he could squeeze through the doorway and out of the oppressively small room.

I followed him, gasping for breath.

He took hold of the heavy bookcase and lifted it.

I shrieked; I couldn't help myself. I recognized the dead man buried under hundreds of books and the heavy shelf.

It was the Asian man I'd seen storming out of Layla's office the first night of class.

"Mr. Soo, I presume," Derek said.

It had to be Mr. Soo. In his hand, he was clutching the *Oliver Twist* I'd restored so lovingly.

In the middle of his forehead was a bullet hole.

Chapter 17

"Another dead body?" I cried, having officially reached the end of my rope. "What the hell is going on with me? Was I a serial killer in a past life? Why do I keep finding dead people?"

Enough already.

"I agree it's all become a bit chary," Derek confessed as he struggled to keep the bookcase suspended.

"Chary? I hope that's another word for totally unfair and highly annoying."

"Something like that," he said, grimacing as he shifted to lower the bookcase.

"Hey, wait, I want my book," I said, pointing to the *Oliver Twist* in the dead man's hand. I began to push books out of my path.

"Sorry, love," he said, and shoved the bookcase back far enough that it no longer crushed the unfortunate Mr. Soo when it crashed to the ground.

"But, Derek, it's worth—"

"Doesn't matter," he said, grabbing my arm and heading for the door. "We're leaving now."

I looked over my shoulder in dismay. "It would only take a second to—"

"We don't have a second, love." He looked both ways down the hall, then took off running for the stairs. "Hear those sirens?" he said as he reached the end of the hall and opened the door to the landing. "The police are going to stop right outside this building, I guarantee it. And since I've already spent several hours under police scrutiny, I don't wish to draw any more attention to myself than is necessary."

"Oh, good point." I'd already determined that the book was well away from that sliver of blood seeping from—*well, never mind*, I thought, shivering at the picture of Mr. Soo lying dead in that room. It bothered me to leave the *Oliver Twist*, but I knew it would end up as evidence and eventually be returned to Naomi, who might still sell it to me.

Derek was more important right now. We had to get him away from there.

We raced down the stairs as police sirens pierced the air, growing louder and louder. Sure enough, they came to an abrupt stop on the side street bordering Mr. Soo's building.

On the ground floor, we walked briskly toward the back of the building and exited onto the narrow one-way street that ran parallel to Grant. A walkway between office buildings and past several hole-in-the-wall eateries took us to the next street over, which was Kearny. From there, we strolled back to Union Square, window-shopping on the way.

Despite acting as a dividing line between the fashionable shops of Union Square and the monolithic skyscrapers of the Financial District, Kearny Street itself was slightly seedy with small discount shops, funky food joints, check-cashing services, and the occasional bar.

But it was a beautiful day in the city, with brilliant blue skies and a lovely breeze drifting through the canyons of high-rises on our left. We seemed a million miles away from the tawdry murder scene in Chinatown, and as we turned up Post Street, it felt as though we had all the time in the world.

"I'm sorry you had to leave your book back there," Derek said as we walked past the Brooks Brothers window, which featured a men's tan suit next to a pale pink crisp cotton dress. The dress was asexual and impossibly conservative, with short sleeves, a tucked bib front and a bow tie at the neck. Seriously, that was a bib. Who in the world would wear it? I had to force myself to look away.

"No, you were right," I said finally. "We had to get out of there before the police showed up. But they'll find the book and use it as evidence to nail these guys."

He brought my hand to his lips and kissed it gently. "Yes, they will."

"I'm sorry I went a little crazy," I said, remembering my tantrum as we waited for the signal to change at Post and Grant. "I saw that man lying there and my brain exploded. One too many dead bodies, I guess."

"I'm surprised you've held on this long," he said, resting his cheek on my hand. "I know it's been traumatic for you."

"It's getting more and more weird," I admitted. "But that's still no excuse to go off like I did."

"Darling, you're a strong woman, but you mustn't be so hard on yourself." He wrapped his arm around me and we crossed the street.

A sea of emotion swirled through me at his kind words. I wasn't sure I deserved them, but they touched me in ways I couldn't begin to describe. Maybe later, when I was alone, I would think back and wonder if this might be the most perfect moment of my life.

And how sad was it that such perfect moments were now defined by dead bodies?

A half block later we turned onto Maiden Lane, and I stopped to stare at a twelve-thousand-dollar cameo in the window of Gump's. The ivory carving of the woman's face was flawless, precise and elegant. It was mounted on a piece of amber so dark and rich it appeared midnight blue. Tiny diamonds encased in platinum circled the ivory and crisscrossed into a bow beneath the woman's face.

"I wonder who called the police?" I mused, tearing my gaze away from the cameo.

"Somebody was watching that building," Derek said matter-of-factly.

I looked up at him. "Maybe it was just another tenant who heard those two guys screaming and called nine-one-one."

He shook his head. "That wasn't the sort of place where people would willingly invite the police in."

"True."

"And the timing was much too coincidental."

I turned to face him. "So you really think someone saw us go in there and called the cops?"

He shrugged.

"That's downright creepy."

"I couldn't agree more."

Uneasy, I glanced around, then shivered. Was somebody watching us right now? I didn't want to believe it. Maybe someone, namely the killer, had been watching Mr. Soo's place to see who might show up. That made some sense. But to be watching Derek and me? Following us around? Why?

I see things.

I shivered at the thought that Ned might be watching us from somewhere around here. But that was ridiculous. Ned never left BABA. Still, I couldn't shake the feeling that someone had watched us go into that building.

"Those two men who came into Soo's office didn't sound like upstanding citizens, did they?"

"No," Derek said, and left it at that.

We walked another half block along Maiden Lane and stopped to look at the display of yummy foods in the window of a tiny Italian cafeteria-style bistro. It looked a lot prettier than that amazing cameo. I was hungry before in Chinatown. Now I was ravenous.

Derek, bless his heart, ushered me into the cozy restaurant, where we chose a salad and sandwich to split. I decided to have a glass of wine, too. I deserved it. Derek chose a small bottle of San Pelligrino.

"What business would you say Mr. Soo was in?" I asked, once we were seated.

"My guess is book fraud."

"That's what I was thinking. That place was a veritable book repository."

"Yes, it was," he said, tearing at the loaf of thick Italian bread and dipping it in rich olive oil. "I would guess he bought and sold, but mostly brokered the deals. Books, engravings, other related artwork."

"At least he was a good reader," I reflected, as I took a bite of the thick, buttery prosciutto and cheese sandwich.

"Not anymore," he said.

Derek dropped me off early at BABA and promised to come by later to pick me up. Did I dare to dream that tonight would be the night? I wasn't going to hold my breath.

The first thing I saw when I walked inside was Alice and Naomi, whispering heatedly by the guillotine in the lower gallery.

The good news was, at least they were speaking.

When Alice saw me, she waved me over. "Brooklyn, you won't believe what happened to Gunther."

I glanced around warily. Because the Twisted festival was in full swing, visitors were walking through the gallery, checking out the cool displays and perusing the bookshelves.

"Why don't we go to Naomi's office to continue this conversation?" I said, sounding so annoyingly mature I wanted to cringe.

"Fine," Naomi said, and flounced off in that direction.

Once we were behind closed doors, Alice's emotions were let loose. "He's been arrested. Can you believe it?"

"Oh, my goodness," I said. "Really?"

"Yes. Isn't it awful?"

Naomi groaned. "Alice, don't be naive. Brooklyn's acting like she doesn't know, but she does. Her boyfriend is Gunther's keeper."

Wait a minute. Even Naomi could tell I was lying? That was so unfair.

"Naomi, shut up," I said lamely.

Alice wasn't paying attention to either of us. "I've had to cancel Gunther's lithography class, but the auction is this coming weekend. He's our biggest name. People will expect him to be there. What will we do without him? How will we make any money on the auction?"

"Stop whining," Naomi said.

But Alice continued her rant. "What'll we do? We can't cancel it now. All those people. And the food. The caterers will . . . oh, God, the caterers." She stopped and tried to catch her breath, but she couldn't. She began to wheeze uncontrollably.

"Alice, you're hyperventilating," I said, alarmed. "Naomi, do you have a paper bag or something she can breathe into?"

"Why would I have a paper bag? Just . . . make her stop."

Alice's wheezing was louder and more frantic. Her eyes were wide with panic. Just as I thought she might pass out, Naomi stepped in front of her and slapped her across the face.

"There," Naomi said, wiping her hands together. "Maybe that'll chill her out."

"Jeez, Naomi, have a little compassion," I said.

But Alice's breathing immediately began to slow down. She took a few controlled gulps, then nodded to indicate she was okay. She sank down on the nearest chair and flopped over to put her head between her legs.

Naomi and I exchanged a look. Alice was absurdly fragile. Everything set her off. Would she make it in this job? I had my doubts. Especially if she had to work with Naomi every day.

After a few minutes of stiff silence, Alice finally lifted her head, slowly drawing in air and exhaling. "Okay. Okay, I'm better. Sorry. I kind of flipped out there."

"Kind of?" Naomi said, her tone indicating just how appalled she was. Maybe she was a little more like Layla than we'd all thought. But honestly, right now I couldn't blame her. Poor Alice was a basket case.

"Look," Naomi said. "I've just put myself in charge of the Saturday-night gala and auction. You can't handle it. I don't want the paramedics running in here in the middle of everything because you're having a freaking heart attack over a broken fingernail, for God's sake."

Alice waved her hand weakly. "Fine. You handle it. I'll watch this time, then maybe take on the next event."

"Yeah, sure," Naomi said with a sneer. "I'll handle everything like I always do."

I checked my watch. "Listen, I've got a class to teach," I said. I didn't want to get in the middle of another fight if these two took off on each other again.

"Yeah, whatever," Naomi said, and walked out of the office muttering, "Freaks. I'm surrounded by freaks."

Concerned, I looked back at Alice. She raised her head slowly and gazed up at me, a satisfied smile on her face.

Realization dawned slowly. "You did that on purpose, didn't you?"

"Well, I wasn't expecting her to smack me like that." But then she shrugged contentedly. "It makes her happy if she thinks she's in charge. I'll watch to make sure she doesn't get too drunk with power and start thinking she owns the place. But things should run a little smoother from here on out, don't you think?"

* * *

During the dinner break, I decided I needed a little touch of down-home comfort, so I called my mother to see how Gabriel was doing. He'd been at her place since he'd left the hospital.

"He's still having nightmares," she said. "I'm worried."

"Does he know what they're about?"

"He won't talk about it. He sleeps a lot. I've made a healing charm bracelet and he wears it all the time. And I'm trying out a few spells on him. I just can't remember if I do the banishment spell during the full moon or the waxing moon."

"Mom, you're kind of new at this Wicca business. Don't go changing him into a black cat or something."

"Silly, Gabriel wouldn't change into a black cat."

"Good."

"No, he would much more likely turn into a raven."

Oh, boy.

"Anyway," she continued, "your father has been keeping him company, discussing wine and world events and such. And Annie and I are playing nursemaids, so he seems pretty happy about that."

"I would think so," I said wryly, then told her I'd try to get up there the next weekend to visit him.

"He'll be so happy to hear that, sweetie. He's a darling man, isn't he?"

"Yes, he is," I said, laughing. "But, Mom, be sure to count the silverware before he leaves."

What with Layla's death and funeral, my students had lost out on several hours of class time, so during Thursday night's class, I gave them the option of a makeup class on Friday night. It was a sad statement on my personal life that I was available on a Friday night, but at least I wouldn't be alone. All my students were available, too.

After I once again demonstrated the process of centering the boards and spine stiffener on the cloth covers, and gluing the endbands in place, the students progressed to within several steps of completing the traditional journals they'd started earlier in the week.

As promised, Derek picked me up after class and we drove to my place. I had a bottle of champagne waiting in my refrigerator and I could picture us cozied up on my couch, sipping the bubbly and nibbling on warm brie and toast.

He parked his car in the visitors' space in my garage. We took the elevator up to my floor and slid open the heavy metal gate. Hand in hand, we walked to my door. I was nearly vibrating with anticipation.

"Yoo-hoo, Brooklyn?" Vinnie called from her doorway around the corner from mine.

I moaned out loud.

Derek's voice was low and husky. "Don't answer. She'll go away."

The temptation was irresistible, but not very neighborly. "I'm so sorry," I whispered. Wincing, I called out, "Hi, Vinnie. What's up?"

Her light footsteps pattered down the wide hall.

"We have—oh, hello, Derek," Vinnie said, smiling brightly. "How nice to see you again." Derek had met my neighbors a month or so ago after that vicious killer tried to gun me down inside my home.

"Hello, Vinnie," he said cordially. "How are you?"

"I'm quite well. Isn't this a nice surprise?"

As she ran back to her apartment, I unlocked my door and pushed it open.

"Suzie," Vinnie cried. "Brooklyn is at home and Derek—Remember Derek? He is with her. Come quickly and say hello. Bring the wine bottle."

"Oh, dear God," I whispered, then laughed as Derek pounded his head against the wall. I walked inside. He followed close behind me and grabbed me at the waist, turned me around and kissed me. I sank my fingers into his hair as my knees grew weak.

Derek's breath came in ragged gasps as he broke away from the kiss just as Suzie's steel-toed boots clomped against the hardwood floor outside my door.

Suzie walked in. "Hey, Brooklyn, hey, Derek."

"Suzie," he said cordially, and gave her a hug. "You look as lovely as ever."

How he could sound so cool and debonair after a scorching kiss that had left me shaking was a mystery for the ages?

"Uh, yo, looking good," Suzie said, flustered and blushing from Derek's hug. Even a steel-toed lesbian was no match for his charms.

"Come on in," I said, waving them into the living room. "Make yourselves at home while I put my tools away in the office."

"You sure?" Suzie asked. "You guys rushing off somewhere or can we hang for a while?"

"Hang away," Derek said generously, and I flashed him a grateful smile. They were, after all, my favorite neighbors and dear friends.

Still, that whole karma thing was getting on my nerves.

Vinnie walked in a minute later with a large bag of leftover Thai food. As I said, they were my favorite neighbors, and the free food was just one reason why.

I walked with her into the kitchen and she went to work emptying the bag, finding places in my refrigerator for all the little white boxes to fit.

"Anybody home?" a voice called from the door.

"That's Robin," I said, mystified.

"Lovely," Vinnie said, folding the bag. "You're having a party."

"That's what it looks like," I said, flashing Derek a bewildered look before running to the door.

Robin was already inside, hanging her coat up in my front closet, so I grabbed her for a hug. "What are you doing here?"

"Nice to see you, too." She held up a bottle of wine. "My date canceled so I thought maybe you could use a friend to listen to you rant some more. But I can hear you've already got a full house."

"Yes," I said, then whispered, "Derek is here."

Her eyes went wide. "He's here?"

"Yes."

"Should I get everyone out?"

I laughed. "No, we're fine. Fabulous, in fact. Please don't say anything about the other night."

"Why would I do that?"

"You wouldn't do it on purpose. I'm just saying."

"Hmm. Well, now I can't get the idea of blackmail out of my mind."

"Don't even think about it," I advised her as we walked back into the living area.

"You're right," she said with a sad shake of her head. "You've got way more dirt on me than I could ever scrape up on you."

"Which is another sad commentary on my life," I conceded. "Still, don't you forget it."

Everyone greeted each other and more wine was poured. I met Derek's ironic gaze and laughed. He chuckled. What else could we do but accept the inevitable?

"How's Gabriel doing?" Robin asked as she topped off her wineglass. "And how's your little friend, Alice? Did she have fun in Dharma before all the fireworks started?"

I filled everyone in on Gabriel's recuperation, Alice's spa treatment, and the latest body count. Everyone wanted to hear details of the latter, especially.

"Do you think Gabriel's attack is related to these other murders?" Robin asked.

"Absolutely not," I insisted. "I mean, the only thing the

BABA murders and the Dharma attack have in common is me. And I refuse to accept that any of this is connected to me. That would be off the scale."

"Truly, Brooklyn?" Vinnie said. "You're the only one who was in the vicinity of all three attacks?"

"Yes."

"No," Derek said. "Gunther was there, as well."

"Gunther?" Shocked, I turned to him. "Do you really think your client had anything to do with Gabriel being shot?"

"No, of course not," he said, relaxing back in the red chair. "I'm just pointing out that you're not the only common denominator, as you keep insisting."

"Okay, let's leave Gabriel out of the equation," I said. "So you have Minka being attacked. Then Layla is killed, and now the mysterious Mr. Soo ends up dead. They're all connected to BABA. So we have a pot full of suspects to choose from."

"Well, let's figure out who did it," Robin said eagerly as she pushed herself up off the couch. "I'm going to get a notepad and we're going to make a chart."

"I love party games," Vinnie said.

I laughed, then glanced over and caught Derek shaking his head at me.

I shrugged. "Hey, it beats Trivial Pursuit."

"Don't deny it. You're in heaven," he said in a half-accusing tone.

"And I'm glad you're here with me," I said softly.

He reached over and squeezed my knee affectionately. "I wouldn't want to be anywhere else."

"Suzie, aren't they a cute couple?" Vinnie said, gazing fondly at both of us.

"They're freaking adorable," Suzie said drolly. She stood and grabbed the empty wine bottle off the coffee table. "Come on, Vin, let's get some more wine."

Derek tried not to laugh. I felt my cheeks burning. I'd

always hated when couples made googly eyes at each other in front of their friends. Now I was doing it. I'd lost all sense of dignity and didn't mind at all.

"Here we go," Robin said, walking back in with a legal pad and pen. "We're going to solve a murder."

"Two murders," Vinnie corrected, as she put a freshly opened bottle of wine on the coffee table. "Plus the attacks on your friend Gabriel and that evil cow, Minka."

Robin snorted with laughter and Suzie grinned with pride. "Gotta love her."

"Forgive me," Vinnie said, scowling. "I should not speak ill of cows."

After Robin had written down the long list of suspects and motives, Derek stood and took the list from her. He studied it for a moment and a speculative gleam appeared in his eye.

"All right, let's do this," he said decisively, patting the back of the red chair. "Brooklyn, darling, you sit over here so you can concentrate more fully."

I was suddenly apprehensive, but I brushed it off and switched chairs. I tucked my legs under me and shifted until I was comfortable.

Derek touched my arm. "Now, I'm going to take you step by step through both Minka's and Layla's attacks. Will you be okay with that?"

"Sure," I said, hoping for the best.

He glanced at my three friends. "You'll all take notes and point out inconsistencies, won't you?"

Vinnie nodded eagerly.

"Coolio," Suzie said, and settled into her corner of the couch.

"We'll start with the night of Layla's murder," Derek said. "You were in your classroom, correct?"

"Yes. The signatures had dried and we were hammering the spines to round them."

"Fine," he said, hunkering down in front of me and resting his hands on my knees. "Close your eyes, darling, and think back. Who was in the building that night?"

I thought of Naomi and Karalee, Marky and Ned. Minka was back from the hospital, although I didn't see her until later. I assumed all her students were there with her.

"Now, you're in your class," Derek murmured. "Can you see it?"

After a moment of concentration, I could picture my classroom, the students, the smell of PVA glue.

"Now, where were you standing?" Derek asked.

I answered him, and we went back and forth. What tool was in my hand? Who else was in the room? Picture the students. Go around the room and name them. I did as he instructed.

"Now you hear the gunshot," he said. "Who's in the room with you now?"

"All of my students," I said, then frowned. "No, wait. Cynthia Hardesty had left to make a phone call. And Alice had to run to the bathroom. And Gina . . . no, Whitney. No, wait. They're both in the room. They scream and huddle under the table."

"What else?"

"Kylie isn't there. Did she go to the ladies' room? And I can't see Jennifer. But she's probably there. She's quiet." I sighed. "That's all I can remember."

"So, to recap," Derek said, glancing at his own notes. "Cynthia, Kylie, and Alice were out of the room when the gunshot went off."

I closed my eyes and tried to picture the classroom at the precise moment. "Yes, I'm pretty sure."

"You hear the shot and run down the hall," Derek continued. "There you see the body. Who's with you?"

"Mitchell," I said instantly. "He wouldn't stay in the room."

"Who else?" Derek asked, pacing a few feet in each direction as he peppered me with questions. "Where is everybody now? Who do you see next?"

I went down the line, picturing Alice and Gina at the gallery end of the hall. I remembered Mitchell saying he'd assigned Ned to watch the other hallway. But I never saw Ned that night.

I related Tom Hardesty's display of grief and Cynthia's contempt for Layla. And I told them about Minka stomping over and Mitchell forcing her to stay away.

"All right, darling," Derek said soothingly. "Now, where is Naomi?"

I opened my eyes and stared at him. "She wasn't there. She showed up a few minutes later. Said she'd had to run an errand. She went berserk when she saw Layla. She tried to get closer and I had to hold her back, she was so out of control." I hesitated, then added, "It seemed over the top, but I won't judge her on that score."

"What else do you remember?"

"I remember you walking in with Gunther. He was angry, arguing with Inspector Jaglom."

"Yes, I remember that, too."

I looked over at my three friends on the couch, all in a row, riveted to their seats.

"This is so cool," Suzie said. "Keep going."

"Okay," I said, grinning. I looked up at Derek. "If we assume that the same person attacked Minka, then it can't be Gunther. He wasn't in town on Monday."

Derek folded his arms across his chest as he pondered that for a moment. "But he was. He arrived Sunday night with three of my men. They drove him by the book arts center. He had managed to evade my men twice and I was livid. That's why I flew in late Monday."

"So Gunther was already in the city?"

"The plot thickens," Robin murmured dramatically.

I looked at Derek as something dawned on me. "But

Gunther couldn't have killed Mr. Soo because he was in jail."

"Yes, that just occurred to me, as well," Derek said, and we smiled at each other. Were we smiling too much? Were my friends thinking, *Get a room*?

To distract myself, I picked up the legal pad, sat back in the chair, and perused the list again. "So it could still be anyone."

"Not you," Robin said.

"Nope, not me," I said with relief, and made a third column of people who absolutely didn't do it. I put my name on that list, then added Derek's.

After a few fortifying sips of wine, Derek and I went through the same exercise for the night of Minka's attack.

I thought back to the classroom Monday night, then named the people who left the class, one by one. I remembered trying to sneak out to talk to Layla, but being stopped by Kylie, who asked for an explanation of some technique. Threading? Stitching? Something.

"So Alice and Cynthia and Whitney are out of the room during the time Minka is attacked," Derek reiterated.

"Yes," I said.

"That means that Alice and Cynthia are now the common denominators for the two attacks at your workplace," Vinnie said.

"Very good," Derek said, winking at Vinnie, who preened with pleasure. I couldn't blame her.

"And Naomi," I added. "She was supposedly in her office with the door closed when Minka was attacked. She acted perfectly dumb when she finally opened the door."

"She's my guess," Suzie said, and Vinnie patted her leg in encouragement.

"Where did Alice go off to?" Derek asked.

"The bathroom, probably," Robin said, smiling.

"No doubt," I said, thinking back. "She's always in the bathroom. Or off texting Stuart."

"Is she?" Derek said.

Robin laughed. "You couldn't possibly think Alice had anything to do with this."

"I'm not eliminating anyone yet," Derek said thoughtfully.

"You've seen me pass out over blood, right?" I said. "Alice is ten times worse than that."

"She is quite sensitive," Vinnie allowed.

"She couldn't even lift a gun, let alone shoot it," Suzie said, amused. "The noise alone would probably cause her to faint."

"But she was in Dharma when Gabriel was shot," Derek persisted.

"Oh, come on," Robin said. "The girl is a wimp."

"Besides, she was at the spa when it happened," I said.

"Was she?" Derek asked, one eyebrow raised in doubt.

"And don't forget," I said. "The killer would have to know how to break into a hotel room and hide those books."

"Can't you just see her breaking into a hotel room?" Robin said with a laugh.

"She is pretty thin-skinned," Suzie noted. "She was in tears half the night we met her."

I looked at Derek. "It's kind of silly to have her on the list. I mean, where would anyone as young and innocent and sensitive as Alice learn about breaking and entering?"

"Oh, she's not so young," Vinnie said, sitting forward. "Her earlobes are those of a much older woman."

"What?" Robin laughed. "Come on."

"It is true," Vinnie insisted. "My mother, Padma, is a cosmetic facialist with the soul of an artist. She has studied facial structure, bones and skin, and passed the knowledge on to me."

"She wanted Vinnie to open a spa with her in Mumbai," Suzie revealed.

"Really?" Robin asked. "Do you know how to do all that spa stuff?"

"Yes." Vinnie shivered delicately. "And I cannot tolerate it. Can you imagine cleaning toe jam and waxing hairy upper lips all day?"

Suzie snorted with laughter.

"But what were you saying about earlobes?" Derek persisted, bringing us back to the key topic.

"Ah, yes." Vinnie sobered. "If earlobes could talk, they would tell you that your young Alice is no spring chicken. I calculate her to be at least forty years old."

Chapter 18

My mouth gaped open. Robin stared dumbly back at me. We both looked up at Derek, whose eyes were narrowed in speculation.

We all turned to Vinnie, who sat quietly sipping her wine.

"Is that really possible?" Robin said finally.

"This is a well-known fact in my country," Vinnie said offhandedly. "The headband she wears may be an aid to keep her skin taut. It is an old trick."

Could it have been true? Was Alice really that old? Not that forty was all that old, but she didn't even look thirty. And now that I thought about it, her sweet, genteel wardrobe added to her youthful appearance. Was it all an act?

And even if she was older than we thought, why would Alice kill Layla?

"What's her motive?" I asked. "She just started working at BABA a month ago. Layla was so nice to her, it was spooky. She was almost maternal toward her. I never saw any animosity between them."

"Perhaps Alice was holding something over Layla's head," Derek said.

"Blackmail?" I said. "So Layla had to be nice or Alice would reveal something? It's outlandish."

"Don't forget Gabriel," Robin said. "What could she possibly have against him?"

"Maybe we should ask Gabriel," Derek said, staring out the window at the moon cresting over the Bay Bridge.

"Maybe." I rubbed my temple where a headache was starting to throb. The idea that Alice could be a cold-blooded killer was hurting my head. I glanced at Derek. "You're playing devil's advocate and I appreciate that, but you don't know this girl. She's sweet and thoughtful. Sensitive. I just can't see her in the role of killer."

"Remember Ted Bundy," Derek said ominously.

"Oh, come on."

"He was a very attractive man, by all accounts," Vinnie said with a nod to Derek.

"And charming," Robin added.

Vinnie turned toward me. "I am sorry, Brooklyn. It can't be pleasant to realize you've been fooled by someone you believed to be a friend. But you must admit it is possible. Someone is killing these people. We must consider all possibilities."

"Yes, of course, I know you're right." I stared at the names on the legal pad. "But in the interest of considering all the possibilities, I'd like to reassess Naomi. She had much more to gain than anyone else, both monetarily and professionally. Or there's Cynthia Hardesty. She hated Layla."

"But what are their connections to Gabriel?" Derek interjected. "Neither of those women were anywhere near Dharma on Saturday."

"I know, I know. I'm grasping at straws." I stared up at him and grasped at one more straw. "It's still possible that Gabriel isn't connected to the other attacks."

"But, darling," he said gently. "If our killer is Alice, they're all connected."

"But how in the world is Alice connected to Gabriel? And what about Mr. Soo?"

"I can't answer those questions yet," he said. "But we'll start with the fact that she was in Dharma when Gabriel was shot. And she might've known Mr. Soo through Layla."

"Gabriel was shot while she was at the spa," I countered.

"According to whom?"

I had to think. Alice and my sister Savannah had come running shortly after Gabriel was rolled into the ambulance. The timing seemed off. But I could ask Savannah if she'd been with Alice the entire time. I didn't want to interrupt the conversation so I made a mental note to call my sister tomorrow.

"Oh, hey," Robin said brightly. "Maybe Layla was having an affair with Gabriel, and Alice was—"

"Stop right there," I said, thoroughly disturbed by the image. "If I hear that another man I know was having a sleazy affair with Layla, I'm going to join a damn nunnery in Tibet."

My friends laughed while Derek coughed discreetly. Then he laid his hand on my shoulder. "Brooklyn, how well do you know Gabriel and Alice?"

Troubled, I sat back and considered the question. I'd made light of it in the past, but it was clear to me that Gabriel was a thief, pure and simple. High-end, gorgeous, heroic, and sophisticated, but a thief nonetheless. So why had he sought sanctuary with Guru Bob? Who was after him? I knew Guru Bob trusted him and I'd bet my father did, too. And I trusted Guru Bob and Dad. I needed to think about Gabriel awhile longer before I divulged his secrets.

Alice was a different story. If she'd been playing me all this time, I would have no problem throwing her to the wolves.

"All I know for sure about Alice is that she came to BABA through Layla."

"That's suspicious right there," Robin said dryly.

"True," I admitted, then stood up to pace the length of the couch and back. I could think better on my feet. I told them everything I thought I knew about Alice, some of which I'd already told Derek. The Catholic boarding school, the stomach problems, the conference where she and Layla first met. "Oh, and she's engaged to a guy named Stuart," I added.

"Stuart? Who would make up a name like that?" Suzie asked, mystified.

Our chuckles broke the tension.

"According to Layla," I added, "Alice's background is in arts fund-raising."

"Art and money," Vinnie said sagely. "For a wily thief with a clever cover story, it is the perfect world to infiltrate."

I sighed. "Okay, Gabriel's drawn to that world, too, so I'm willing to acknowledge a connection between him and Alice is not impossible. But it's highly improbable."

"But why would she shoot him?" Robin said. "That's so disturbing."

"Perhaps Gabriel recognized her," Derek said. "Or more likely, Alice saw him first, recognized him, and knew she had to get rid of him before he saw her and blew her cover."

"To protect her band of thieves," Suzie murmured, and her eyes widened in amazement. "It's just like *Oliver Twist*. Far out."

"Oh, my God," I said. "Layla was Fagin."

"But Alice is Sikes," Suzie said, wagging her finger at me. "Talk about a psychopath."

I shivered. Bill Sikes was the personification of evil in the story of *Oliver Twist*.

"It's all speculation," I said halfheartedly.

"Oh!" Vinnie wiggled with excitement. "This reminds me of an old episode of *White Collar* with a similar plot. The bad guys dealt in Asian antiquities, but rare books would work just as well. So, Alice wants to take over Layla's territory and Mr. Soo was Layla's middleman. Alice had to dispose of them both in order to move her own people into place. The center where Brooklyn teaches classes was similar to the private museum depicted in *White Collar*. Both provide the perfect front for nefarious activities."

Suzie gazed fondly at Vinnie. I caught Robin's eye and we both smiled. Vinnie was in love with American television and pop culture.

"I guess anything's possible," I conceded finally, and turned to Derek. "So what do we do now?"

"This is Derek Stone, everybody," I announced the following night at the start of the makeup class. "He's my ride home."

"Nice ride," Whitney whispered.

I had to agree. "He's going to hang out and see what we do here. Hope nobody minds."

"Fine with me," Gina said, her voice suddenly sultry. She exchanged glances with Whitney, who dipped under the table, pretending to fiddle with her purse. When she surfaced, she wore pert red cheeks and fresh lipstick.

Similar behavior was repeated by many of the women around the table.

"How you doin'?" Mitchell said, bobbing his head in acknowledgment of Derek.

"I'm well, thanks," Derek murmured. "You?"

Mitchell grunted, thus giving his male seal of approval to Derek's intrusion into his domain. That was it. The male ritual dance was concluded.

I stole a glance at Alice, who stared at me meaningfully, then wiggled her eyebrows and winked. I returned her smile, praying I was acting as natural with her as I had in the past. I felt like a complete impostor.

We'd stayed up late the night before to work out our plan of attack. Derek was to wander around my class and occasionally pretend to check his e-mail while he actually took pictures of my students. Then we'd show the photos to Gabriel to see if he recognized anyone.

Since Robin had indulged in several glasses of wine,

Derek had insisted she spend the night, and he'd driven back to his hotel. As far as Derek and me getting together went, I was beginning to feel like the punch line of a bad joke.

Tonight, as my students completed their second journal book, I threw in a lesson on how to mix PVA glue with certain powders and pastes to achieve different textures and results.

"The thinner the PVA," I explained, "the more useful it is for restoration work, patching delicate tears and securing frayed threads."

Thickening was another story. I showed them what happened to the glue when wheat paste was added to the mix. Then a different result occurred when methyl cellulose was used. Essentially, the addition of another compound tended to slow down the drying process, allowing the bookbinder to manipulate the textblock or pastedowns as desired.

"Methyl cellulose can also be used to thicken the water bath when marbling paper." I held up a small bag of the compound. "It's important to always check the pH balance of any solution to determine its effect on the paper you're applying it to."

At that moment, I noticed the blank look on Mitchell's face and knew I'd given the class more than enough information.

"Okay, I've said too much."

Everyone laughed and I suggested we all take a break.

During the dinner break, Derek ran to the corner café and brought back lattes and a panini to share.

When he walked back in with Inspector Lee, I tried my darnedest to appear serene and normal instead of showing how stunned I was to see her. I guess that was a mistake.

"What's wrong with you?" Lee asked, her eyes narrowed in suspicion.

"Nothing," I said, three octaves too high. "What's new with you, Inspector?"

I could see Derek rolling his eyes, but it was his fault for bringing the cops back with him.

Lee leaned against the table and crossed her ankles. "You wouldn't know anything about the demise of a Mr. Soo, would you?"

"Why does that name sound familiar?" I asked. I could hear the BS in my own voice. Oh, when would I learn to lie effectively?

Lee scoffed. "Maybe because Naomi Fontaine mentioned his name two nights ago when you were standing right there."

"Oh, yeah. Maybe."

She watched my face as she said, "He's dead."

I blinked a few times, then said, "You're kidding."

"Jesus, Wainwright, don't take it to Vegas."

This wasn't the first time I'd heard that warning, but it was still annoying that everyone I knew could tell when I was lying.

Lee pulled her notebook out of her pocket and flipped through it until she found a photo paper-clipped to a page. "You've got to be the world's worst liar."

"But that's a good thing, don't you think?" I said.

"Yeah, whatever." She handed me the photo. "Here's his picture. Look familiar?"

I took a quick glance, shuddered and looked away. Hell, yeah, he looked familiar. I'd just seen him the day before, lying dead under a bookshelf. Wincing, I forced myself to look at the photo again. "Yes, he's the guy who stormed out of Layla's office the first night I was here. The one I told you about."

She slipped the photo back into her notebook. "We found a key in his pocket with a Bay Area Book Arts logo on it. Turns out it's the key to Ms. Fontaine's office."

"Really?" I said. "I guess they knew each other pretty well."

"That's one theory."

"Do you think the same person killed both of them?"

She folded her arms across her chest. "What do you think?"

"Seems more than likely." I sipped my latte casually, praying I wouldn't spill it down my shirt. "Can you tell if they were killed with the same gun?"

"Call me cuckoo, but I'm not gonna reveal that just yet." She turned and strolled around the room, pausing at the large brass book press. She grabbed the handle and turned the screw an inch. "You've got some cool shit in here."

"Yeah, we do." I watched her warily as she made her way back to me.

She stuck her hands in her pockets. "One thing I will tell you is that I think Ms. Fontaine and Mr. Soo were trafficking in stolen or forged rare books."

"Huh." I smiled.

She nodded. "Yeah."

"So," I said, measuring her, "how's my sting operation looking to you now?"

She laughed, then gave me a look that told me not to hold my breath. "I'll have my people call your people."

Alice came running into the room after the break and grabbed my arms. "You'll never guess."

"What's up?" I asked.

"I'm overjoyed," she said. "They let Gunther go."

"Oh, good," I said, feigning surprise. "So that must mean he's innocent."

"Yes, and he's agreed to teach a class Saturday afternoon. But there's more. I talked to a few of the board members and they're absolutely thrilled about Gunther going to jail. I guess word got out and the ticket sales for the gala are up more than twenty percent."

She did a happy little jig around me, and when she finally slowed down I had a few seconds to study her face.

Fine lines around her eyes were carefully masked with a natural but thick matte foundation. And there were the tiniest little folds by her earlobes. She really did look older than I'd originally thought, and that realization chilled me straight down to the marrow.

"That's great," I managed to say with a smile, then reminded myself that just because she was trying to look younger didn't mean she was a vicious killer.

"Thanks," she said, catching her breath. "I know it's crazy, but I guess the idea of cozying up to a possible felon has brought donations and requests pouring in from all over the city. It's going to be a huge success."

I had to bite my tongue to keep from commenting on her "cozying up to a felon" remark.

"I'm so happy for you," I said in the most sincerely perky voice I could muster.

The other students straggled in from dinner and everyone got back to work. Derek made a show of circling the room and feigning interest in each student's progress. He talked quietly to almost everyone, asking questions and voicing encouragement. When he was finished, he leaned against the front counter and checked his e-mail. The women in the room, including me, stole furtive glances his way at every opportunity.

A sociologist would have a field day here, observing female behavior as a new alpha male was introduced into the group.

My ladies' chests were thrust forward, shoulders pulled back, hair fluffed more often, and laughter a bit more high-pitched. And maybe it was just me, but you could cut the tension with a bone folder. It felt as though an eternity passed before class was finally finished for the evening.

Alice was the last to leave. She waved excitedly, then flashed a stealthy look at Derek and gave me a thumbs-up. It was something a girlfriend would do.

I smiled and waved, but as soon as she was out the door, I slumped against the table, exhausted. Either she was a psychopathic killer or I had just betrayed a budding friendship. Either way, I felt sick at heart.

Derek stood behind me and massaged my shoulders. "You'll feel much better once we've cleared her of any wrongdoing."

I turned around and faced him. "You promise? Because right now I feel pretty awful. I wouldn't blame her if she never spoke to me again."

"She need never know," he whispered. "And it's all for a good cause." He planted a kiss on the corner of my mouth. "Are you ready to go?"

"Yes." I grabbed my bag and we walked out arm in arm. In the gallery, Karalee was finishing up a small group tour of the facilities. There had been a lot more visitors this week because of the Twisted festival, and the hours had been extended. Refreshments were served all day, as well, and the caterers were starting to clean up.

Leaning close to Derek, I whispered, "Did you get some good photos?"

"I managed to get a number of close-ups of all the key players," he said, his lips close to my ear. Tingles resonated across my skin as he moved his mouth along my neck. It took me a minute to recall that we were in the middle of the gallery in full view of people, talking about him taking pictures of possible murder suspects.

"Good job," I managed, and exhaled. "The sooner Gabriel can look at the shots, the sooner we'll be able to put an end to this charade."

Derek drove to my place and parked the Bentley in the visitors' space in the garage. "Do you think we can sneak in without anyone noticing?"

I laughed. "Not if we take the elevator."

"Where are the stairs?"

"Right over there."

"Good." He touched my cheek, his hand warm on my skin as he turned my face toward his. He leaned in and kissed me and I savored the sensation. I was disarmed by his gentleness as his hands slipped through my hair and he pulled me closer.

His phone trilled loudly in the quiet of his car.

Derek groaned. "I'm going to throw that thing away."

"It's me, I'm cursed," I said, flopping back in my seat. "Don't blame the phone."

He answered the call. After a minute, he hung up and leaned back against the headrest. With eyes closed, he said, "The prime minister's jealous son-in-law just tried to kill Gunther."

I spent another restless night alone. At four a.m., I couldn't stand it any longer. I called Derek to get the scoop on Gunther and his would-be killer.

"Gunther is shaken but safe," he said, his voice weary. "The son-in-law and his accomplice are both being held in jail until they can be processed for extradition."

"Do you know what happened?"

"Yes, Gunther was club-hopping in North Beach and met a woman. She wanted to leave and Gunther didn't want my men following him, so he pretended to use the toilet but instead snuck outside through the kitchen. When he circled around to the front sidewalk, he was assaulted. The son-in-law stood nearby as his henchman tried to stab Gunther."

"That's horrible," I said, not adding what I thought of a man who paid thousands of dollars for protection and refused to use it.

"Yes, it is," Derek said. "It's lucky that my men are used to Gunther's stupidity. They were there in time to rescue him and apprehend his attacker."

"I'm glad it's over," I said.

"Yes, so am I."

So this was it. He would leave town in the next few days and that would be the end of our budding friendship—or whatever it was. I wished him sweet dreams and we hung up. I was certain I wouldn't sleep another wink, but I managed to doze off after a while.

Saturday morning, Derek picked me up at nine o'clock and we drove to Sonoma in record time. As we wound our way through Sausalito and into San Rafael, I finally related Guru Bob's story of Gabriel.

"And this happened five years ago?" Derek said.

"Yes."

He thought for another moment. "And Robson said Gabriel came to him asking for sanctuary?"

"That's what he said. Why?"

"I'm not sure." He shrugged. "It's one big long shot, any way you look at it. If Gabriel doesn't recognize anyone in the photos, we're back to square one. And even if he does recognize someone, will he be willing to leave the security of Dharma to help us set a trap?"

"I think he will," I said. After all, a man who would climb a mountain in Afghanistan during a tribal war to save people wouldn't let a little threat of death slow him down.

We discussed a wager over whose photo Gabriel might recognize. My money was on Naomi. Or Cynthia. Or Ned. Anyone but Alice. The thought that I might've brought a brutal killer into my home and introduced her to my friends caused me physical pain.

Derek told me that he'd actually considered calling the police the night before to give them the benefit of our brainstorming session. But at the last minute, he'd decided against it. He was still feeling the burn of his own recent interrogation and we weren't sure anything would come of this plan. So for now, we would operate on our own. If something broke open, we would turn things over to Inspectors Lee and Jaglom immediately.

I was only now realizing how traumatic it must've been for him to be taken in for questioning. Days later, I could tell it still disturbed him, that the very institutions he'd pledged his life to serve had refused to believe him. Talk about betrayal.

I hoped the drive to Sonoma would help ease some of the tension he was feeling. As I stared out at the rolling, vine-covered hills, I could feel my own stress seeping away from my shoulder muscles. My neck was looser than it had been in a few days. Then Derek took hold of my hand and everything smoothed out. I felt at peace. I knew it wouldn't last, but at the moment, life was perfect.

"Have you spoken with Savannah?" he asked, interrupting my perfect thoughts.

I gasped. In all the hubbub of the last twenty-four hours, I'd forgotten to ask Savannah about Alice. I pulled out my cell phone, pushed her number, and waited. When she answered, I asked the question. She had to think back for a few seconds.

"It was an odd moment, now that you ask," she said.

"How so?"

"Alice and I were walking back to Annie's to find you. Then I saw you standing outside of Annie's store a block or so away and I pointed you out to Alice. That's when I saw Gabriel walking into town. He's a pretty one, isn't he?"

I mumbled my agreement.

"Okay, so just then, Alice grabbed hold of her stomach. I thought she was going to be sick right there."

"Was she?"

"She said she needed to find a bathroom and went tearing off. I yelled at her to go to China's, because she has one at the back of her store, but I don't think she heard me. She ran across the street and disappeared down the walkway between the baby shop and Peregrine."

Peregrine was a French bistro on the Lane.

"What did you do?" I asked.

"I went on to Annie's," Savannah said. "I figured Alice would end up there eventually. It was maybe another ten minutes later that we heard someone had been hurt. By then, Alice had returned and we all ran down to find you."

It was my turn to feel sick. I blew out a breath and looked at Derek. He watched me with concern in his eyes.

If Alice had seen Gabriel walking toward me, she would have had ample time to hide between two of the stores on the other side of the street and take aim at him.

In my heart, I knew that Alice had tried to kill Gabriel. I just didn't know why.

That would mean she'd had a gun with her the whole time. All during our drive up to Dharma, the few minutes she'd spent with my mother, all the while she'd been at the spa, at the hospital, at my parents' home for dinner.

It was my worst nightmare come true. I'd brought a ruthless killer into my family's home. It wasn't easy to admit, but I knew what I had to do now.

"Will we see you later?" Savannah asked, her tone gentle.

"I'll be at Mom's for a little while but then I have to get back to the city."

We ended the call, and I related to Derek everything she'd said.

He nodded once, his jaw rigid. "Let's go talk to Gabriel."

Chapter 19

Gabriel lay pale and groggy under a fluffy white blanket and crisp blue sheets, a stack of soft pillows beneath his head. His left temple was swathed in a large gauze bandage crisscrossed with white surgical tape. It hurt to see him laid out like this.

Around his wrist was a ratty-looking bracelet made of yarn and strips of cloth woven together with sticks and willow twigs and a bundle of something. Herbs? Bat-wing powder? Was this Mom's attempt at a Wiccan healing bracelet? If so, it was kind of gross.

Derek had stopped to talk to Dad for a minute, but then he walked into the bedroom and I watched his eyes widen, then narrow as he got his first look at Gabriel. His jaw flexed and I wondered what was going through his mind.

I looked down at Gabriel, then back at Derek, whose expression was now impassive.

"Maybe we shouldn't wake him up," Mom whispered, nervously clasping and unclasping her hands against her chest. "He didn't sleep well last night. He's still having nightmares."

"It's important," Derek said.

"I'm awake," Gabriel mumbled. His eyes remained closed, but his mouth was set in a scowl.

"I'm so sorry," I said softly.

His eyes blinked open. "Hey, babe."

Derek frowned.

I smiled. "Gabriel. How are you feeling?"

"Like I got hit by a bus."

"Poor baby," I murmured.

He tapped his left cheek. "It hurts right here. Maybe you'd like to . . ."

"Easy, tiger," I said with a grin. "I don't think you've met Derek Stone."

Gabriel stared up at Derek with one eye open. He blinked once, then held his gaze steadily. After a long moment, he said, "Haven't had the pleasure."

"Nor I," Derek replied.

"Derek Stone," I said, "this is Gabriel . . . uh, Gabriel." I still had no clue what his last name was.

"Gabriel's good enough," he muttered, and with what seemed like superhuman strength, given his current condition, he whipped the blanket off and sat up. I figured he wasn't about to remain in bed when another alpha dog stepped into the room.

Gabriel shoved his hand forward and Derek gripped it in a tight handshake. "Nice to meet you."

"Pleasure's mine," Derek said.

"Well, isn't this lovely?" Mom said, as she gazed affectionately at both Derek and Gabriel. "Everyone's friends now."

She really needed to find a hobby.

"Gabriel," I said, sitting on the small chair Mom had placed by his bed, "Derek has something we'd like you to take a look at."

"Yeah?" he said slowly and gazed up at Derek, his forehead furrowed in suspicion.

Derek tapped his smart phone until he found the best shot of Alice, then handed the phone to Gabriel.

Gabriel blinked to clear his vision, then stared at the screen. He shook his head, blinked again. "Mary Grace?"

"Mary Grace?" I frowned at Gabriel, then at Derek, then back at Gabriel. "Who's Mary Grace?"

He glared at me, then Derek, then back at the phone. "What the hell is Mary Grace Flanagan doing on your phone?"

"Who's Mary Grace?" I persisted.

He ignored me and looked straight at Derek. "What's she done now?"

"She may be implicated in a double murder," Derek said straight out. "And she may have been the one who shot you. Can you tell us how you know her?"

Gabriel blew out a heavy breath. "I married her."

"What?!" I might've shrieked it because he winced, while Derek stroked my shoulder as if I were a spooked horse.

"When?" Derek asked.

"Why?" I demanded.

Gabriel shook his head, then laughed without humor. "She was running a scam. We needed to appear married. It's not important, but you should know that Mary Grace is very, very good at what she does."

"Which is what, exactly?" Derek asked.

Gabriel told an amazing story. Mary Grace Flanagan had indeed been raised by nuns in a Catholic orphanage and she was a bad seed from the start. Gabriel had met her more than ten years earlier in Bahrain, when he was involved in a Tylos pearl scam and she was smuggling Russian iconic antiquities through the Middle East and into Western Europe. He was twenty-two years old and she was ten years older. They became lovers, but never trusted each other. The thrill wore off quickly as it turned out that there was, after all, no honor among thieves. Gabriel stuck close to her, though, as she geared up to move a shipment of forged Dead Sea Scrolls into France. She hoped to pass them off as newly discovered Qumran cave scrolls, but the shipment never went through and Mary Grace disappeared off the face of the earth.

I couldn't get a clear picture of Gabriel and Mary Grace together. Gabriel refused to elaborate. What did she mean to him? Had he been trying to set her up or had he been in on the deal?

"I'm not surprised to hear it's Mary Grace who shot me," Gabriel said darkly. "It wouldn't be the first time."

"She shot you before?" I asked, fascinated.

"She tried," he said. Then he cast a look at Derek. "If you're setting a trap, I want in."

"I'm not sure you're up to it," Derek said mildly.

Gabriel stood. "I'm up to it."

"I've made sandwiches," Mom announced from the doorway. "There are chips and cookies, too."

"Let's do this," Gabriel said, then took one step and wobbled. Derek and I both grabbed him, but he held up his hands. "I've got this."

He led the way, slowly, to the spacious dining room and sat down at the large, dark wood Craftsman-style table where my family had eaten together for years.

My dad joined us, insisting that we try sips of a new batch of chardonnay he'd extracted from the barrel for the occasion. As we ate sandwiches, Derek and I brought Gabriel up to speed on the attacks at BABA. Mom and Dad listened, occasionally adding bits of insight I found remarkably useful. I guess they'd had some experience with some unsavory elements in their lives. Not all Deadheads were about peace and love, it seemed.

After lunch, Dad went back to work in the barrel room and Gabriel and Derek discussed logistics while I joined Mom in the big sunny kitchen.

"Tell me more about the gray aura you saw around Alice," I said.

Mom set her sponge on the rack near the sink. "I was so bothered by it, I had to look it up to be sure." She walked me back to my parents' office off the kitchen, where she pulled a thick old book from the wall of bookshelves. Laying it open on the desk, she flipped to a bookmarked page. "See? Look at this."

I began to read about auras and their meanings, skimming through all the colors of the rainbow until I reached the various shades of gray and black.

Gray auras were indeed often a sign of disease. Usually the grayness would appear spotty and clustered around those parts of the body most affected by tumors or cellular abnormalities. But the book also warned that a gray aura could indicate dark thoughts, or the dark side of a personality.

"That's why her aura was so dark," Mom said. "I thought it was disease but it was just plain old evil. If I'd been more aware, I might've prevented Gabriel's . . ."

"It's not your fault," I said, gripping her arm. "She fooled us all."

"Sweetie," she said gently, "it's not your fault, either."

"Mom, I invited her into my home, introduced her to my friends. Then I brought her here. I brought that evil to Dharma." Tears stung my eyes. "I'm not sure I can ever forgive myself for that."

She rubbed my back and gripped me in a hug. "Well, I for one am glad you didn't recognize her dark side."

"What do you mean?" I pushed away from her and tossed my hands up in dismay. "If I'd known—"

"No." She gripped my arms and forced me to look her in the eye. "You must never become so cynical that the first thing you see is the negative rather than the positive."

"But I could've—"

She shook me. "Promise me."

"Okay, okay," I said, giving in to the inevitable. "I promise I'll be a naive twit for the rest of my life."

"That's my good girl," she said, smiling. "My little twit."

"Yeah, thanks."

"Come on, sing with me," she teased. "You know the words, 'Look for the silver lining . . .' "

I laughed. "Oh, my dear God."

After Derek and Gabriel worked out the scenario they would follow to trap Alice (or whatever her name was), we settled in my parents' quiet office. Gabriel collected his thoughts, then called Alice from his cell phone.

"Hey, babe," he drawled.

It seemed Alice recognized his voice immediately.

"Of course I knew it was you," he said a moment later. "I hate to mention it, but you're still missing your target."

She responded, and he chuckled. "Yeah, you always were a good shot. If you really wanted me dead, you wouldn't have missed."

She spoke for another few seconds. Gabriel rolled his eyes and said, "Yeah, I love you and miss you, too." He looked at me and winked.

Derek watched, his mouth twisted in a tight grin.

"Here's the thing, Mary Grace," Gabriel said finally. "I want in on the book deal."

He listened to her protests for a full minute.

"You've shot me twice now, Mary Grace," he said at length, his tone hardening. "I'm not letting this one go. I'm in, or I take it to the cops."

They spoke for another minute. Gabriel told her he'd meet her at BABA late the following afternoon. Then he disconnected the call and we finalized our plans.

That night, after Gabriel fell asleep in my guest bedroom, I brought linens and blankets out to the living room, where Derek insisted on sleeping. He met me halfway and took the bundle from me. "A blanket is all I need."

I spread the sheet over the couch and began to slip the ends under the cushions. "You'll sleep better if you have sheets and a pillow."

"I daresay nothing will help me sleep well tonight."

Concerned, I asked, "Do you want some warm milk?"

"No." He tucked the sheet under the last thick cushion, then sat on his makeshift bed and reached for me. "Come here."

With a smile, I climbed on top of him, cradled his face in my hands, and kissed him.

He grabbed hold of me and returned the kiss, his lips more demanding, more fervent than ever before. I groaned as he slid his cool hands under my thin T-shirt and stroked my skin.

Footsteps slapped against the floor of the hall, then Gabriel's weak voice called out, "Babe? Can I have some water?"

"Christ in heaven," Derek muttered against my hair. "We're doomed, I tell you."

I laughed to keep from crying. "Yes, we are."

"No, you're not."

"What do you mean, no?" I asked, as I paced around the living room the next day.

"I mean, you're not going to be in the room with Gabriel and Mary Grace." Derek went back to testing the tiny microphone at the end of the wire he would tape to Gabriel's back. Gabriel had agreed to wear the wire in order to tape Alice—or Mary Grace, whatever her name was—admitting she'd killed both Layla and Mr. Soo.

The previous night, after we were so rudely interrupted by Gabriel, Derek and I had stayed up and talked for hours. We'd laughed over the realization that we'd both tried collecting stamps at a young age but found it unspeakably boring. Derek confessed that he'd wanted to join the Royal Navy ever since he saw the Sharks, the Royal Navy's elite helicopter team, perform at an air show when he was six years old. Sadly, by the time he was old enough to enlist, the team had been disbanded, but he was determined to fly helicopters anyway.

My heart had melted as I pictured a starstruck little boy staring up in awe at the wildly exciting maneuvers of those daring helicopter pilots.

Finally, I had dozed on the couch while Derek placed a phone call to his people at Scotland Yard to find out what he could about Alice's adventures in Bahrain. According to his sources, she still had a number of outstanding international warrants for her arrest. Once they realized exactly who we were dealing with, Scotland Yard, through Interpol, took control of the investigation, and Derek was duly authorized to run the sting operation. The local police were to follow his lead.

That hadn't gone down well with Inspector Lee.

And now, as I continued my pacing, I was feeling a little cranky myself. "It's not like I'll be in the same room with them. I just want to be part of the action, back where you all are. There's a small closet inside that workroom. I could just sit in there and—"

"Absolutely not."

"You can't keep me away."

"I believe I can," he said mildly, as he tested the earbuds attached to the micro recorder.

"But why?" I winced at the whiny tone of my voice. "I'm part of this."

"That doesn't mean I'll allow you to—"

"Allow me?" I glared at him. "You don't *allow* me to do anything. I do whatever I want."

He looked up. "Of course you do, darling. But you'll recall that I've already seen you at the wrong end of a psychopath's gun, more than once. It's not good for my heart."

He patted his heart for emphasis.

I stomped my foot. "That's so unfair."

"I'm glad we agree," he said. "It would be quite unfair of you to put me through that misery again."

My shoulders slumped. "That's not what I meant."

His smile was affectionate. "I know."

Gabriel and Derek had already decided that I would be their "front man." I was not impressed with the job title or the description. My duties would predominantly involve schmoozing with Alice at the gala, keeping a sharp eye on her as I drank expensive champagne, nibbled on blinis and caviar, and partied with the rich and famous of San Francisco.

Talk about unfair.

I sat down next to Derek, scooted my chair closer, and put my hand over his. "Derek, I'm serious about this. Alice used me. She pretended to be my friend and wormed her way into my home and my heart. I feel sick about that and . . . and soiled."

"Darling, no, you mustn't." He turned in his chair and wrapped me tenderly in his arms. "I would do anything to wipe those feelings away."

I sniffled. "I brought her to Dharma and introduced her to my family. To my mother. They welcomed that negative, destructive force into our lives. I'll never forget the look on Guru Bob's face . . ." My lips trembled.

"Oh, sweetheart," he whispered, as he stroked my hair. "Shush now. I know, I know. It's very painful."

I nodded, unable to speak.

"Poor darling." He leaned back and tilted my chin up so I could see him. "But there's still no way in hell I'm letting you hide in that closet."

My mouth opened, then closed.

He winked. "Nice try, though."

Gabriel was still weak but determined to carry on with the sting. I had changed his dressing so that instead of the eight-inch-wide white sterile patch that had covered half his head the day before, he now sported a subtle two-inch-wide tan bandage.

Two hours before departure time, Gabriel had to stretch out on the couch and rest.

I took a good look at him, then glanced at Derek. "I'm concerned his strength will be gone before we ever get to BABA."

"I'll rally, babe," Gabriel protested.

"You'd better," I said. "I don't want to give Alice the chance to finish the job she already started on you."

He groaned. "That cuts to the core."

"Sorry," I said, scowling. "But your ex-wife is at the top of her game and you're weak as a kitten."

"The weakness might play in his favor," Derek said.

"What?" I said. "You think you'll appeal to her maternal side?"

"That's what I'm counting on," Gabriel said.

"You think she has one?" I asked.

Neither of them answered.

"I just hope the police will be close by," I muttered. I had a lot less confidence in Alice's maternal instincts than these two did.

"The less obvious the police presence, the better," Gabriel said, his voice gruff. "Mary Grace can smell a cop from a mile away."

Gabriel slept for a half hour, then showered and dressed in his best black-on-black gunslinger's outfit. I was wiping off the kitchen bar when he walked out to the living room. I stuttered to a halt.

The man looked like something off the cover of an extremely hot romance novel, meaning he looked damned good. It just went to show that Alice wasn't as smart as she thought she was. If I were her, I never would've let him go. Just saying.

Then Derek walked in from my front office wearing an old leather bomber jacket over a navy T-shirt tucked into faded jeans, his muscular thighs hard beneath the denim.

I'd never seen him in such casual clothes before, so I guess you could say he caught me off guard.

My feet froze to the floor. I fumbled for the sponge. Time slowed down as he turned, saw me, and smiled. My breath rattled in my throat and my heart tumbled into a place it had never been before.

Something flickered in Derek's eyes. He walked across the room and slid his hand around my neck, then leaned in and covered my mouth with his. The kiss was openmouthed and heart-stopping. My lower stomach tightened and my knees threatened to give in. His lips inched along my cheekbone, planting kisses until he reached my ear. There, he whispered, "You dropped your sponge."

I laughed in surprise and my heart began to beat again. He bent down to retrieve my sponge, smiling wickedly as he handed it back to me. After another quick, hard kiss, he moved to the dining table, where his equipment, and a grinning Gabriel, waited patiently.

While I watched, Derek wired Gabriel for sound and they tested the equipment for a few minutes longer.

All systems were go, except my own.

Overwhelmed by a flood of emotions, I walked unsteadily into the kitchen and leaned against the cool surface of the refrigerator to regroup.

So much for acting like the sophisticated urban animal I fancied myself to be. Yes, I'd gone in with both eyes wide open, knowing Derek would leave town as soon as Gunther's stint at BABA was completed. I'd been engaged before and I'd survived the breakups just fine. Truth be told, I'd done most of the breaking up myself because I'd had no business saying yes in the first place.

But now I knew I would be losing a great big chunk of my heart when Derek left. I would miss him more than anything or anyone I'd ever missed in my life.

All this time I'd been worrying that my karma was keeping us apart, when I should've been worrying about my karma bringing us *together*. Because now he would leave and I would be a complete, miserable, slobbering mess.

I sucked in a deep breath of air and pushed myself away from the refrigerator. I couldn't afford to think about all that right now. I had a job to do, a book to avenge, and a killer to unmask.

Chapter 20

I walked into BABA and was slammed by the wall of sound that greeted me. It rattled my nerves and made me want to turn around and go home. For a few seconds, I wondered if Naomi had hired a live band, but no. It was the same old stereo system, set to an ear-bleeding level. I could take it. I could take anything. I held my shoulders high and plunged into the crowd.

The Sunday afternoon soiree had been Naomi's idea and it was a good one. The time of day suited the large gallery space to perfection. Sunshine poured in through the wide skylight, casting crystalline shards of color and light over the crowd. And instead of the usual black-clad bodies, many of the women were dressed in jewel tones and even in a few pastels. It made for a lovely, bright palette and lent a lightness and joie de vivre to the normally dour, artsy crowd.

I waved to a few acquaintances and caught snippets of conversation as I made my way across the crowded room. Art, books, music, films, the weather, the environment, climate change, the latest scandal erupting at City Hall. One conversation faded into another until I reached my destination. The bar. Naturally. Where else would I be going?

I cast a glance at the short but impressive wine list, then decided to live dangerously and ordered the party's signature drink, the TNT. It stood for Tart 'n' Twisted. Nice that they got that "twisted" thing in there.

I took a sip and found that it was, in essence, an ice-cold vodka gimlet, one of my favorite drinks. They served it in a martini glass with an extra slice of lime. Very refreshing.

Not that I was nervous, but I downed that drink in two gulps and ordered another. I planned to nurse the second one for the next hour or so, though I was sorely tempted to get tanked up and pass out on one of the office couches. Derek would wake me up when it was over and we could drive off into the sunset.

But as I turned from the bar, I spotted Alice on the opposite side of the room and knew what I had to do. She was tight in conversation with Cynthia Hardesty. It was an interesting pairing. I wondered what nonsense Alice was filling the board member's ears with. Perhaps they were bonding over their shared concerns about Naomi. If Alice weren't unmasked today, would she try to implicate Naomi in Layla's death? Or worse, would she eventually kill Naomi, too?

Why not? She'd already killed two people in her quest to take over Layla's book-fraud ring. The more power she got hold of, the easier it would be to knock off anyone who stood in her way of gaining total control.

Watching Alice from my vantage point, I felt a shiver of anticipation trill across my shoulders. Today was the day that power grab would end. Today, we would take her down.

My thoughts drifted to Gabriel, who at this moment was sneaking in through the back door of the building with Derek. I imagined Inspectors Lee and Jaglom had met them back there, as well. I hoped so. I hoped they'd brought a full battalion with them. My worry was that however many cops made up a battalion, that might not be enough to protect Gabriel from Alice's malevolence.

Gabriel was my main concern. He was still so weak. Seeing Alice now and knowing what she was capable of, I knew Gabriel would be no match for her if he couldn't harness his inner forces to make up for his lack of outer strength.

I skirted the lower gallery and made a show of studying each item in the silent auction. I wrote my name and the amount of my bid on a few of them. I particularly coveted a leather-handled set of Jeff Peachey knives. The brilliant bookbinder and craftsman had created a set of cryogenic steel-bladed knives that were hand-honed to surgical precision and beautifully beveled to work with the thinnest calfskin.

I sighed. Even in the midst of danger, I could geek it up with the best of them.

"That's a very nice bid," Alice said behind me. She'd caught me off guard and my stomach dropped twenty feet.

I turned and laughed, hoping I didn't sound too hysterical. "Hey, you. These are some fabulous auction items."

She smiled. "I thought those tools might appeal to you."

"Peachey is a genius," I murmured, nodding. Abruptly, I reminded myself I was here on a mission and shook myself out of my daydreams. "This party is a real hit, Alice. Congratulations."

"Thanks," she said. "Much as I hate to admit it, Naomi gets most of the credit."

"That's got to hurt."

We shared a laugh despite the wave of depression running through me. Alice and I could've been such great friends, if only she hadn't turned out to be a stone-cold murdering bitch. I forced a smile back onto my face, knowing I needed to maintain illusions for a while longer.

She leaned closer and said in a teasing tone, "So, where's that hunky British dude who can't stay away from you?"

I tried to giggle along with her. "Derek should be here in a little while."

"He's a lucky guy," she assured me.

"Aw, thank you." I gritted my teeth and gave her a hug. "You're so sweet."

Her gaze wandered off. I tried to follow it, homing in on Cynthia Hardesty as the board member grabbed another glass of champagne off the tray of a passing waiter.

"I saw you talking to Cynthia earlier," I said, lowering my voice. "What's going on?"

Alice continued to stare across the room, then finally looked up at me. "She wanted to talk about Naomi. She thinks Naomi killed Layla, but frankly I still have my doubts. Cynthia could be trying to deflect attention from the fact that she did it herself."

"I hate to say it," I said, "but I'm not sure I can blame her after seeing how Tom reacted every time Layla walked into a room."

"I know," Alice said, shaking her head. "He's kind of disgusting. But can I confess something to you?"

I blinked. "Okay."

"I'm not really sure about Karalee anymore, either. She's been acting so weird lately, and I caught her in Layla's office earlier today. I could swear she was about to steal something."

"You're kidding." I couldn't take much more of this. I placed my empty glass on a nearby service tray. "Tell you what, I'll keep an eye on her and let you know if I notice anything odd going on."

"Would you?" She gripped my arm. "Thank you. I hate to be so suspicious, but I can't help it. Sometimes I work late at night and I'm so worried there will be another attack."

"You poor thing," I said, patting her hand. "You must be under a lot of strain." *What with the unbridled murder and mayhem and all,* I added silently.

"Oh, don't worry about me," she said bravely. "I'll be fine."

"I hope so." And I hoped she'd get a lovely cell with a nice view of her neighbor, Big Beulah. "I'm going to run to the ladies' room. Then maybe I'll grab another one of those TNTs. Have you tried one yet?"

"Just a taste. I figured I'd better stay sober."

"Too bad, because they rock. I'll be back in a few." I waved and headed for the bathroom. Once inside, I sagged against the door and exhaled in relief.

I should've been exhausted, but my outrage energized me. The fact that she could keep up the pretense so easily made me realize we were dealing with a true sociopath. She was perfectly willing to implicate anyone—Cynthia, Naomi, Karalee, to name a few. I had to wonder if she'd brought my name up to the others as a possible suspect. It wouldn't have surprised me.

I used the facilities, then took another deep breath and walked out. The bathrooms were down the hall from the workroom where Gabriel and Alice had agreed to meet. I checked my watch. Less than ten minutes to go. I had to assume the good guys were in their places.

The room they'd chosen was one of the individual workrooms BABA rented out to bookbinders and artists who needed space to work. Some rooms were used for individual studies and small group classes. I'd taught a few master classes with three or four students in these types of rooms and knew their design. They all had a small anteroom leading to the main workroom, with a closet off the anteroom.

They would never know I was in there. I'd played my role out front, kept an eye on Alice for as long as I could stand it. Now I belonged back here.

If Gabriel was already in there and saw me, that would be the end of it. But if I could sneak inside unnoticed, I would be able to hear everything and know that Alice was Layla's killer. I would feel vindicated, and at the same time, no one would have to know I was there. Derek wouldn't worry and all would end well.

Without further deliberation, I tiptoed farther down the hall to the workroom. The door opened without a sound and I crept inside. The room was empty.

My heart pounding, I carefully opened the closet door

and slipped inside. The small space was dark but not completely black, thank goodness. My eyes slowly adjusted and I could see the shelves above my head. I crouched in the corner and waited.

Less than five minutes later, I heard the outer door open and shut quickly.

Five minutes after that, it opened and shut again.

"Hey, babe," Gabriel said, his tone a casual drawl.

"Well, look what the cat dragged in," Alice said, her voice huskier than usual. So even her voice was fraudulent? Unbelievable.

"I'm digging the pixie look," Gabriel said derisively. "What's with the Alice in Wonderland charade?"

"It's working for me," she said. "You're looking a little pale. Feeling okay?"

"I really appreciate your concern, considering it was your bullet that nailed me. Have a seat."

It was a smart move to get her to sit down. That was the only way Gabriel could get off his feet.

"So, Mary Grace," he said. "I was surprised to hear you'd moved into my world. You're getting into books."

"It's where the money is."

"So you're finding it lucrative?"

"I'm doing okay," Alice demurred.

"Come on, babe. I hear you're making a killing."

"Oh, that's a terrible pun," Alice said, giggling.

I shook my head in disbelief at the fact that she could admit to a pun about making a killing. It was practically a confession of murder as far as I was concerned. And I was still annoyed by the radical change in her voice from the way she'd talked to me. She really was diabolical.

Gabriel asked her how she'd stumbled onto the book-fraud gig. Alice told him she'd been cooling her heels after a fine art con in Belgium went south, so she'd skipped over to San Francisco and put out feelers here. She caught a whiff of a rare-book scam going down and followed her nose to BABA. After a few months of careful planning and several efforts to prove her street cred, she finally came to the attention of Layla Fontaine.

I wondered if committing murder was one way she'd proved her "street cred" to Layla. I made a mental note to ask Inspector Lee whether any recent unsolved murders might be connected to Layla's ring of thieves.

Alice went on to boast about how eagerly Layla had glommed onto her. The hotshot executive director had taken "young Alice" under her wing, bringing her into BABA to learn all about the business so Alice could be Layla's partner in both the legitimate and criminal sides of the biz.

"Sadly, familiarity breeds contempt," Alice complained. "The more I got to know Layla, the more I realized I'd never be able to work with her long term. She was a pain in the butt."

Look who's talking.

"Not only was she a bad manager who desperately needed my expertise," Alice said, "but she knew it. And yet, when I told her I wanted half the business, she wasn't willing to pay the price."

"So she had to go," Gabriel finished.

"Yeah, she had to go. Now I'm in charge and things will be different around here."

"But how're you going to keep the scam going, now that you've got the police sniffing around?"

Alice laughed. "You let me worry about that, pretty boy."

I could imagine Gabriel's hackles rising at that comment. But his voice was mild as he said, "Rumor has it your associates are dropping like flies. What's that all about?"

"Price of doing business in tough times."

"And what's your racket?" he asked. "You playing the little schoolgirl, Mary Grace?"

"Hey, I've got a good gig going on here," she said, her voice dripping with sarcasm. "They think I'm as sweet as sugar pie. I'm all artsy-craftsy, making books and crap, and I've got a wonderful fiancé, too. Check this out."

"Nice bling," Gabriel said, and I could picture Alice flashing her beautiful diamond ring in his face.

"I like it," she said, and laughed.

"I assume the fiancé is as fake as that ring is real."

She simply laughed again.

So there was no Stuart, and I had no doubt she'd stolen that beautiful ring from somewhere. What other lies had she told us? She probably had a perfectly fine digestive system. All those health issues were more figments of her fertile imagination. She'd sucked us in royally. For some reason, her lack of stomach problems burned me more than some of the other lies she'd told.

I wondered why the police weren't coming in to arrest her by now. Hadn't she made it clear that she was the one who'd killed Layla and Mr. Soo. Did they need even more evidence?

"Let's cut to the chase, Mary Grace," Gabriel said. "I want in. I know books a hell of a lot better than you do. I'll play the middleman or the seller."

"It's an interesting offer," she said slowly.

"It's not an offer—it's a done deal. And we split things fifty-fifty."

"What?" That was followed by a few expletives and I could hear her pushing chairs around. Guess she wasn't happy with his offer.

"Is there a problem?" Gabriel said.

"Yeah, there's a problem, you slug. I'll give you twenty percent and you'll like it. You're in no position to make demands, Gabriel. I was there at the hospital after you were shot. I know you're still weak."

"Not that weak, pixie. I can pin your ass to those murders, not to mention your little attempt to put a hole in my head. I don't mind telling you, that just pissed me off. Fifty-fifty's the bottom line or I call the cops."

The tension was growing palpable. Gabriel couldn't have been happy knowing she'd been so bold that she'd come to the hospital after shooting him. If she was that bold, she would stoop to anything to protect her cut of the book ring profits.

Now I was worried that Alice had her gun with her. I knew Derek was listening in and probably shared my worry. Was he rallying the police to get ready to charge? Maybe Gabriel had told them to wait until he'd riled her up enough to pull a gun on him. I was not happy about that possibility.

I had no doubt that flying bullets could go through the plasterboard wall separating me from Alice's gun. Nervously, I glanced around the dark closet. That's when I noticed the stack of books perched dangerously on the shelf above me. They were set to fall right on my head at the slightest shake-up. If Alice started shooting, I wouldn't have to worry about bullets. I'd be knocked out by flying books.

With extreme care, I reached up and pushed the stack back from the edge so it wouldn't tumble. A heavy sharpening stone lay on the top book and began to totter, then started to fall directly toward me. I reached to grab it but only managed to deflect it. It slammed against the wall and fell to the floor.

"What the hell was that?" Alice sputtered.

Seconds later, the closet door was yanked open and I stared into the flashing eyes of Alice Fairchild. Gabriel stood behind her, staring at me in horror.

"Well, look who's here," she said, and turned to glare at Gabriel. "It's your little friend. This your idea?"

"I barely know her," Gabriel said. He grabbed my arm and pulled me out of the closet. "What're you doing in there?"

By the time I brushed off my pants and Gabriel shoved me into the room, Alice had her gun out and pointed in my direction. Gabriel quickly stepped in front to protect me.

"Still playing the hero, Gabriel?" she said with scorn, and jerked the gun toward the chairs lined up along the wall of windows. "Sit down, both of you."

We moved in that direction.

"Put the gun down, Mary Grace," Gabriel said. "Are you going to keep killing everyone who works here?"

"If I have to." She glared at me. "Brooklyn, what the hell were you doing in there?"

"I came out of the bathroom and heard a noise down here. I came to check it out. Then you walked in and started talking. Book scams? Layla's murder? What's going on here, Alice?"

"Shut up." She paced in front of me. "I need to think."

I chose to take it as a good sign that she had to think before shooting. I stole a look at Gabriel. He stood leaning against the side counter with his arms folded tightly across his chest and his jaw clenched. He glowered at me and I couldn't blame him. We both knew Derek was going crazy right now. I expected him to storm the room at any second.

"Look, Alice," I said, "I know the police inspector on this case. I can talk to her. You can plea bargain—"

"Shut up, Brooklyn," she said. "There's no way I'm going to prison."

As she paced, a waft of incense flitted my way, jogging my memory. Incense was what Karalee said she had smelled the night Minka was attacked. Incense. I recalled a small can of patchouli-scented spray on the sink in the bathroom. Alice had haunted the bathroom constantly. She must've used the spray that night.

The door burst open, but it wasn't Derek or the police.

It was Minka. "Is my coat in here?"

Alice whipped around, her gun pointed directly at Minka.

"Where the hell did Ned put our coats?" Minka asked, then noticed the gun. "What the fu—"

"Minka!" I shouted. "Alice is the one who attacked you. She hit you with a hammer and left you for dead."

Alice turned around and shoved me. "I told you to shut the hell up."

"That was you?" Minka said, her eyes bulging.

Alice whirled back at Minka, waving the gun. "You shut up, too! What's with you bitches? Move over there and sit down. I need to think."

Minka gasped and repeated, "That was you?"

"I said, get over there!" Alice jerked the gun in my direction, but Minka didn't care. Bullheaded, she stomped right up and punched Alice in the face.

"Ooh," I said, cringing. I'd been on the receiving end of that left hook. Minka packed a wallop.

Alice wavered, stunned. Then she rallied, lifting the gun and aiming it directly at Minka. "You cow!"

But Minka was like a caged beast let loose. She jumped on Alice and screeched, "You could've killed me!"

"Stone," Gabriel yelled. "Get in here."

Seconds later, Derek raced into the room, gun drawn, followed by four or five cops. He saw me and shouted, "Get over here."

But I was trapped. Minka was now on Alice's back and she was kicking her legs every which way. I couldn't get past them.

Minka grabbed hold of a good chunk of Alice's hair and pulled with all her might. Alice screamed as her head jerked back and she dropped the gun.

I scrambled to retrieve it, then scurried back to avoid being kicked in the head by Minka's deadly feet.

Gabriel moved closer and tried to grab Minka, but it was impossible to get hold of the two women locked in writhing combat.

Alice kept turning and bucking, fighting to get Minka off her back, but it was like trying to remove a giant tick. Minka wasn't letting go. She got her hands around Alice's neck and started squeezing. That did it. Alice was so enraged that she finally flung Minka off.

Minka flew right into me and the gun went off.

The bullet shattered a window. Alice screamed and ducked.

Gabriel jumped and wrestled Alice to the ground. One of the cops grabbed Minka but quickly regretted it, as Minka was still in swinging mode. Her fist caught his ear. The cop staggered back, to be replaced by two more. Finally, they subdued her.

Derek jogged around the piles of bodies and grabbed the gun lying on the floor. He shoved it into the waistband of his jeans, then yanked me into his arms.

"We're going to have a long talk later," he whispered against my hair.

"I understand," I said, shaking. "Just please get me out of here first."

Chapter 21

The police insisted that we stay.

It was just as well, because I wanted to see with my own eyes that Mary Grace Flanagan, aka Alice Fairchild, was led away in handcuffs and thrown in jail for as long as possible. I savored the fact that, as she departed, she was snarling and feisty, no longer the demure princess she'd pretended to be for the past month.

And talk about snarling, Minka was still complaining to anyone who would listen. She told the police she planned to press charges and insisted they take pictures of her head wound for evidence.

The door was open and I could hear party sounds down the hall. Had anyone heard the gun go off or the window shatter? I almost hoped they hadn't. I would hate for anyone to be fearful of coming to BABA, now that the true threat was gone.

"Stone."

We both turned. Gabriel had his hand held out and Derek shook it firmly. "Gabriel. Well done."

"Maybe," he said. He appeared more tranquil. Tired around the eyes, but stronger physically. He'd acted so heroically, leading Alice into a perfect trap, then standing in front of me when she drew her gun. Now he glanced at the empty doorway and bared his teeth. "Mary Grace will have her lawyer cut her loose within hours and she'll disappear again."

"She'd better not," I said intently.

Gabriel looked at me. "She did a number on you, didn't she?"

I shrugged, trying to brush off the lingering sense of betrayal. "I was a little too trusting, but it won't happen again."

"Babe," he said, and reached out to touch my cheek. "Trust looks good on you."

I shook my head, not quite believing him, then grabbed him in a fierce hug. "Thank you for saving me."

He chuckled without humor. "I almost got you shot."

"I mean that first time. On Fillmore."

He gave me a brief squeeze and I breathed in his distinctive scent of earth and spice. Then I stepped back, close to Derek, who put his hand on my back.

"Do you need a ride to Dharma, Gabriel?" Derek asked.

"Got it covered," Gabriel said, then winked at me. "Nice little town you've got up there, babe. I might stick around." He flashed me a sexy grin, then walked away. At the doorway, he stopped and turned, then held up his arm to show me he was still wearing my mother's tacky herbal healing bracelet. We traded smiles, and I whispered a quick prayer that he would indeed stick around.

"Are you all right?" Derek asked, pulling me close in a protective embrace.

"Yes," I said, staring at the now empty doorway. "Derek, was it my imagination or did you know Gabriel before two days ago?"

His mouth curved as he smoothed my hair away from my face. "Your imagination is vast."

That was a nonanswer if I'd ever heard one, but I let it go for now. The police continued wrapping things up. One of the crime scene guys slipped the gun in an evidence bag and carried it away. Awhile ago, I'd seen both Ned and

Naomi walk by the open door, accompanied by officers, to be interviewed. And Minka was still whining.

I gave Derek a meaningful glance. "I can't take her anymore. Can we please leave?"

"I think it's safe to go."

But we stopped as the classroom door swung open and Naomi came running in. When she saw me, she gave me a gentle hug. "Oh, thank God you're safe!"

"Thanks, Naomi."

Then she saw Minka and gasped. She headed straight for her and grabbed her in a bone-crushing bear hug. "Oh, Minka, I just heard the news! Alice was arrested, thanks to you! And you saved Brooklyn's life!"

"Get away from me," Minka balked, pushing her back.

"But you're the hero of the day!"

"Don't you ever shut up?" Minka groused, then did a double take. "Wait a minute. What did you just say?"

"I said, you're the hero of the—"

"No, before that."

"You mean the part where you saved Brooklyn's life?" Naomi asked. "I heard all about it. You could've been shot but you forged ahead anyway. And Brooklyn is alive, thanks to you!"

"Oh, screw a moose." Minka flashed me a murderous glare. "I did *not* just save her life."

"You did!" Naomi cried, and hugged her again. "You're a hero."

"Stop saying that!" Minka yelled, and squirmed out of Naomi's grasp.

"But, Minka, it's—"

"Shut up!" Minka slapped her hands to her ears so she wouldn't have to hear the dreaded words, then shrieked again, "Shut up, shut up, shut up!"

"Jeez, Minka, scream a little louder," I said, rubbing my own ear. "I don't think they heard you in Saskatchewan."

She shook her fist at me. "You shut up, too!"

"Look at the bright side," I said, waving her off. "Now we're even. I don't owe you and you don't owe me."

"Well, that works, too," Naomi said cheerfully.

On impulse, I gave Naomi a hug. Even though she'd tried to be the bitch and thief her aunt was, she would never make it. She was just too good-hearted to pull it off. "Thanks, sweetie."

Naomi smiled tentatively as she let go of me. "I'm sorry about all the controversy. I'll sell you the *Oliver Twist* for a fair price as soon as the police let me have it."

"Oh, that's wonderful," I said, satisfied with the sense of closure I felt. The book would be a fitting memento of the ring of thieves we'd all had a hand in breaking up.

"You deserve it," she said, then smiled at Minka. "So, I guess everything works out for the best."

"Whatever," Minka said, then turned and snapped at me, "And I don't owe you a damn thing."

"Works for me." It felt more than right to go back to being enemies, as if we'd ever stopped. I gazed at Derek as I wound my arm through his. "I think we're done here."

Naomi tilted her head and studied Minka. "You know, Minka, I've tried and tried to be nice to you, but I've finally figured out what the problem is."

Minka pretended interest. "Oh, do tell."

Naomi planted her hand on her hip. "You're just a mean bitch. And I'm sick of dealing with mean bitches."

Minka's laugh was harsh. "Whatever. God, you're lame."

"Fine. I may be lame, but you're fired." Naomi swiveled on her toe and walked out.

And the crowd went wild! Well, I did anyway. Internally. After all, Minka was still in pummeling range and I didn't want to make myself a bigger target for her wrath than I already was.

And I would never admit this to Minka, but it had done my heart good to watch her riding Alice Fairchild like a rodeo star. I would always look fondly on the memory of Minka LaBoeuf clinging to that psycho little blonde like the blood-sucking tick that she was.

It was almost surreal to see that the party was still going strong. People laughed and toasted and mingled among the shelves of books and displays.

As I stood arm in arm with Derek, I could see Gunther Schnaubel signaling to him as he pushed his way through the crowd. What did he want now?

Karalee ran up and hugged me. "You won the Peachey knives. Congratulations."

"They already announced the auction winners?"

"Awhile ago," she said. "I shouldn't really congratulate you since we were bidding against each other for almost every prize."

"Sorry," I said, not really meaning it but trying to be nice.

She grinned. "That's okay. I won the other Peachey knife."

"The ergonomic one?"

"Yes, it's so cool."

"I'd love to try it out sometime," I said.

We talked more about the auction, and bookbinding equipment and classes, all the normal stuff. Then our conversation switched to Alice and Layla. Karalee wanted to know what had happened and I wanted to tell her. But I couldn't concentrate because Gunther was talking to Derek now, discussing their plans to return to London in the morning.

My chest felt tight. Derek was leaving and we still hadn't managed any real alone time. And now he was mad at me for sneaking into the closet against his orders. He didn't look particularly angry, but he also hadn't mentioned the two of us heading off for that deserted island anytime soon.

Unable to hear any more of their travel conversation, I

grabbed hold of Karalee's hand. "Let's go see who else won the auction prizes."

"Okay," she said cheerfully.

I snagged a glass of champagne from a passing waiter's tray and stared blindly at the list of auction winners.

So, Derek would leave tomorrow.

I took a long, stiff swallow of the bubbly liquid. I'd known from day one that he would go eventually, and I'd been determined from the start to stay strong. I could handle this. I would smile and wish him a safe flight home, back to where he belonged. And then I would go on with my life. I had friends, a great job, a wonderful family.

I would miss him, of course, but I would survive. It might be touch and go for a little while because, after all, I'd grown rather used to having him around. We'd become close. Very close. Not close enough, but I liked him a lot. I suppose you could say I liked him more than any man I'd ever known before.

But still, he was a dangerous habit I would have to break myself of. It should be simple enough. After all, he was geographically undesirable, to say the least. Thousands of miles and an ocean separated us and nothing could change that. I'd cured myself of bad habits before. I could do it again. And I would. Eventually.

Karalee drifted off to talk to others and I sipped my champagne alone.

"There you are, Brooklyn."

I turned to greet Cynthia Hardesty.

"I'm in total shock about timid little Alice," she admitted. "But I have to tell you, I still won't mourn Layla too much."

"I understand," I said. And I was right there with her, but I wasn't going to say it out loud.

With the party still in high gear, rumors were flying. The police had tried to be subtle, but with the catfight between Alice and Minka and the gunshot and the police interviews going on, it wasn't surprising that word had gotten out about what had gone down in the back room.

She continued, "We've already told Naomi we want her to be the acting director for the next three months."

"Good."

"We'll see how she does. Then we'll make our final decision. I have a feeling she'll do just fine."

"I think you're right," I said, and meant it. Naomi had been a pill but she'd also been under duress. Maybe with Layla gone and Alice dragged off to jail, Naomi would have a chance to shine.

"See you in class tomorrow," Cynthia said, and turned to greet another friend.

Wow, class was tomorrow night already? It felt like an age had passed since I'd been in the classroom. But now I figured teaching might be one good way I could fill my time for the foreseeable future. Maybe I could sign on to do classes every night. Then I might not feel Derek's absence quite as keenly.

Ned walked up and lifted his chin in greeting. "Huh."

"Hey, Ned, how's it going?"

He stared across the room at one of the police officers who had taken Alice away. "She was bad."

I was watching Alice, so Ned's words took a moment to sink in. "Wait, were you talking about Alice when you said that before?"

"Huh."

"Alice? Not Layla?"

He shuffled his feet, nervous now that I'd raised my voice.

"You couldn't just say her name?" I chided. "It might've saved us all a lot of trouble."

"Huh," he said, and his mouth curved up. "You're smart."

I rolled my eyes. Yeah, I was real smart. "See you around, Ned."

Before he could wander off, I heard, "Meow."

I looked down and saw Baba the cat, another creature who *saw things*. Guess he wasn't talking, either.

"Hey, buddy, there you are," Ned said. "I was wondering where you ran off to. You hungry? Me, too." He reached down and picked up the cat, who nuzzled his neck ecstatically.

"Yeah, you're my friend, aren't you?" Ned held the cat up in the air and stared at him. " 'Specially when you're looking to get fed."

"Meow."

"Come on, then. Let's go chow down." He clutched the cat close and lifted one hand in farewell to me, then wandered off down the hall.

I walked away, shaking my head. Ned talked to the cat more than he talked to humans. Maybe he was on to something.

"I was looking for you," Derek said, wrapping his arm around my waist. I pressed myself against his solid chest and felt the soft leather of his jacket against my cheek. His uniquely masculine scent filled my senses. I breathed in deeply before breaking contact.

"Ready to go?" I asked brightly, determined not to be an idiot in front of him. I would make our last evening together a cheery one. I refused to cry, to make a scene, to make him uncomfortable. I would wish him well and let him go. End of story. Piece of cake.

We walked toward the front door and I glanced around, desperate for conversation starters. Why did I feel so lame, all of a sudden?

"Are you packed?" I asked.

"No."

"Oh. Did you get something to eat?"

"No."

"Did you want to go by your hotel?" I asked.

"No."

"Okay. Well, all righty then."

He pushed the door open and I stepped outside, directly into the path of a frigid evening breeze. The fog had rolled in over the water and dusk shrouded the city in shadows. I shuddered and he pulled me closer as we walked to the Bentley.

I rested my head against his shoulder and tried to sound casual. "Just when I'm getting used to having you around, it's time for you to leave."

"Are you?"

"Am I what?"

"Getting used to having me around?"

"Well, yes." I patted his chest. "But I couldn't help overhearing your conversation with Gunther. I know you're leaving tomorrow."

"Oh, you do?"

"Yes, that's why I was asking if you were all packed."

"Ah." He studied my face and asked, "How do you feel about my leaving?"

He had to ask? I took a deep breath, then tried for a tone of casual friendliness. "I'll miss you, of course, but I know you have to get back. You have a business to run, and I'm sure your family must miss you."

"Yes, I'm sure they miss me terribly."

"And the people at your company must miss you, too."

His lips twisted in a smile. "I have no doubt all eight hundred and twelve of them miss me every day."

"There you go." What a brave little thing I was. Then I realized what he'd said and my jaw dropped. "Wait. You have over eight hundred employees?"

He shrugged. "Security is in high demand."

"I guess."

He studied me as he pulled a small thin case from his inside pocket. "Let me give you my business card so we can be sure to keep in touch."

Keep in touch.

Now, why did he have to go and say that? I felt my throat close up completely, which caused my eyes to water. It was just a physical reaction to the weather. Nothing more.

"I'd like that," I whispered, hating that my voice trembled. I slipped his card into my pants pocket, then looked away, not able to make eye contact, unwilling to make more of a fool of myself than I already had.

"Yes, I'd like that, too," he said.

I cleared my throat. "I remember when you first arrived, you said you'd tried to stay away, so I'll understand if you do this time."

"You'll understand if I do."

I knew my smile was wobbly but I forced myself to continue. "Stay away, I mean. It's hard to stay in touch when there's such a distance separating us, but if you do happen to come through town sometime, it would be lovely to see you again."

Could I have sounded more lame? Tears were blurring my eyes but I blamed it on the cold air.

"Would it?"

"Yes, it would." I turned away to dab my eyes.

He took my chin in his hand to steer me back to look at him. "Are you all right?"

I sniffled, then shook away this maudlin nonsense and smiled tightly. "The cold is making my eyes water. No big deal. So, it's your last evening in town. Anything special you'd like to do?"

"A few things," he admitted, still watching me. "But, Brooklyn, I'm not pleased by the way you brushed off my suggestion that we keep in touch. You didn't even look at my new business card, and I'll have you know I paid a pretty penny for them."

Disappointed, I glared at him. "You're annoyed with me because I didn't look at your business card?"

"Well, yes. You shoved it in your pocket without giving it a proper glance. I'm quite put out."

I stopped in my tracks. Was he trying to pick a fight with me? "You're kidding, right?"

"Read the damn card, Brooklyn."

"For God's sake." Frustrated, I brushed away angry tears. My heart was breaking and he wanted me to read his stupid business card? Selfish man! I pulled the card out and forced myself to study it. My eyes widened and I read it again. "Is this . . . are you . . . is this some kind of cruel joke?"

"Hell, no, it's not a joke." He yanked open the Bentley's passenger door, then blocked my way into the car. "Why would I joke about this? Those cards are damned expensive. Top-quality stock, engraved by the Queen's own royal stationers. Cost me an arm and a leg, but it was worth it, I think. And you ask if it's a joke? It most certainly is not a—"

"Shut up," I whispered, and planted my lips on his.

"Rude wench," he muttered against my mouth.

I laughed. I must've dropped his extremely expensive hand-engraved card as I wrapped my arms around his neck, but that was okay. I'd already memorized the Nob Hill address that would serve as the new San Francisco headquarters for Stone Security.

"You asked if there was something special I'd like to do tonight," he said. "There is."

"What's that?" I asked.

"You," he murmured.

Delighted, I smiled up at him. "Then let's go home."

Brooklyn's Glossary

Parts of the Book

Boards—Usually made of stiff cardboard (or, occasionally, wood) and covered in fabric (cloth, paper, leather).
Covering—Cloth, paper, or leather fabric used to cover the boards.
Endband—Small ornamental band of cloth glued at the top and bottom of the inside of the spine, used to give a polished finish to the book (also called a headband or tailband).
Endsheets—The first and last sheets of the textblock that are pasted to the inside of the cover board; the pastedown.
Flyleaf—First one or two blank pages of a book, not pasted to the inside of the cover board. These pages protect the inner pages of the textblock.
Foredge—The front edge of the textblock opposite the spine edge. The edge is usually smooth but may, on occasion, be rough, or deckled. The edge may be gilded or, in rare instances, painted. Fore-edge painting gained popularity in the seventeenth century when religious or pastoral scenes were painted onto the foredge to embellish the book's content. The painting was invisible until the pages were fanned in a certain direction.
Grain—The direction in which the fibers are aligned in the paper. When grain direction runs parallel to the spine, the paper folds will be straighter and stronger and the pages will lie flat.

Head—The top of the book.
Hinge—Inside the book cover, this is the thin, flexible line where the pastedown and flyleaf meet and is the most easily damaged part of the book.
Joint—Outside the book at the point between the edge of the spine and the hard cover that corresponds with the inside hinge. Its flexibility allows the book to open and close.
Linen tapes—Strips of linen sewn onto the signatures and used to hold the signatures together. The tapes run perpendicular across the spine edge and are pasted down between the cover boards and the endsheets.
Pastedown—*See* Endsheets.
Signature—A gathering of papers that are folded and sewn to make up the textblock or the pages of a book.
Spine—The back edge of a book, where the pages are sewn and glued.
Swell—Term that indicates the way paper lies after folding. Generally, the folded edges of a stack of paper will be thicker than the outer edges. Consolidating and rounding the textblock will reduce swell and allow the book to lie flat and even.
Tail—The bottom of the book, where it rests when shelved upright.
Textblock—The sections of paper sheets or signatures sewn through the fold onto linen tapes.

Other Bookbinding Terms

Conservation—The care and preservation of books, often at a total resource level—that is, a library or the archives of an institution. Conservators will take into consideration the damaging effects of age, use, and environment (including light, heat, humidity, and other natural enemies of paper, cloth, and leather) and strive to apply their knowledge of bookbinding, restoration, chemistry, and technology to the restoration and protection of the collection under their care.
Consolidation—Once the textblock is sewn and pressed, the spine should be consolidated (that is, compressed, in a

press) and coated with adhesive (PVA). When consolidation is completed (the glue is dry), the texblock is rounded by pushing and pounding against the sections, first one side, then the other, with a bookbinders hammer.

Kettle—The kettle actually refers to the first and last holes (usually found at each end of the page) where the stitching together of the signature pages begins and ends (or reverses back to the beginning). The kettle stitch refers to the stitch used to sew one signature page to the next, linking the next page to the previous one, as well as binding the linen tapes to the textblock.

Restoration—The process of returning a book to as close to its original condition as possible. A book restoration specialist will pay close attention to the materials and techniques in use at the time the book was first made, and will attempt to follow those guidelines in terms of resewing, rebinding, and reconstructing the book. This is in contrast to book *repair*, which does not encompass restoration or conservation but focuses strictly on bringing a book back to its basic functional level (which may or may not involve duct tape).

Rounding—The process of hammering or manipulating the textblock spine into a curved shape after gluing and before backing. Rounding diminishes the effect of swelling and helps to keep a book standing upright on a shelf.

Some Basic Bookmaking Tools

Awl—Used for punching sewing holes in folded paper.

Bone folder—A tool used for making sharp creases in folded paper and smoothing out surfaces that have been glued. It is generally made of bone and is shaped like a wooden tongue depressor.

Bookbinders hammer—Used for rounding the spine of a book, a bookbinders hammer is smaller and lighter than a carpenter's hammer, with a large, flat, polished pounding surface.

Book press—There are various types. One small type of wood press can be used to hold the textblock while gluing.

With a newly finished book, a large brass press will help strengthen, straighten, and fuse the book together.

Punching jig or Punching cradle—A V-shaped piece of equipment with a slim opening at the bottom for cradling signatures in order to punch holes in them.

PVA (polyvinyl acetate)—Preferred adhesive in bookbinding, it is liquid and flexible and results in a permanent bond. It dries colorless and is pH neutral, so it is recommended for archival work.

Turn the page for a sneak peek at Brooklyn Wainwright's next mystery adventure in

Murder Under Cover

the fourth Bibliophile Mystery, available from Obsidian in May 2011.

"You're having sex!" my best friend, Robin, cried as soon as I opened the door. "I mean, not currently, thank God, but recently. Oh, I'm so happy for you!"

"Say it a little louder, why don't you?" I yanked her into my apartment and quickly shut the door behind her. "I don't think they heard you in Petaluma."

She dropped her bags on my worktable and pulled me into a hug. "Your closest neighbors are two gay guys. Do you really think they care?"

"It's nobody's business," I grumbled. "I'm not even going to ask how you can tell."

"It's a gift." She patted my cheek. "Besides, just look at you. You're glowing."

"Don't be ridiculous," I said, feeling my cheeks warm up. So maybe she was right—maybe I was glowing. But did she have to point it out to the world?

Robin Tully had been my BFF for years, ever since we were eight years old and our parents joined the same spiritual commune in the hills of Sonoma County. We first bonded over Barbie dolls, Johnny Depp, and a mutual disgust of dirt. Since then, all that dirt had transformed itself into the upscale town of Dharma, a wine-country destination spot for Bay Area foodies. But back in the day, it was backwoods enough to make two fastidious little girls go berserk.

Robin grinned, amused by my reaction. Then she scooped up her bags from the table. "I brought wine and presents."

"I ordered pizza," I said, leading the way down the short hall to my living area.

"I'd kill for pizza."

"No need. I'll share." I pulled two wineglasses from the kitchen shelf and set them on the smooth wood surface of the bar that separated my kitchen from the living room. "I missed you a lot. How was India?"

"India was exotic and wonderful and smoggy, and I missed you, too." She pulled a bottle of wine from one of her bags and handed it to me to open. "And I missed showers. And ice cream. And hamburgers."

"The pizza's got sausage and pepperoni."

"Oh, God, meat." She closed her eyes and sighed. "It sounds like heaven."

"I have ice cream, too."

"I love you—have I told you lately?"

With a laugh, I poured the wine and handed her the glass. "Welcome home."

"Thanks." We clinked glasses, and she took a good long drink. "You have no idea how happy I am to be back."

The doorbell rang, and I ran to pay the pizza deliveryman. After piling pizza and salad onto plates and pouring more wine, we sat in the living room to eat.

Besides Robin's work as a sculptor, she owned a small travel company that specialized in tours of sacred destinations all over the world. Stone circles, pyramids, Gothic cathedrals, harmonic power centers. Her tours catered to the adventurous seeker of esoteric knowledge who had tons of cash to throw her way. She had just returned from a three-week tour of India.

So for three long weeks I'd been gnashing my teeth, unable to share my exciting news—specifically, the news about me and my mysterious British boyfriend—with my closest friend. And Robin had guessed it the very first second she saw me. I supposed that's what the whole BFF thing was all about.

We opened another bottle of wine as she regaled me with the highlights of her India trip and I filled her in on all the news about me and Derek Stone, the hunky British security expert I'd met a few months back during a murder investigation. Yes, we'd done the deed, as she'd shouted to the world earlier. And yes, he was opening a San Francisco branch of Stone Security. So yes, he was currently staying with me, but no, he wasn't home just now. He was currently flying back from Kuala Lumpur where he'd provided security for an installation of priceless artwork from the Louvre.

And yes, I'd been threatened by another vicious killer. Robin had been packing to leave for India at the time and wasn't around to hear the entire story, so I filled her in on all the gory details. The killer was safely tucked away in jail now. And that was my last three weeks in a nutshell.

As we cleared the dishes, I figured it was time to ask Robin the burning question I'd avoided long enough.

"So, did you see your mother?" I asked cautiously.

Robin scowled. "Yes, and she's as annoying as ever."

That was no big surprise. She and her mother, Shiva Quinn, had always had issues.

Shiva's real name was Myra Tully, and she had been raised by missionaries. Suffice to say, Myra had a real savior complex from the get-go. In the 1970s, Myra had accompanied the Beatles to India to see Maharishi Mahesh Yogi. While there, she changed her name to Shiva Quinn. No one was sure where *Quinn* came from. As for *Shiva*, Robin always thought it was telling that her mother had named herself after the supreme god of Hinduism.

When Robin was really irritated with Shiva, she'd call her Myra.

It didn't help that her mother was tall, glamorous, and model thin. She was sophisticated and interesting, and everyone loved to be around her. Her missionary upbringing had given her a sense of awareness of the world and its problems, which led her to become the spokesperson for a humanitarian organization called Feed the World.

By the time Robin was ten years old, her mother was traveling constantly, returning home every few months for only a day or so. But that was okay with me, because when Shiva left the commune, Robin would stay at my house. We had a slumber party every night. I would've been happy if Shiva stayed away permanently, but I could never have said that to Robin.

"How long did you visit with her?" I asked as I started the dishwasher.

"Three excruciating days." Robin laughed dryly. "She's such a drama queen. She couldn't settle in London or Paris. No, she had to go live in Varanasi. I swear she thinks she's Mother Teresa in Prada. Never mind. I promised myself I wouldn't bitch about her, but it's always so tempting. Anyway, Varanasi itself was awesome. I'll probably return with a tour group sometime. I saw the Monkey Temple and walked for hours along the ghats overlooking the Ganges. It was amazing. I have pictures. I'll send you the link."

"Great. It sounds fascinating."

"It was, and my mother sent you something."

"Me?"

"Yes." She held up one of the bags she'd brought with her. "Do you want to see it?"

"Of course I do."

"Let's go to your workroom."

My curiosity piqued, I followed her to the front room of my loft where I did my bookbinding work. I pulled two tall chairs close together, and we sat at my worktable. Robin turned the bag on its side and slid the contents out onto the surface. It was a worn leather satchel.

"It's . . . a bag," I said. "How thoughtful."

Robin chuckled. "Wait for it. You know my mother. We must build the suspense."

She unbuckled the satchel and pulled out a wadded old swath of Indian-print material.

"Um, is it a scarf?" I said, touching the faded, scratchy woven fabric. Once, it might've been dark green with burgundy and orange swirls of paisley, but it was so old and thin now, I could almost see through it. Colorful beads, tiny brass animal shapes, and bits of mirrored glass were woven into the fabric. "Is this really for me?"

"Hell, no." Robin wrinkled her nose at the matted material. "That's just to protect what's inside. It's my mother's idea of wrapping paper, I guess."

"Ah."

"But do you know, she actually thought I would love to wear it? She just doesn't get me. Never did." Resigned, she flicked one of the silvery beads.

"No, she never did." The threadbare fabric had an ethnic style that was intriguing, but I knew Robin wouldn't be caught dead wearing it. I fingered the cloth again, then said carefully, "Maybe your mom's been in India a little too long."

"You think?" She shook her head as she gingerly unwrapped the cloth. "Okay, get ready." She pulled the last of the fabric away. "This is for you."

"Oh, my God," I whispered.

It was a book. The most exquisite jeweled book I'd ever seen. And possibly the oldest. It was large, about twelve inches tall by nine inches wide, and maybe an inch and a half thick. I suppressed the urge to whip out my metal ruler.

The solid red leather binding was decorated with heavy gilding and precious gems. Chunky red teardrop-shaped rubies were affixed to each corner. Small round sapphires lined the circular center where a gilded peacock spread its tail feathers. Tiny diamonds, emeralds and rubies were encrusted into the feathers. The borders of the book were thickly gilded, but some of the gold had flaked off, and the red leather was rubbed and faded in spots.

"Peacocks are the national bird of India," Robin said. "Did you know that?"

"I had no idea." I picked up the book and studied the fore-edge. With the book closed, the pages were deckled, or uneven. I could tell without opening the book that the paper itself was thick vellum.

I checked the spine. It read *Vatsyayana*. I looked up at Robin. "What is this?"

"Open it and find out."

"I'm almost afraid." But I opened the front cover and turned to the title page. "You're kidding."

"Nope."

"The Kama Sutra?"

"Yes." Robin grinned. "Mommy dearest wants it refurbished and evaluated."

My eyes widened. "I can take it apart?"

She laughed. "I guess, but you don't have to sound so excited about it."

"Are you serious? I live for that."

"Good times." She sipped her wine.

"It is for me." I stroked the spine, counting the ribs. "But I wonder why she wants me to do the work."

"Apparently, Abraham visited her a few years ago and talked you up."

"Really?" I smiled. Abraham had been my bookbinding teacher for years. I turned another page slowly, unwilling to disturb the binding too much. The book was at least three hundred years old, and I was shocked to see that it was written in English. But then, the English had ruled India for centuries, so I supposed that made sense.

I turned to a page near the middle of the book and saw an illustration of a couple having sex in a most fascinating style. I closed it quickly. Then I couldn't help but sneak another peek.

"Wow, it's all hand painted," I said after clearing my throat. "Isn't that interesting?"

"Yeah, it's all about the strokes. Paint strokes, I mean. Beautiful."

We both began to giggle. It must've been the wine.

Robin let out a deep breath. "Well, hey, speaking of sex . . ."

"Were we?"

She laughed. "Well, sort of." She waved her hands as if to get rid of that thought. "And I'm not talking about the sex you're having. It's about me. I met a man."

"Oh." That got my attention. "In India?"

"No, here in San Francisco, on the way home from the airport. I was starving, so I stopped at Kasa to get some food to go. He was waiting for his order, and we struck up a conversation."

"You went to Kasa after coming back from India?"

She laughed again. Kasa was part of a small local chain of good Indian restaurants. "I still had a taste for the food. But that's not important just now."

"You're right. So who's this guy?"

"He's . . ." She looked baffled. "He's . . . wonderful."

"Okay," I said slowly. "What's his name?"

"Michael." She smiled softly. "He's an engineer—can you believe it? He was born in Ukraine, but he's lived here forever. His family calls him Mischa. Isn't that cute? He's great. Really handsome and funny. And smart."

"You found all that out while waiting for to-go food?"

"We ended up grabbing a table and eating there together. It was a great conversation, and we found out we actually have a lot of stuff in common. He's wonderful, you'll see. We're going out tomorrow night."

I stared at her in surprise. "Oh, no, you're blushing. You never blush. You really like him."

"Give me a break." She rolled her eyes. "I blush sometimes. But yeah, I like him."

Disconcerted, I glanced down at the Kama Sutra and decided that further inspection could wait. I closed the book and looked up at Robin. "Okay, he sounds great, but I have to ask why you're seeing Mr. Wonderful when you're in love with my brother."

Her lips twisted into a frown. "Austin hasn't made any moves in my direction lately."

I frowned, too. "Well, it's not like you live in the same neighborhood anymore. He's going to have to make an effort to come after you."

"Yes, he is," she said wistfully. "Look, he traveled and partied for years, and now he's ready to settle down back home in Dharma and run the winery. But I'm not ready to do that, yet. Not that he's asked me to."

I sighed. "I don't want my brother to blow this."

"I don't want him to, either. But I'm not going to sit at home waiting for the phone to ring, either."

She looked like she could have used a hug so I jumped off the chair and wrapped my arms around her. "You know I love you, no matter what happens. So for now, I'll just hope you have a good time with Mr. Wonderful."

"Yoo-hoo!"

We both jolted in surprise. I turned and saw my neighbors Jeremy and Sergio poking their heads through my open door. I guess I hadn't locked it earlier.

"Hi, guys," I said. "Come on in. You remember Robin, right?"

"Of course," Jeremy said, waving both of his hands at us.

Sergio gave me a hug, then said, "Hi, Robin."

"We're sorry to bug you," Jeremy said, pacing around my workroom, staring at the shelves. "But I'm preparing for my performance art debut at the Castro Street Fair, and I'm hunting for accessories. Do you have a boa or any girlie hats or big jewelry?"

"Big jewelry isn't really my style," I said, "but I probably have a hat you could use."

"I have lots of pretty things at home," Robin said.

"Your stuff is probably too nice for what he wants," Sergio said. Then he whispered, "He's presenting an homage to the homeless."

"Yeah, the tackier, the better," Jeremy said. "Ooh, what's this?" He grabbed the funky Indian scarf and wrapped it around his neck.

"It's yours if you want it," Robin said.

"I love it. It's so scruffy."

"I have other stuff you can look at," I said.

"No, this is perfect. Shabby but colorful." Jeremy scurried over to the small mirror hanging near the front door and tossed the length of the scarf back and forth and over his head. "I love the sparkly beads. It's kind of me, don't you think?"

"Yes, it's you," Robin insisted. "Take it. I'll never wear it. My mother is insane to think I would."

"Would you guys like a glass of wine?" I asked.

The men exchanged a look; then Jeremy shrugged. "If you insist."

"I'll get the wine," Robin said, laughing. "You show them your sexy new book."

"You have a sexy book?" Sergio said, moving closer to the worktable. He was fascinated with my bookbinding work. "Is this it?" He touched the spine of the Kama Sutra.

"Yes, and wait till you see it," I said, excited all over again. I opened the book and turned to the page Robin and I had been peeking at earlier.

Jeremy began to squeal and slapped my arm. "You naughty girl."

"This is fantastic," Sergio said in awe as he carefully touched the outer edge of the book. "Maybe I'll take that bookbinding class you teach after all."

The following night, Derek returned from his Kuala Lumpur trip. I made pasta with a creamy tomato-vodka sauce, and we drank an Etude pinot noir I'd been saving for a special occasion. Our relationship was new enough that Derek coming to stay at my house definitely qualified as a special occasion.

After dinner, we snuggled on the couch. In my wildest imagination, I never would've used the word *snuggle* in regard to the ruggedly masculine Derek Stone. But there we were, snuggled. And I felt completely satisfied with life.

Of course, the next thing I knew, Derek was sound asleep. Jet lag had hit him hard. I dragged him off to bed where he continued to sleep like a dead man.

It was five o'clock in the morning when the pounding began.

"What the hell is that?" Derek muttered.

"I don't know," I said, sounding whiny as I punched my pillow. Were they cleaning the streets? The pounding continued, so I finally tossed the covers back, sat up, and mumbled, "I hope it's not the little kids that just moved in down the hall. That won't make for good neighborly relations. I'd better go find out."

I grabbed my short robe and threw it on, then stood on wobbly legs as the pounding grew louder. It wasn't coming from outside, I realized. There was someone knocking at my front door.

Then I heard the screaming.

Derek jumped out of bed. "Stay here."

Ignoring his command, I raced after him down the hall, through the living room and out to the workshop. I skidded to a halt behind him as he threw the door open.

It was Robin and she continued to scream as tears rolled down her cheeks. She was covered in blood.

Kate Carlisle

Homicide in Hardcover

A Bibliophile Mystery

The streets of San Francisco would be lined with hardcovers if rare book expert Brooklyn Wainwright had her way. And her mentor wouldn't be lying in a pool of his own blood on the eve of a celebration for his latest book restoration.

With his final breath he leaves Brooklyn a cryptic message, and gives her a priceless—and supposedly cursed—copy of Goethe's *Faust* for safekeeping.

Brooklyn suddenly finds herself accused of murder and theft, thanks to the humorless—but attractive—British security officer who finds her kneeling over the body. Now she has to read the clues left behind by her mentor if she is going to restore justice...

Kate Collins

The Flower Shop Mystery Series

Abby Knight is the proud owner of her hometown flower shop. She has a gift for arranging flowers—and for solving crimes.

Mum's the Word
Slay It with Flowers
Dearly Depotted
Snipped in the Bud
Acts of Violets
A Rose from the Dead
Shoots to Kill
Evil in Carnations
Sleeping with Anemone
Dirty Rotten Tendrils

"A sharp and funny heroine."
—Maggie Sefton

Also Available

Leann Sweeney

The Cat, the Quilt and the Corpse

A Cats in Trouble Mystery

Jill's quiet life is shattered when her house is broken into and her Abyssinian, Syrah, goes missing. Jill's convinced her kitty's been catnapped. But when her cat-crime-solving leads her to a dead body, suddenly all paws are pointing to Jill.

Soon, Jill discovers that Syrah isn't the only purebred who's been stolen. Now she has to find these furry felines before they all become the prey of a cold-blooded killer—and she gets nabbed for a crime she didn't commit.

"A welcome new voice in mystery fiction." —Jeff Abbott, bestselling author of *Collision*

Available wherever books are sold or at penguin.com

OM0009